MURDER BAY

MURDER BAY

A BEN CAREY MYSTERY

DAVID R. HORWITZ

TOP FIVE BOOKS

2008

A TOP FIVE MYSTERY

Published by Top Five Books, LLC
521 Home Avenue, Oak Park, Illinois 60304
www.top-five-books.com

Copyright © 2008 by David R. Horwitz, LLC

Library of Congress Catalog Number: 2007906738

ISBN: 978-0-9789270-2-8

Book and cover design by Top Five Books.
Cover images (clockwise from top right): police officer courtesy of Corbis;
battlefield, U.S. Capitol building, and Johnson's 1862 map of Georgetown and the
City of Washington courtesy of the Library of Congress; Confederate flag courtesy of
Corbis; U.S. flag courtesy of the Library of Congress.

Printed and bound in the United States of America
10 9 8 7 6 5 4 3 2 1

To Deirdre with love
Que sera, sera

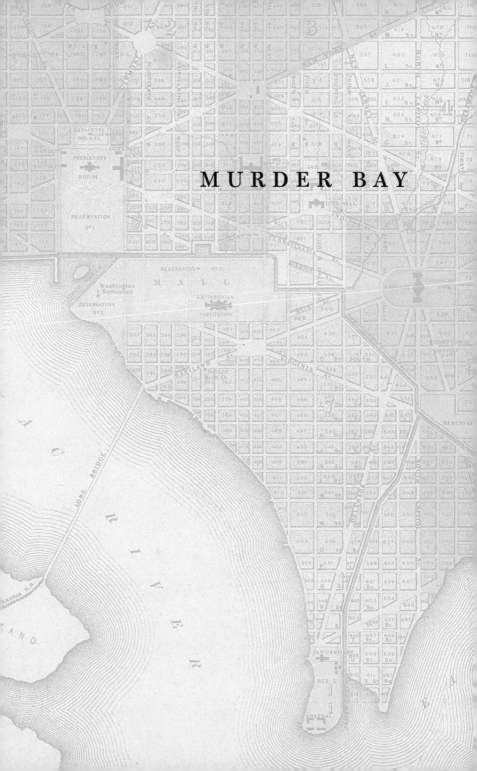

MURDER BAY

PART I

CHAPTER 1.

North of Warrenton, Virginia
Thursday, August 28, 1862

THERE WAS SOMETHING OUT THERE, crackling in the leaves, snapping twigs. Deer, the young private guessed. *Maybe if I stay quiet, I'll get to see a deer up close*, he thought. A city boy, he had only ever seen them recently, bounding away from a marching formation and into the woods, but never up close.

The day had taken its toll on the men. They were quiet, tense, knowing the enemy was near—they'd passed dead pickets from both armies as they marched through the humidity of the rain-sodden August day. On command, they set up camp alongside an unfinished railroad track, wanting to eat and rest while they could. The young soldier had made coffee with water from his canteen and chewed a previously cooked bit of beef. He had watched a dozen men, their turn for picket duty, climb over the partially graded rail bed and march toward a creek, a small river really, the locals called Bull Run.

After dinner, while the others wrote letters, rummaged in their packs for pipes and tobacco, or drowsed, the young soldier had pulled out his bowie knife and whetstone and sharpened the knife with a practiced motion. Then he had set off into the nearby woods in hopes of finding a good stick for whittling. He intended to whittle a little wooden soldier, musket and all. He had seen one of the other fellows do it—he had whittled a locomotive, complete with smokestack and wheels. It didn't seem too hard, and his first attempt at whittling—a shoehorn—had not proved much of a challenge.

An old elm tree, its base split by lightning, provided him a comfortable resting place, and he eased his tired body into its caress. The lightning had blasted a hole in the tree nearly the size of a pup tent. The young man surveyed the vicinity from his new perch and saw that he could still see the general's tent, and the cannon, and a hundred little campfires in the distance. He heard the order for the men to pitch their tents—a bugle call followed by a drum roll—they were here for the night. He closed his eyes and listened to the night sounds. It was calm, no wind. Then he heard the snapping of twigs again.

The hairs on the back of his neck pricked. There's more than one deer, he could tell, as the delicate sounds seemed to come from all around now. Perhaps he'd get to see a whole family coming near to sniff at what the army was eating. They were coming from behind, and he peered warily around the burnt edges of his tree stump.

What he saw caused him to drop the stick he had been whittling. One brief glance had shown him that he was surrounded by Confederate soldiers, all staring intently into the Union encampment, all unaware that he was in their midst. If they noticed him, he would be shot at once. He pushed himself deeper into his crevice, gripping his knife with both hands, and tried to figure out how many of them there were. Two right in front now, still moving toward the right, and two others just behind and to the left. A few more up ahead were loading their muskets and scurrying on their bellies to line up a shot into the oblivious Union camp. The Rebels were mostly barefoot and looked skinny and dirty. Many wore bloodied clothes, some of them U.S. Government issue, and the young soldier recoiled at the thought of these men stripping clothes from dead Yanks. He resisted the temptation to bolt into the dark woods—he would surely be shot in the back.

There was a footfall, this one very near, and suddenly standing before his tree was a Rebel officer, his back to the young man, a long cavalry sword dangling from his belt, a shiny Colt .36 holstered at each side. The officer was not four feet in front of him, whispering orders to the men ahead—"Take aim...pull hammer..."—*and here is my chance*, he thought—"Fire!"

There was no time to think. At the explosion of the muskets, the area was enveloped in smoke, and the young man rose from his hiding place, took one step, and leapt onto the officer's back with the bowie knife at his throat. The older man recovered quickly, grabbed his arm, and with the knife an inch from his throat, stopped the upward progression of the blade. The young man realized that the Rebel was stronger than he, so he shifted his left hand up to threaten the officer's eyes, and the man instinctively moved a hand up to protect his face. With his right hand, the private plunged the knife into the side of the man's throat and pulled it firmly across the flesh above his larynx. The Rebel commander grunted and grabbed the back of his attacker's head. He struggled and fought and pulled the young man's hair, as blood ran down the front of the Confederate officer's uniform. The private was thrown off the man's back and found himself lying face-up, staring into the barrel of a pearl-handled revolver. Blood gushed from the wound in the officer's neck, and the young man kicked desperately at the officer's legs, managing to knock him off balance. The gun wobbled in the officer's hand and fell onto the private's chest. He grabbed it and began rolling in the dirt.

Another roar from a dozen muskets—the troops were still firing into the camp, clueless to the struggle going on a few yards away, obscured by the smoke and the dark and the sounds of battle.

And yet the officer still stood, woozily reaching now for the left-handed holster, but the young private was on his feet now and behind him. He grabbed the officer around the chest, pinning his left arm against his body. He could feel the officer weaken, and the man started to topple over. He held the swaying man up with his left arm. There was a huge sound, a cannon firing nearby. The private could feel the vibrations of a solid shot bouncing across the camp, destroying everything in its path. He could see, in the distance, that the Rebs were coming up from over the railroad embankment, a classic encirclement, the pickets long since silenced, and no one ever thought to find out why. The Union camp was in complete chaos.

The young man smelled the officer's blood and felt its warmth penetrating his shirtsleeves. He became dizzy, disgusted, wanted to retch. In his right hand, the private held the nickel-plated revolver, sticky with blood, and with his left arm, he was now holding up a dead man. The soldier to his right was watching him with furrowed brow, trying to figure out what he was seeing in the near total darkness, and the young man did not hesitate to raise the revolver and fire it into the Rebel's chest. But there was another enemy soldier behind that one, and he raised his musket and fired, striking the corpse that the private still held upright with his left arm. Two shots from the revolver took down that Rebel. He heard noises to his left, and swung the dead man in that direction. One, two, and then three minié balls thumped into the lifeless body of their commanding officer. He fired the remaining three rounds, knocking down two more Rebels. He threw down the empty gun and began searching for the commander's other gun. His left hand got a grip on the other revolver, and the dead officer began to fall away. Then he saw the skinny kid, aiming with his ancient musket, hands shaking. The private began to raise the revolver, but it was too late—the kid fired, and he felt the round slap into his belly. The kid was frantically reloading, fumbling with paper cartridge and lead ball, but the private shot him through the throat with his left hand, and then turned his attention to who else might be alive near him. There was no one. He was terribly disoriented and became aware finally of the pain in his side, the blood pouring from the hole in his stomach and mixing with the Rebel's blood on his trousers. He took off his shirt and tied it around his midsection, then collapsed onto the body of the Confederate officer.

Stay awake. Breathe in, breathe out. Head spinning, got to clear my head. Breathe in, breathe out.

He heard footsteps now, tried to play dead, with no idea where he dropped the second revolver. Then the footsteps were gone, and he was still conscious, breathing, alive. He opened his eyes but could see nothing in the pitch black. He pushed himself to his knees. *Got to get back to camp, can't die out here in the woods.* One hand covering his wound, he began to crawl toward the distant flames, the sounds of men screaming and horses whinnying. The gunfire was a continuous blur of pops and bangs, most of it in the distance as the Union troops withdrew from the camp. After a few yards, he pulled himself to his feet with the help of a birch tree and walked the remaining twenty yards to the clearing.

It was awful. Everyone was dead and everything was on fire, the air thick with smoke. In the dark, he stepped on someone's leg and instinctively apologized, but there was just the leg, no one to apologize to. He saw some men standing by the officers' tents and stumbled in that direction, avoiding the bodies of the wounded and dead as best he could. Had to talk to an officer, and there's one standing up ahead. But he reached the man and saw that there wasn't much left; a shell had exploded at his feet, and the shrapnel had nailed him to the telegraph pole against which he had been leaning. The young man swooned, and now he was on his back, staring up at the dead officer still standing at attention, and as he blacked out, he heard the footfalls of cavalry.

CHAPTER 2.

On foot beat in Georgetown, Washington, D.C.
Monday, December 16, 1957

THE MAN STAGGERED TO the middle of the street, flailing his arms and screaming until he slipped on a patch of black ice and hit the pavement. The man—too drunk to quit—got to his knees and began pounding on the hood of the black Packard stopped before him. Officer Ben Carey, who had run to the scene, stumbling and sliding himself on the frozen sidewalk, could see the wide, terrified eyes of the woman behind the wheel as he grabbed the man by the collar and tried to pull him toward the curb. The man spun around, and something hit Carey in the face. He fell backward, and the drunk stumbled away. Carey got to his feet and reached for his baton, but the man had already fallen to the curb. There was the sound of breaking glass. The man was trying to get to his knees, but Carey pushed him down and yanked his arms behind his back. In a moment the man was handcuffed. He smelled of gin. Carey dragged him to the sidewalk, where the drunk collapsed face-first.

A thin layer of ice had coated the city, lending a sparkle to the night sky but making life miserable for anyone needing to get from one place to another. Now freezing rain began to fall, bouncing on the pavement, the sound as quiet as salt being sprinkled onto china. Under different circumstances, Carey would have found it calming. But not tonight.

Carey left the man lying there and walked around to the

Packard's driver-side window. "Are you all right, ma'am? What happened here?" She was staring at him, above his eyes, and he touched his forehead. Blood.

"I didn't hit him," she said. "He was standing in the middle of the street." She dug through her purse with shaky hands, found a cigarette, and lit it with a gold lighter. She was older, probably about his mother's age, and she looked like money. He wondered why she would be out driving at three in the morning. "I was lucky to have stopped in time." She blew smoke in his face absently, and he blinked.

Carey thanked her for the information and sent her on her way. He waved another car past that had slowed to gawk. He approached the drunk, who had turned on his side, in a fetal position, the jagged neck of a liquor bottle inches from his face. "Let's go, sir, on your feet," Carey said.

The man wore a dark business suit, black raincoat, and rubber boots over his shoes. He was about forty, blond, heavyset, five-foot-ten or so. A black fedora lay in the street where it had been run over by the Packard. Carey walked over and picked it up. "Come on, buddy, I don't wanna have to drag you to jail," he said. The man was sobbing now, coughing, mumbling incoherently. Carey put one arm under the man's shoulder and tried to pull him to his feet, but the man would not stand and fell to his knees, then to his side.

Carey lifted his cap and dabbed at his forehead with a handkerchief. The man would have to have been drunk to take a swing at Carey, who stood a good four inches taller than him. And despite the baby fat that still rounded out his young face, his body was fit and trim. His blue overcoat hung straight down from his broad shoulders and tended to conceal the fact that he had remained thin while so many officers his age had already grown soft around the middle. Carey turned his gray eyes up to the corner and replaced the hat atop his head of unkempt black hair.

He could see the street signs at the nearest intersection: Fox-hall and Reservoir. The closest call box was at MacArthur Boule-vard, a quarter mile down Foxhall toward the river.

He searched his suspect for weapons. The man had none, and Carey shoved the fedora inside the man's coat. He grabbed the drunk's collar with his leather-gloved hands and began dragging. *So this is why the New York City police call it a "collar,"* he thought.

The ice was falling sideways, stinging his cheeks, undeterred by the three-pointed rim of his uniform cap. Despite two pairs of socks, dress shoes, and rubber overshoes, his toes were freezing, almost numb, and he remembered the frostbite. The doctors in Korea had told him that his toes would forever be vulnerable to further damage and to keep them warm, but he couldn't do any-thing about that now. He wondered how many more winters his toes could endure before they turned black and had to be clipped off like dead tree branches.

He was dragging the drunk downhill now, past turn-of-the-century duplexes inhabited by young government workers and col-lege students from nearby Georgetown University. It was usually a quiet beat; in fact, this was the first incident of any kind he had encountered in a week. His prisoner was snoring as they reached the call box and did not wake when Carey gently lowered the man's head to the sidewalk. He chipped away the ice covering the lock with his key, unlocked the box, and picked up the receiver.

"Hello, Carey here. I need a scout car to transport a prisoner. Yes. Drunk and disorderly. Foxhall and MacArthur. Northwest. Great. Thanks." He hung up the phone, locked the box, and waited.

He stamped his feet and rubbed his hands together. Soon he heard a car, sputtering and coughing, its gears grinding as it strug-gled uphill. Scout 71, an old, battered Dodge, pulled to the curb under a cloud of exhaust smoke. It was a late 1940s model, black, the word POLICE spelled out in stenciled white letters on the door. Along the wheel rims and the bottoms of the doors, rust had eaten away the original contours of the vehicle. Officer Rick Tabian got out to help Carey with his prisoner.

"What happened to you? It looks like he clobbered you," he said as they stuffed the man into the back seat of the car. "Well, it seems he got the worst of it."

"I didn't touch him. He's been unconscious since he hit me with a bottle." Carey got in the front seat passenger side and placed his feet on the two-by-four that constituted the floorboard of the police car. The original floorboard had rusted away, and someone had tied the two-by-four into place with wire. The car lurched forward, and Carey could smell the exhaust rising from the hole in the floor and mixing with the general stink of the vehicle.

"He's kind of well-dressed for a drunk, isn't he?" Tabian asked, as he ground the gears on the dash-mounted shifter.

"So's the chief," Carey said with a sardonic grin, staring at the pavement rushing by below his feet.

CAREY HAD BEEN FIGHTING exhaustion the last few hours of his shift; the hours before sunrise were always the hardest. He finished the paperwork on the drunk by six A.M. and had to go back on his beat for two hours before being relieved. He walked the quiet, frozen streets of Georgetown until the morning sun rose high above the mansions of the wealthy sleeping warmly and safely in their beds. At the No. 7 Precinct house at Volta Place, his sergeant expressed concern for the cut on his eyebrow as Carey signed out, but Carey insisted that it was not worth a visit to the hospital.

It took him twenty minutes to walk to his apartment building, across the street from the perpetually unfinished Washington National Cathedral on Wisconsin Avenue NW. The Chancery

was down to one elevator again. One or the other seemed always
to be broken, and he waited several minutes for his ride to the seventh floor. He pulled his knit cap as low over his forehead as possible, hoping to avoid the inevitable questioning that would follow
once Marie saw the cut. But, as he knew, Marie noticed everything, and he made it only three steps into their apartment before
she stopped him.

"Ben, what happened to you? You're hurt!" Marie was in her
gray wool suit, a brass pin on the lapel. A pair of nylons was draped
over a chair, and she was barefoot.

"I'm fine, honey. It's just a scratch," he said as he raised his
hand to his brow and pressed lightly on the forming bruise. Their
comfortable one-bedroom was immaculate as always—a small
aluminum Christmas tree sparkled on a corner table, along with
a few other tasteful decorations Marie had put up. A dining-room
window was open a few inches to let air in. He could hear the traffic on the street.

Marie took him by the hand and led him to the bathroom,
where she dampened a washcloth and began to dab at the cut
above his right eyebrow. "You're going to get a black eye, you
know," she said.

"I know." He walked to the bedroom.

"What happened?" She followed.

"A drunk. He hit me with a bottle." Carey began to undress,
stowing his service revolver and badge in the metal lockbox on
the top shelf of the bedroom closet.

She stood with her arms folded, lips tight. Her bouffant hairdo
looked somewhat incomplete.

"It was sort of a fluke. I wasn't in any real danger," he said, sitting down on the edge of the bed to remove his socks. "This guy
could barely stand, and he swung his bottle when I grabbed him.
I don't even think he was aware—"

"I thought Georgetown would be a safe beat. Isn't that what you said?"

He looked up at Marie but didn't speak. Somewhere along the line, what had seemed like her concern for his safety had transformed into disdain for his job. As if it were beneath him. Or her.

"You always said this was temporary until something better came along—"

"I never said that, Marie. I said I'd keep my options open, but I never promised you this would be temporary." He sighed and tried to collect his thoughts. Sitting there in his boxers and undershirt, with Marie standing over him in her suit, he felt like a little kid. He was being defensive but didn't know why. "I like being a cop, Marie," he said. "I think I have a future in the department."

"I know," she said, and turned away from him.

He stood up, trying to change tactics. He didn't want another fight, especially before she left for work. He put his hands on her shoulders and could feel her body stiffen. He lightly kissed her on the back of the head and said, "I won't always be walking a beat, honey. I'll be moving up someday."

"Someday," she said flatly and wriggled away from him. "I just wish you could've found a job that didn't involve getting beaten up. You had—you have such potential..." She trailed off.

"What does that mean?"

She turned and stared at him in silence for a moment. "Nothing," she said. "I'm going to be late for work." Her round face became emotionless, indifferent almost, and she muttered something under her breath. She hurriedly slipped on her hose and black pumps, gave him a final cold stare, took her purse and blue cloth coat, and left. The door slammed behind her.

Carey sat there a while, trying to figure out what had just happened and thinking of a reason to get up. Finally, out of habit, he rose from the bed, collected the newspaper on the bedroom dresser, and took his Kiwi kit from the closet shelf. He drew a bath and polished his uniform shoes while the tub filled. He took the rest of the newspaper into the bathroom to read while he bathed. Outside, he could hear a siren, an ambulance. He lowered himself into the hot water and turned off the spigot with his toes and thought of his wife.

He knew things had not been right for some time. They had married two weeks before he left for Korea, and when he came back, she was different. Or maybe he was. In any case, though they had never talked about it, they were trying to make it work. Five years now, and increasingly, she seemed to resent his night hours, his weekend work, his job. Carey rubbed soap on his neck and face, and gently fingered the wound above his eyebrow. She was too good for him. She was educated. He walked the streets all night arresting drunks. He rinsed his face, leaned back into the warm sudsy water, and began to drift off to sleep.

Marie had gone to the University of Maryland while he was in Korea, emerging with a degree in economics that had won her a job at the Social Security Administration. Personally, he did not envy her sitting in an office all day long, but he knew that she loved her job, and it had given her a confidence, an independence, that few women enjoyed. And she earned as much as he did.

But then, Carey hadn't been raised to value money quite as highly as Marie. His father, a carpenter, was a man who had worked with his hands all his life. A doughboy during World War I, he'd met Ben's mother in the spring of 1918 while stationed outside Paris, a corporal with the Army Corps of Engineers. When the war ended, he returned—to the dismay of his family—with a child bride who barely spoke English.

By the time Ben arrived, his parents were already in their thirties. Never well-off enough to spoil him, they compensated by being too easy on him. Ben mitigated their leniency by being harder on himself than they ever could be.

As a boy, Ben spent more time with his dad than most kids ever did, even tagging along on construction jobs during the summer once he was old enough to help out.

When his father died while he was in Korea—though he'd never had a chance to say so—Ben was certain that his dad was proud of him. With Marie's parents, things had never been that simple or straightforward.

The phone rang, and he awoke. The water was chilly, and he climbed out of the tub and wrapped a towel around his waist. He trailed water across the wood floor as he tiptoed to the phone.

"Hello."

"Ben. Did I wake you?" It was the voice of Inspector James Price.

"No, sir, I've been...yes, you woke me."

"Well, it'll be worth it. You've made sergeant. Congratulations."

"Uh..." Carey's mind raced to catch up with the new information, and a smile crossed his still-boyish face. "Thank you, sir."

"Unfortunately, you've got to come in. Headquarters. You're on day shift now, and you're late."

IT WAS JUST BEFORE NOON, and Sergeant Ben Carey was sitting in the office of Deputy Chief Herbert Correll, tapping his fingers on the armrest of the chair and smiling nervously at Inspector Price. The two of them sat in silence. Finally Carey spoke. "So what's the new assignment, sir?"

"Correll wants to tell you. I wasn't even supposed to tell you about making sergeant. Act surprised," Price said, incongruously.

They sat in silence again. For several minutes, Carey drummed his fingers under his chair seat and regretted the two cups of coffee he had consumed in the last hour. Between the caffeine, the lack of sleep, and his nagging insecurity about the shape of his marriage, he was finding it nearly impossible to focus. He stood and looked at the framed photographs on the wall. Correll with the chief. Correll shaking hands with Harry Truman. Correll accepting an award on behalf of the Metropolitan Police Department.

Carey sat back down just as Correll walked in. "Sorry to keep you waiting," Correll said, and the men stood and exchanged salutes. "Please, sit back down," the deputy chief said as he took his seat behind the oak desk. "Well, now. What the hell happened to you?" Both men stared at Carey.

An uncomfortable silence. "You mean this?" Carey pointed at his right eye. "Nothing. Minor altercation with a suspect. It's all in my report from last night, sir." He clasped his hands in his lap. Another uncomfortable silence. Correll spoke again.

"Officer Carey, congratulations are in order. You've made sergeant. And not only that. You scored highest on the exam of anyone who took it this sitting. That's very impressive." Correll shuffled some papers and read from one. "Strong organizational skills, it says. Exceptionally high score in the management section. You should be pleased."

"Thank you, sir. I am." Carey waited for the other shoe to drop.

"Son, how would you feel about getting off the night beat? Working nine-to-five?"

Carey allowed a slight smile to form on his lips, then straightened. "Yes, sir, thank you. I'd be —"

"Wonderful," Correll said. "There's a project I think you would do well. The MPD has won a grant from the Department of Justice. It's sort of an experiment. The funds are to be used exclusively to create a planning unit." Correll tossed a folder across the desk. "Start reading this, it's got the details. They're pretty particular about how the money is spent. You start immediately. You will recruit and oversee a staff of three."

Price chimed in, obviously eager to get in on the conversation. "MPD has an office in a building down the street. An old Victorian house, actually. Third and C." Price shifted in his chair, clearing his throat. "You'll also be working with a consultant on this project, Captain Wallace. He's been working out of that office for a while."

"Captain Wallace?" Carey asked. "I don't think I'm familiar—"

"Everything you need to know is in the file," Correll snapped and leaned back into his faux-leather chair. "I'm not sure what kind of shape the facilities are in. But you can take care of those things yourself."

"I didn't even know the department had an office over there. What's it been used for?"

Correll ignored the question. "You will be under the command of Inspector Price. The project will be evaluated by DOJ at the end of the year. They will decide on a continuance." The chief folded his arms.

"If the project goes on for a second year, we'll have to find another office. The house is scheduled for demolition by the end of next year," Price said.

"How much is the grant?" asked Carey.

Correll cleared his throat and stood. "It's all in there," he said, nodding toward the folder. "I've got a meeting with a community group, so you'll have to excuse me. Congratulations again, Ben. I'm sure you'll do fine with this project." The other men stood and saluted.

Outside the office, Carey waited until his superiors were just out of sight, then opened the folder, and began flipping through the papers, looking for an answer. *Who the hell*, he wondered, *is Arthur Wallace?*

•   •   •

THREE BLOCKS NORTH and west of the U.S. Capitol, Sergeant Ben Carey stood before an antebellum Victorian house of brick and wood built eighty years before he was born. The house at 301 C Street was lovely from a distance, with an inviting wraparound porch that gave it a certain Southern charm. Closer, its neglect became apparent. The current layer of white paint must have been twenty years old, and he could see at least one broken window on the second floor. Facing south was a tower, looking odd indeed in a neighborhood of sedate brownstones and vacant lots overgrown with weeds and trash. Carey knew that the federal government owned most of the lots and had big plans for the neighborhood. Soon enormous office buildings, like the Municipal Center around the corner that housed police headquarters, would dominate this area.

He climbed the cast-iron steps. The rusty railing wobbled at his touch, and the porch buckled slightly under his weight. The floorboards were rotten. He stepped to the door with key in hand, but found it unlocked. He entered.

It opened into a hallway, with a stairway immediately before him. The air was thick with dust and the moist stink of soft wood. Off to the right, a door was ajar. He pushed it open. There was a small office area, dimly lit, smoky. Carey could see a newspaper, fingers, feet on a desk. A coffee mug, some magazines, a phone. An uncovered light bulb hung from the ceiling.

"Hello?" Carey removed his cap. Silence from behind the newspaper.

Carey cleared his throat. A corner of the newspaper curled inward, slowly, and he could see a receding hairline, a bloodshot eyeball examining him. The eye went straight to the stripes on Carey's shoulder. The newspaper straightened out, and the face was hidden again. Carey presumed that the eye outranked him. "You must be Captain Wallace," Carey said as he walked around the desk. "I don't believe we've ever met. I understand we'll be working together." Carey saluted. It was not returned.

Wallace was a tall, lanky man with a grossly bloated stomach. His gray hair was receding in an exaggerated widow's peak, with wisps of hair struggling to hold on to the top of his forehead; the rest of him was equally disheveled. His flesh was a pasty color, the veins in his nose and under his eyes tracing a spidery blue web across his face. He wore a uniform, but the belt and pants were unbuckled to allow his gut some room behind the desk. His cap was on the dusty floor, upside down behind his chair.

He tilted his head slightly and eyed Carey uneasily, looking through, rather than at him. He extended his arm as if to shake hands, but instead jabbed his index finger into Carey's ribs. Satisfied, he returned his eyes to his paper, but did not focus on the page. "Sergeant? Didn't you mean to say that you'd be working under me?"

Carey scrambled for words and backed away from the desk. "My understanding is that you will be a consultant to this project, isn't that what you were told?"

Wallace glanced up at Carey, took a drag from his cigarette, and spit out some smoke. "What project?"

"I'm sure Inspector Price will be discussing it with you. Do you mind if I have a look around?" Wallace stared at Carey this time, squinting to focus on him. Carey went on, "I'll be working here, too. And a couple of other officers. Starting next Mon—"

"Here?" Wallace growled, hacking out smoke. "What the hell do you mean, working *here*?" Carey shrugged his shoulders at Wallace. "I was supposed to transfer out of here after my last assignment. I've been in this dump for over a year. They promised me—" he broke off.

"That's just what I was told," Carey said after a moment, shrugging again.

Wallace grunted and hid behind his newspaper. After a minute, he spoke again. "Do whatever you like. Just stay the hell out of my way."

"Does that phone work? I might be needing to use it next wee—"

Wallace got up suddenly from behind the desk, startling Carey. The captain picked up the phone and walked around the desk with it. "Fine. We'll put the phone out here. You can have it." He walked past Carey and tossed the phone to the floor of the adjoining hallway. It clanged loudly, and its handset bounced across the floor. The cord was short, and the phone would go no further than three feet past the door. Wallace reached for his pants, which were falling around his thighs, and buckled them as he walked behind his desk, assumed his seat, and returned his attention to the paper.

Carey felt as if he'd been dismissed. "Um…I'll just have a look around…"

No reply.

The rest of the building was no surprise. Crumbling plaster, hanging light bulbs—many of them burned out—and rotting wood. There was no furniture except the desk and chair in Wallace's office. The rooms were small and cold, the windows shaded by dirt. Wallace had dropped the phone at the foot of the stairs, and Carey began climbing them. When he stepped on the fourth step, he thought his foot might go through it. He backed slowly down the stairs. He thought, *I've got a lot of work to do.*

HE MET SERGEANT Norman Crawford for coffee at three that afternoon, at a coffee shop on 11th Street. They had served together in Korea, and Crawford had helped Carey after the war in getting a job with the MPD. Crawford was a short, wiry man with intense eyes hidden behind black-rimmed glasses. He was a smart guy, a couple years older than Carey, and he was working on a degree in accounting at night. Carey knew that he wanted Crawford on the job; he trusted him, and he was the only cop he knew who had a head for numbers. He told Norm of his meeting with Captain Wallace and the condition of the office space.

"You don't know the story behind Wallace, I take it," said Crawford between sips from his cup. His glasses fogged momentarily from the coffee.

"You know me, Norm, I don't pay much attention to the grapevine."

"I know this guy—civilian, works in personnel."

Carey nodded.

"Anyhow, he told me about this guy who went nuts several years back. Seems he was in command of the second precinct, night shift. There was a civil disturbance after a police shooting. Back in '54." Crawford was stirring his coffee.

"I remember that," said Carey. "Captain was called to the scene but went home instead."

Crawford shook his head. "That's not the whole story. Wallace went to the scene. There were ten cops trying to hold back about forty civilians. They were throwing fists, rocks, bottles, whatever they had. Wallace walks up to an officer who's being held down and pounded by two guys, doesn't help him or anything. Like he was waiting for the guys to finish so he could talk to him."

"Oh."

"Then he went back to the precinct house and hid in his office for a while, behind his desk, gun drawn. That's the way his lieutenant found him. He told Wallace to go home. And he did. Lieutenant had to call in help from other precincts."

"Sounds like he's ready for retirement," Carey said.

"He wouldn't retire. Didn't have enough time in. They tried to get him a medical but couldn't find a doctor to play along."

"So they warehoused him. And now we're stuck with him," Carey said as he removed papers from a folder. "Let's talk about the planning unit. Are you okay getting off the street for a while?"

"Yeah, Ben, no problem."

"Okay. So let me fill you in. We have this grant. From the Justice Department. Unfortunately, we can't just go out and buy what the department really needs, which is new police cars equipped with two-way radios."

"Why not?"

"Because the feds have this way of structuring their grants. They don't want to see their money spent on physical benefits, like things we can actually use. They want to see management improvements, strategic challenges addressed, new administrative methods, stuff like that. Then they evaluate us, decide what we're doing right, and start paying other cities to do these things."

"Sounds like the army," said Crawford as he poured more cream into his coffee. "Though I can see how it would be an interesting challenge, in a way."

"Exactly. We're going to try to get the things the department needs anyway. The idea is to package it to the feds so that it satisfies their needs, and ours."

"What's your plan?"

"Look." Carey was pointing to a paragraph from the grant paperwork. "'Grantee may purchase matériel and equipment necessary to carry out or implement a strategic plan within the framework...' blah, blah. So we identify some problem and then write a detailed proposal for solving it, and explain carefully how these squad cars will help in its implementation." Carey leaned back in his seat. "And if that flies, then we purchase the cars and the radios."

Crawford looked intrigued. "And what problems do we identify?"

"Well, it could be anything we want. That's where we get to be creative. The goal is to get the equipment we need. The rest is essentially just paperwork." The waitress walked by, and Carey asked for the check.

"No charge, officers, just be sure to stop by again." She smiled sweetly and was gone.

They left a big tip.

BEN WAS CONCERNED that his new desk job might become boring, but he was also relieved. As much as Marie professed to worry about him walking a beat, she didn't know the half of it. Between his days in the service and with the department, he'd experienced things he couldn't share with her, things she would never want to know. And aside from the stuff he wished he could forget—the screams of boys wounded in battle, the streetwalkers who'd been cut, beaten, and bruised, the junkies who OD'd—Ben was sure even his most colorful stories would absolutely horrify Marie.

He had once responded to a call on a burglary in an apartment near Catholic University. The elderly widow living there awoke to find a man crawling through her bedroom window. She took her late husband's revolver from a drawer and shot the intruder through the top of the head. Fretting that his blood was ruining her clean white carpet, she took a stainless steel mixing bowl and placed it underneath the gushing wound. Then she called the police. Before Carey and his partner had arrived, the bowl had filled, so she had pulled it aside and put another, larger bowl beneath the dead man's head. This is how they found him: half in, half out of the window, drained of blood, with a neat hole in the top of his head. They discovered the next day that he had been a bus driver who lived two blocks away, and theorized that he had been drunk and tried to sneak into the house without waking his wife, but had picked the wrong house. No charges were filed.

Marie couldn't share any of these events that made up his life — her image of his occupation was seen from a view so distant that, he suspected, he barely even existed to her when he wasn't within sight. She had grown up in a somewhat sheltered existence. Her parents, proprietors of an apartment building in Foggy Bottom, had sent her to private schools, then to college, where they no doubt expected she would find a prosperous future lawyer or doctor to marry. Instead she met Carey, a working-class kid who didn't know what he wanted to do with his life.

When they'd first met, it was as if they both knew what they wanted from the other and could read it in each other's eyes. Marie was the first beautiful girl Ben had met who had anything resembling a sense of humor. She was smart and quick-witted, but mixed in was a vulnerability that touched Ben in a profound way. She put up a front to mask her tender, nurturing side, and only let it down when alone with him. It only made him love her more.

Marie fell in love with the loyalty and honesty that Ben wore on his sleeve, and saw in him the potential for great things. He was the tall, dark, silent man of her dreams. Though he was solidly blue collar, he was also gentle and thoughtful, an unpolished gem. With her by his side, she thought there was nothing he couldn't achieve.

They sparred in conversation — she teased him about his lack of refinement, he chided her about being a social climber — but there was nothing contentious about their physical relationship. They'd both been virgins when they met. Neither had even considered sex before marriage. But they drew out the repressed libido in each other. After two weeks of dating, of constant companionship and frequent, frantic lovemaking in cars, friends' apartments, and cheap motels, Ben couldn't imagine living his life without Marie.

He proposed one night while they lay naked under a rough wool blanket in the back seat of his father's Studebaker. He had no ring, no prospects but for a halfhearted apprenticeship to another carpenter on a construction crew. But he had no doubt about her answer. From the way she looked at him, and how she held her body close to his, he knew she felt the same way.

It wasn't until they told their parents that anyone raised concerns—about how short a time they'd known each other, about their future plans, about money. So it was a combination of inevitability and good timing when Ben received his draft notice. Being sent overseas solved the problem of needing a vocation, and it gave Ben a reprieve. Maybe by the time he returned, he reasoned, his future in-laws would have grown used to the arrangement, even happy with it.

They were nineteen.

Ben and Marie wed in a simple ceremony presided over by a justice of the peace—since he was nominally Catholic, she Presbyterian, it was the path of least resistance. Their honeymoon lasted one weekend, and they discovered that sex prohibited by God and society was twice as exciting as that sanctioned and approved, if no less productive.

It was only in retrospect, with Ben in Korea and a life growing inside her, that Marie began to wonder what marrying the first man she'd fallen in love with might have cost her. She'd foregone a picture-book wedding for Ben. Now she wondered for the first time if he would make a good father. Would he even make it back to be a father?

So when Marie miscarried six weeks into her pregnancy, she was worried to find herself relieved. And so she never told Ben, or anyone, about the loss.

They'd been little more than children when they married, and they spent the formative early years of their adulthood apart, in proving grounds as different as any can be. When Ben returned from Korea, a veteran caring for his newly widowed mother, his expectations of life were somewhat less grandiose than his college graduate wife's.

Ben's vision of success—having enough money to put food on the table for a happy family—had never quite matched the definition that Marie's parents had instilled in her, and college had only reinforced. But Marie encouraged Ben to join the police force, and had tried hard to make him happy and to make their life together work when he came back from the war. His decision to go straight into the MPD after his return didn't please his in-laws. His decision, after several years, to stay on the job walking the night beat seemed to have had the same effect on his wife.

As such, Carey expected surprise when Marie came home from work and heard of his promotion and new assignment. More specifically, he expected her to be pleasantly surprised, now that he was back on day shift. This would seem to be what she had wanted from him—normal hours, a desk job, weekends off, even more money. But despite her congratulations, he could see something else in her eyes, a certain discomfort, fear almost. While he polished his uniform shoes, he talked of his ideas for the planning unit. She feigned interest in his new project, and he wondered what it was she wanted from him.

They ate dinner in a strange silence. Ben complimented Marie on the lasagna, which they were eating for the third night in a row. She looked at him quizzically, as if she were mentally cataloguing his inadequacies.

You're just overreacting, he told himself as he watched his sleeping wife, listened to her breathing. *How excited was she supposed to get? Did you expect her to dance around the room?* He knew she was still angry about the black eye. Such a trivial thing to be angry about.

He turned on one side now. *She's eight inches from me*, he thought, *but it feels as if she's a mile away.* Early in their marriage, even when he first came back from Korea, she was incapable of sleeping unless touching him, head on his chest, arms and legs intertwined. Now she hardly touched him at all, and sometimes pulled away from his hand. He could not remember the last time they had made love. Or even carried on a conversation that did not end with one or the other of them annoyed.

The hours and the risk that went along with his job had been tough on his marriage. It was his fault, he decided; he knew the night shift was hard on all police marriages. And he had pulled more than his share of this duty. *It will get better now that I've got a normal nine-to-five. We've just got to get used to each other again.*

He thought about the planning unit and the building. He'd need some help getting that place into decent condition. Rip out those rotten boards on the porch and fix the stairs. Paint the walls. Clean the windows. He had already placed an order for furniture and phones, but it might be a few days before they showed up. Administration always dragged its feet on these things.

He had decided on two men, had made the transfer offers to them, and both had accepted. Officer Don Mullins had been his first partner. They had walked a beat in Southwest, along the waterfront, for about eight months. He was very quiet but smart, and had common sense. Sergeant Brian Kelsey was an older cop, worked behind a desk at precinct, and knew the bureaucratic ropes.

Carey lay in bed, his mind racing, until nearly three in the morning, and slept fitfully for a few hours.

. . .

BY NOON THE NEXT DAY, Carey was pulling rotten wood out of the staircase of Substation C, as the building was now formally known. In another room, Lorna, the Mexican cleaning woman, was scrubbing the windows, and upstairs, Billy, an older black man, was painting the ceiling and walls. Both were contract laborers employed by the department.

Wallace sat in his usual perch, writing something in a black hardcover notebook, not at all happy about the activity surrounding him. What he was writing, Ben could only guess. He glared at Ben every time he walked by. Ben ignored him.

He worked with a crowbar, ripping the rotten boards from the stairway. He knew more than a little about carpentry, having worked with his father as a kid. When Carey began hammering the new floorboards into place, he turned to see Wallace standing in the doorway, hand on hip, flushed in the cheeks, his hastily fastened belt failing to disguise the fact that his zipper was undone. Again, Carey ignored him, and after a moment the captain returned to his desk.

By five P.M., Carey was ready to quit for the day, the staircase now safe for humanity. Billy, the guy painting the upstairs, descended the stairs and voiced admiration for Carey's work. Then he said, "Who was that guy? He work for you, Sarge?"

"What guy?"

"Blond kid, skinny, sideburns. Checking out my work, I figured. Peered through the doorway, didn't say nothing. Came downstairs, I thought." Billy looked tired, dots of white paint on his face and arms, but there was a look of unease in his eyes, Carey noted.

"Nobody came down the stairs. I've been here for hours." Carey closed his toolbox and set the latch.

"Maybe he's still up there somewhere." Billy was rubbing spots of paint from his dark skin with a rag, looking strangely introspective. "Anyway, it's quitting time. See you in the morning." He walked past Carey and stuck his head into Wallace's office. "Evening, Cap," he said, and Carey could hear no reply from Wallace as Billy pulled the front door shut.

Carey inspected the upstairs, four large rooms connected by an L-shaped hallway. Billy had painted one room—the one with the broken window—and it looked pretty good. He noticed a splatter of white paint on the ancient brick fireplace and scraped it off with his pocket knife. Nearly every room had a fireplace, essential in the days before central heating, although this building had been retrofitted with oil heat sometime early in the century. He didn't know if it worked, but most every room had radiators connected to a pipe system.

Plumbing had been retrofitted, too, and there was a tiny, filthy bathroom on the first floor, near the back door. The bathtub was cast iron, with curled feet in the form of lion's paws, and outfitted with a moldy, semicircular shower curtain. The porcelain was worn away around the edges. The toilet had an elevated water tank, five feet in the air, with a chain flush. Down the hall, there was a narrow kitchen, really only a room with a dirty sink and ancient cabinetry. There were no appliances.

Carey finished his tour of the house. He found no skinny guy with sideburns. He wished Lorna, the cleaning woman, a good evening after complimenting her work on the windows, which were now transparent. Wallace had already gone, carelessly leaving his kerosene heater burning. Carey turned it off.

He opened the door to the basement and looked in. He carefully made his way down the stairs and could see the boiler and the oil tank outlined in shadows. The only source of light came from a single bulb in a corner of the room, but it had burnt out long ago. Without a flashlight he couldn't do more tonight.

Carey locked the house and went back to headquarters to sign out. The sun was setting, and it was getting cold. On the long walk home, he stopped for Chinese takeout. He entered his darkened apartment at six P.M. but waited for Marie until seven before finally eating his share of the now-cold lo mein. Twice he called her office, but the phone went unanswered.

When Marie finally walked through the door at 8:30, Ben was steaming. Had to work late, she claimed, and forgot to call. She was defensive and looked flushed. Little more was said that night, and by 9:30 he was again watching her sleep from across the vast expanse of their bed, wondering why she hadn't asked about dinner.

THE NEXT DAY, Carey paid his apartment building superintendent $10 to check out the boiler at Substation C. He got it lit and told Carey the tank was half-full, enough to last a month or so. The cleanup continued. The glass contractor came and fixed the broken window. Carey replaced the rotted boards on the front porch. Lorna scrubbed the bathroom and kitchen; Billy was still painting upstairs. Wallace, gray and tight-lipped, was looking through his notebook with his feet on the desk.

The office furniture arrived from the warehouse that afternoon and was distributed among the three vacant rooms on the first floor. Carey kept the largest office for himself, nearest the stairway. Mullins's and Kelsey's office got a typewriter.

Soon after the moving crew left, Carey heard a clanging sound reverberating throughout the building, seeming to come from everywhere, from inside the walls. He went into the basement, which was now quite warm, and the rhythmic clanging grew louder. It was the pipes expanding from the heat of the furnace.

It sounded like someone banging a wrench against the pipes; it would start softly and grow louder, and then become softer again. There would be a pause of a few moments, then the cycle would start again.

He went back to his office and touched the radiator. It was getting warm.

He checked the hall radiator and, seeing that Wallace's office was open, knocked on the door, popped his head in, and asked, "Is the heat coming on in here?"

Wallace was sitting in his chair, his back turned to his desk, his notebook lying on the floor. "Captain," Carey said.

Wallace turned partway around and glared at Carey. "How the hell am I supposed to get any work done with that goddamn noise?" he said.

"We can't use kerosene heaters anymore, Captain. It's a major fire hazard."

"The hell it is," Wallace snapped.

"You can speak with Inspector Price, if you don't like it, sir," Carey said, curtly. Wallace stared at Carey, stunned at his insolence. His cheeks grew red and he stammered, obviously trying to think of an authoritative, commanding response. "Maybe I'll do that," said Wallace. An empty threat if Carey had ever heard one. Wallace turned away from Carey, clenching a pencil in his left hand. "Please shut the door, will you, *Sergeant*."

The crew from the phone company arrived about four P.M., and by five P.M. there was a phone on each desk. Carey took Wallace's phone from the hallway floor and placed it back on the captain's desk. But Wallace was gone, having left moments before the clock struck five.

He turned off Wallace's kerosene heater and his desk lamp. As he was headed back to his own office, he encountered Lorna descending the stairs. "*No vuelvo a entrar en esta casa otra vez!*"

she said as she gave herself the sign of the cross.

"What? I'm sorry, I don't speak Spanish," Carey said, wondering why she had lost her halting English. She opened the door and stepped outside, her hand gripping the doorknob as she stared into Carey's eyes.

"*Usted debe alejarse de aquí!*"

The door slammed behind her, rattling the newly cleaned windows.

CHAPTER 3.

Saturday, August 30, 1862

THE YOUNG SOLDIER AWOKE on the battlefield. It was dark and drizzling into his open mouth, and he swallowed hard and gasped. The pain was unbearable, and he screamed, one long, plaintive wail, and then another, then stopped, bit his cheek until it bled, and he tasted blood. He was alive.

He screamed again, unable to stop, and began to detach himself from the sound of his own anguish. He tried to figure out who and where he was, how he was injured, what hurt the most. His right ankle was in agony. He propped himself on his elbows, crying, and examined himself in what little moonlight there was. He could see, all around him, the tracks of horses. His right leg was pushed into the soft wet earth, amid the distinct impression of a hoof. He had been trampled.

He felt his side now. A few inches to the left of his navel, a black hole, clotted with blood. A few more inches, a lump under his skin, the minié ball, hard against his ribs. He collapsed back into the mud and began weeping, his leg mercifully numb now. He wondered if it was bleeding.

Gingerly, he tried to pull himself out of the mud. The pain came alive as the mangled foot emerged from the muck. He saw the foot turned at an unnatural angle, saw it bounce left and right as if it were dangling from a rubber band. He cried out for help, and became aware now that others were calling out, that the field was strewn with sluggishly moving forms and others that did not

33

move at all. Near him, an army wagon burned, and before it lay a dead horse. He began to crawl, pulling himself forward on his elbows, but didn't know where he was going, or why. So he lay his head down in the mud and fell asleep.

When he regained his senses, it was daytime, and he was being carried off the battlefield by two shirtless men, one of whom had a bloody bandage around his head. One had him under the arms, and the other was between his legs, holding his thighs. They walked for what seemed like a mile, then set him down in a carriage of some sort, set him down right on the body of another wounded man. There were four of them in this little cart, stacked like firewood, and as the cart began moving, the man under him began screaming, and he tried to find some way of taking his weight off the poor fellow, but there was no way.

The cart had only one axle, and it tilted and jolted and knocked the men against the wooden slats. The young soldier was quiet as the men around him screamed and cursed and whimpered and prayed. It quickly became horribly hot in the little enclosed space. The air was thick and soupy, and the sweat ran off his brow in streams. He was crazy with thirst, and descended into a strange delirium, thinking that he was dead and in hell. The cart hit a particularly hard bump, the men all bounced into the air, and when they landed, the man below him screamed again, then stopped.

He heard the man draw in two long breaths, and then nothing. Then the cart was filled with a familiar stink, as the dead man vacated his bowels.

An hour, or two. He did not know how long. The cart pulled up hard, its little wooden gate was lowered, and clean young faces were peering in at them. He noticed now there were only three in the cart; the fellow next to him had bounced out along the way. The clean men pulled him from the cart, and he glanced back into it as he was led away. The fourth man was dead, too. He was the only soldier to survive the journey.

He was placed on a cot, right in the hot sun, and there he remained for what seemed an eternity. A young boy came by, twice, to offer him water from a tin cup. The young private greedily drank every drop he was given.

A man in a bloody smock walked by, and the private tugged the doctor's sleeve and asked to be taken out of the sun. The doctor examined him critically, gestured to some orderlies, and the young man was carried, cot and all, into a gray tent.

An orderly gave him something to drink, a full glass, but it was not water. It tasted alcoholic, but there was a strange, metallic quality to the drink he did not recognize. Then he saw the pile, and he gasped. A scream emanated from somewhere. He looked around, getting groggy now, but he was alone in the tent, his cot lain across a wooden table, and he looked again at the pile. The room spun about him, and sleep was coming quite involuntarily, inevitably, inexorably. With his last conscious moment, he looked again at the pile.

It was a pile of arms and legs, boots still attached.

HE REGAINED CONSCIOUSNESS gradually, becoming aware, for instance, that someone was holding his hand. He tried to open his eyes but could not. His breathing became panicked as the pain came back in waves, from his stomach, from his right leg. He cried out, and someone placed a wet cloth on his forehead beneath a tangle of grimy, matted blond hair. It was hot, very hot, and his head was swimming, and he could hear her voice now, she was squeezing his hand.

He had been in a battle, the events coming back as screams and flashes of light. He remembered now, the fight in the woods, the minié ball thumping into his belly. He remembered stumbling back to camp, lying in the mud, waiting for someone to come and help him, and then the cavalry—was it the Rebels' or our own?—that came crashing across the field. The shocking, vicious pain when the horse stepped on his leg. The men around him were calling out, whimpering, some of them crawling past him on their way to God knows where. He remembered lifting his head to look at his shattered right calf. He could see shredded cloth, and bloody chunks of his muscle, and the bright white of his bone, and then he could see only blackness.

She was turning him on his side now, and it was hurting him. He could feel a cold wet cloth on his rear end, probing, wiping. Now he could feel dry cloth down there and he was turned again on his back. He just wanted to rest, he tried to tell her, but she was busy again, tugging at the bandage, just below the rib cage on his left side. Next came a sponge bath, on his neck, and his chest, under his arms. The warm, wet sponge was drawn down his left leg, under his knee, and along the sole of his foot. He could hear the sponge dipped into a bucket, squeezed. Down his right leg, over and under the knee, and here the sponge stopped. He waited for the sponge to massage his right foot. But the sponge went back in the bucket and the woman went away.

He tried to wiggle his toes, but the effort made him pass out again.

CHAPTER 4.

Friday, December 20, 1957

SERGEANT CAREY ARRIVED HOME Friday at 5:45 P.M. to find his suitcase packed. Marie told him that she wanted him to move out "temporarily." She needed some time to think about their relationship. She hoped he would understand, she said, as she dabbed her eyes with a handkerchief.

Shocked, speechless, he took the suitcase, walked into the hall, and stared at her as she pushed the door shut. He could hear her chain the door behind him, and see her eye in the peephole. She stayed there, on the other side of the door, until he turned to go. On the street, he hailed a taxi and told the cabby just to drive around for a while. He didn't know where to go.

Carey spent Friday night at the ritzy Hotel Washington at 15th and F Street NW. At the hotel bar, he drank scotch. He talked to no one in the crowded lounge. Normally a light drinker, he was drunk before his fourth drink was served, and he had two more. He staggered to his room around midnight and managed to strip down to his shorts before passing out.

He had troubling dreams.

Back in Korea, in a field hospital recovering from wounds. Shrapnel from a grenade ripped through the flesh of his left shoulder and lodged in his back. He can't feel his left arm and he can't move. His doctors are Korean, but speak to him in perfect English. There are bars on the windows. When the doctors finish with him, he wanders from room to room, confused, fearful, trying but unable to read the hand-lettered signs posted in every corner. The words are unintelligible, foreign. Then he is flat on his back, mortally ill, struggling for breath, while the doctors surround him, holding him down. He feels a sinking sensation, like he is slipping away into darkness, the world of light and sound getting further and further away as he spirals down. Sweating, writhing in his cot, his arms reach toward the ceiling, grasping, hands closing on empty air.

It was still dark when he awoke, and his heart was pounding. He sat up in bed and tried to think through the haze. A hotel room. *My gun and badge—where are they?* He turned on the lamp by the bed, wincing at the sudden light. His vision cleared, and he looked around. There was a chest of drawers, a bed table, and a desk. He rose from his bed and slowly pulled open the desk drawer. Empty, except for a Gideon Bible. *My God, I hope they're in the bed table drawer,* he thought to himself. The gun and badge were in the drawer, along with his keys, watch, and wallet.

The sense of panic did not leave him. His heart was racing, and his stomach was filled with acid. His mouth tasted foul. He went to the bathroom and brushed his teeth.

He sat on the edge of the bed with his face in his hands, his bare feet chilled. *Is she having an affair?* Behind his tightly shut eyes, involuntary images of Marie in bed with another man. He stood suddenly and began to pace in tight circles. *Should I follow her?* He could talk his buddies into helping. There was a detective, Borgman, who would do pretty much anything for a bottle of twelve-year-old scotch.

The brown bag on the chair caught his eye, and he stopped in his tracks. He must have bought a bottle to go last night, at the bar.

It was four A.M. and not even a coffee shop would be open for two more hours. He could not imagine pacing around this room for two hours, heart pounding and hands shaking. But drinking before dawn? Maybe it would put him back to sleep. In any case, it would stop his heart from beating so hard.

The bathroom faucet ran for twenty seconds before the water became cold. He poured two fingers of scotch into a hotel glass and filled it with tap water.

He pulled the blinds up and opened the window a bit. Cold air rushed in. He sat before it and sipped his drink, staring into the darkness of an alleyway. He felt better.

After a while, the wall of the adjoining building became visible. A thin line of sunlight appeared at its top. Gradually, the line drew downward, and now he could hear the traffic on Pennsylvania Avenue.

CAREY HAD BREAKFAST at a diner on G Street NW, eggs and bacon, toast, and coffee. Unable to drink the coffee, he ordered a glass of milk, and that seemed to settle his stomach. He had a newspaper but did not read it.

What to do? Call his wife? He didn't want to appear desperate. She seemed pretty determined last night. Too soon to call. Give her some time. She would start to miss him, he hoped.

Marie and Carey kept separate bank accounts. They generally paid the rent out of his account at Riggs National Bank. January's rent had been paid early, meaning he had precious little money left. He could not stay in hotels indefinitely. He considered calling his mother in Bethesda. She'd jump at the chance to take him in and mother him again, which is why he quickly ruled that option out. He knew he'd see her soon, with Christmas just days away, but the thought of dealing with her questions and advice, and most of all, her disappointment, required more energy than

Ben could muster now.

The diner began to fill up, and the waitress asked again if there was anything more she could get him. He thought about asking for his dignity, or the last five years of his life back, but just said, "No, thanks." He paid the tab and returned to his hotel room. He stayed there for several hours, read the paper, sorted through his options. Around ten A.M., he headed out, walking nine blocks to Finkel's department store. In the sports department, he bought a sleeping bag, the kind outdoorsy people use while camping. Upstairs, in bedding, he bought a pillow.

He walked back to the Hotel Washington with his purchases slung over his shoulder. He asked the bellhop to summon a taxi while he went upstairs and gathered his things. He checked out at the front desk, then dragged his suitcase and bags to the street. He climbed into the cab.

"Third and C, please. Northwest."

BEN CAREY SPENT SATURDAY afternoon painting. He wondered how many other police sergeants across the country were painting their station house that afternoon. None was his guess, and certainly not without overtime pay.

Billy had done a good job, but there was plenty more to do. Carey started by sanding the sections of the porch where he had replaced the boards. Then he slopped on white paint with a roller, not too concerned about the quality of the job he was doing. After all, the building was to be torn down in a year; he just had to ensure that it didn't injure anyone before then. The wet paint stood out against the faded, peeling paint on the rest of the porch. He moved on to the second floor hallway. He opened all the windows while the paint dried.

He swept out an upstairs room, the circular turret room, and spread out his sleeping bag on the floor. The room looked cheerful now, bright and sunny, birds singing outside the open windows. For a moment, the heavy darkness lifted from his mind, as he stood at the window, surveying the city. He could see the dome of the Capitol in the distance, and the Supreme Court, and farther, off to the left, Union Station. Each building was obstructed somewhat, but he could make out the line of taxis waiting at the station through the trees. To his right, he could see the top of the Library of Congress building.

Later, after the sun had set, Carey stopped his work and took a walk around the neighborhood to see what there was to eat. Not much, was his conclusion—a Chinese takeout place, an Italian restaurant, a burger joint.

Carey crossed the street to Mac's Grill and went inside. He ate a burger and french fries at one of the small tables in front of the counter. There were only a few other people scattered around the dining area. In one of the booths against the front wall of windows was a man with his two children. The father was a stockily built man with a light brown complexion and a receding hairline. His daughter, a daintily dressed girl of about ten, sat opposite her father, and beside him was his son, a boy no more than three or four years old. The little boy kept looking over at Carey, sticking his tongue out and laughing, while his father ate, oblivious to the boy's foolishness. Carey smiled and made faces at him in turn, engaging in the silent conversation, to the boy's delight.

The little boy grabbed a french fry and pointed it at Carey, waving it around as if it were a sword. Carey picked up the straw beside his soda and pretended to stick it all the way into his ear— the only "magic trick" he knew. The boy looked on, eyes wide, as Carey pulled the straw from out of his nose and held it up with a small flourish. The little boy started giggling and fell backward onto his father's lap, as the man just shook his head and told the boy to sit up and "quit acting a fool."

The boy stared back at Carey, and Ben shot him a look of mock disapproval. The little boy smiled and returned to eating his french fries.

As a rookie cop, Carey had walked a beat near Logan Circle for most of one summer. Over time, he'd gotten to know most of the kids who hung out on the streets in front of the ornate town homes that now served as small apartments, dingy rooming houses, or worse. That first summer on the job had convinced him then—and continued to remind him—that he was meant to be a cop. Although he knew he could never share with his wife the darker aspects of his job, he realized he had never shared with her the good things, either. He regretted it now. Aside from the bronze statue of a soldier on horseback, all Marie had known of Logan Circle was hookers and dope fiends. For the most part, despite its rougher aspects, the people living there cared about the same things he and Marie did. Or at least the same things he did. He was no longer sure what Marie cared about. He wondered how well he had ever really known her.

Carey would never forget two little girls, sisters, who lived on Church Street. They teased him every morning on his rounds— testing him, he knew—and he always joked back with them and stopped now and again to hold one end of a jump rope or settle a debate. And when their older brother was caught shoplifting, it was Carey who intervened with the store owner and sat down with the boy and his mother. Carey and Marie had talked about having children when he first got back from Korea. But there had been little talk of that recently. And he wondered now if her withdrawal from him was simply a reflection of his own remoteness.

Carey had always been reserved. Even as a boy, he seldom spoke up if someone didn't talk to him first. But he was good at sports and possessed a quiet leadership other kids were drawn to. An avid reader of pulp comics, illustrated histories, and true crime, Ben displayed a brilliant memory for facts and figures at an early age. If school had interested him half as much as obscure battles and baseball, he'd have done well. But his mother and father took special pride in their son's gifts, despite his academic indifference. They knew, from having lost every argument with him since the age of twelve, that Ben was smart enough and he'd find his way.

His shyness around other grownups had remained with him as an adult, something Marie used to tease him about. But Carey had always been more at ease with children. Adults, he'd discovered, weren't always so easy. Kids didn't require clever conversation or extravagant gestures. A little attention was enough. Marie may have been childish at times, but she wasn't a kid.

A waitress interrupted Carey's thoughts with the offer of pie. He passed, noticing he was the last one in the place. He finished his meal, paid the bill, and resisted the temptation to find something else to do. The neighborhood was an island of boredom, with Capitol Hill and the H Street Corridor hardly a mile away. He knew of some ritzy nightclubs on Capitol Hill, and the mostly black area around H Street had some great jazz venues.

On the other side of town, Pennsylvania Avenue got more lively where it encountered 16th Street and Connecticut Avenue. The place was full of nice restaurants, where one could encounter Cabinet secretaries or Congressmen as they were wined and dined by lobbyists. Up Connecticut were some grand old movie houses, like the Uptown Theater.

But here, just three blocks from the Capitol, Carey was living in a graveyard of vacant lots and abandoned buildings.

●   ●   ●

IT BEGAN that Saturday night.

Carey sat at his desk on the first floor, examining the grant paperwork by the light of a desk lamp. A thick blanket of fog had settled over Washington. Looking out his office window, he could barely see the fireplug by the sidewalk. He returned his attention to his work and soon became lost in the grant, taking notes, scribbling diagrams, scratching his neck with his pencil. He would not have heard the sound of the front door opening were it not for the cold draft at his ankles. He looked up when he heard the footsteps on the stairs. Someone was in the house with him.

Carey shivered involuntarily. He rose and drew his service revolver. The footfalls ascended the steps, slowly, unevenly, but unmistakably human. The house looked as though it were vacant. Maybe someone was squatting here? He walked over to the closed door of his office and pressed his back against the wall next to it. He slowly turned the doorknob with his left hand. The door opened with a scraping sound and the footsteps stopped.

Carey held his breath. Through the crack in the door, he could see the base of the stairway, dimly lit by the hallway light, and he imagined he could hear the other person breathing. He must be near the top of the stairs.

Suddenly, the heavy footsteps resumed, at a quickened pace, along the upstairs hallway. Carey tiptoed to the base of the steps, his gun held with both hands, pointing at the top of the stairs. The footsteps stopped at the end of the hall, and entered the room where Carey had spread his sleeping bag. Carey raced up the remaining stairs and halted at the top.

The hallway was dim, illuminated only by the reflected light from downstairs. His hand searched the wall for a light switch but found none. Carey stood in the darkness, gun at his side, and contemplated his next move. He spoke, his voice a whisper at first.

"That you, Billy?" he asked meekly.

After a moment he spoke again, this time a commanding, bullying tone.

"This is the police! Come out of that room!"

Silence from the other end of the hall. Carey held his breath again and listened for the intruder. He took two steps forward, his right hand gripping the revolver, his left searching the wall for a light switch. He found it, and turned it on. The bare bulb, hanging on its wire six inches from the ceiling, was inexplicably swaying in the still air.

He took two more steps forward.

From the room at the end of the hall, a gray cat with a white nose emerged and walked nonchalantly toward him. How did he get in? Carey and the cat passed each other in the hall as Carey approached the room, gun held with both hands in a firing stance. The room was empty. There were no closets to check; the windows were shut. Could a ten-pound cat have sounded like a man climbing stairs? He checked each upstairs room and found them all empty. He holstered his pistol and went downstairs to find the cat sitting by the front door, apparently waiting to be let out. Carey unlocked and opened the door—it was still locked—and the cat trotted away into the foggy darkness. Just to be sure, Carey checked the entire downstairs for any unexpected visitors. He was undeniably alone in the house.

Another two hours of paperwork, and Carey was ready to sleep. He walked upstairs, down the dimly lit hallway, this time showing no hesitation. He left the hallway light burning and undressed in what had become his bedroom, suddenly aware that there were no curtains, that he could be seen from the street. He turned out the bedroom light and climbed into his sleeping bag. Enough light reflected from the hallway that he could see everything in the room: his suitcase on the floor; his gun, badge, watch, wallet, and keys on a chair he had borrowed from an empty office. After a few minutes staring wide-eyed around the room, he got out of his sleeping bag, turned out the hallway light, and climbed back into his bag.

SUNDAY BEGAN AS A beautiful, bright December day, cool and breezy, and at midmorning Carey walked to a Waffle Shop and ate a stack of pancakes with maple syrup. He watched the traffic through the windows, the shopkeeper sweeping the sidewalk, the smiling couples on the street. *Maybe I should call. Maybe she wants to talk, but can't find me….Maybe*—his thoughts turned to images of Marie waking up in the arms of another man, and he tried to wipe the picture from his mind. He rubbed his chin, which was thick with stubble.

Carey threw a dollar on the table and walked out.

Back at Substation C, he mixed himself a cocktail of scotch and cold tap water and drank it while reading the newspaper he had picked up on his walk. It occurred to him that Christmas was approaching—Wednesday, and he didn't have a gift for his wife. Considering the circumstances, it was hardly his most pressing concern. He thought of calling his mother, decided to put it off.

Carey looked at the empty glass in his hand. He was dirty and unshaven and felt as if unhappiness was being pumped into his veins from some unseen IV drip. It felt foreign to him, depression. Even in Korea, where he sat in the frozen mud holding an M1 carbine for months at a time, he had felt better than this.

In his suitcase, he found the soap and towel he had borrowed from the Hotel Washington, grabbed his straight razor and cream, and headed downstairs to the bathroom. The sink was ancient, much of the enamel gone, patches of rust eating away what was left. The hot water ran brown and smelly at first, eventually clearing and warming. He washed his face and rubbed the shaving cream into his beard. In the mirror, his eyes were baggy and his straight black hair was sticking up all over the place.

The razor cut him almost immediately, before traveling two inches. Carey cursed and concentrated on the task, finishing without another nick. He bent over the spigot and splashed water on his face and watched the shaving cream and blood run down the drain.

After washing up, he dressed in blue jeans and a dirty work shirt, poured another drink, and sat on the front steps. He watched the world go by for a few minutes until it occurred to him that it probably didn't look too good for a policeman to be sitting in front of his stationhouse drinking scotch on a Sunday afternoon. So he grabbed a flashlight and went to the basement and poked around there for a while, finding nothing much but old gardening implements and a child's toy cannon. It was at least eighty years old, a five-inch-long, Civil War–style brass cannon with an exquisitely carved wooden carriage. He took it into the kitchen and rinsed off decades of dust under the tap. He dried the toy with a rag.

Carey was at his desk again, aglow from the scotch, not knowing what to do with himself. He stared at the toy cannon, now a paperweight on his desk, and wondered about the child who once played with it—no doubt an old man, or one off to his great reward. The heating system cycled on now, and with it the incessant clanging, which Carey was beginning to find profoundly irritating. He mixed another drink. The rest of the day was a blur.

CHAPTER 5.

Wednesday, September 10, 1862

WHEN THE YOUNG SOLDIER AWOKE, she was holding his hand, as she always seemed to be. His pain was still great but no longer overwhelming. Looking around, he saw other men from his regiment, some awake, some sitting up. He looked into the face of the woman by his bed, a girl really, perhaps seventeen or eighteen. He tried to speak, but his mouth was dry, and, as if reading his mind, she brought a cup of water to his face. He drank, looking around the cavernous room, noticing—stained glass. He was in a church.

"My name is Louisa," she said. She was quite lovely, with strong brown eyes and a white cap atop her dark bundled hair. There was a silence of a few moments, and he managed a weak, "Mordechai."

She smiled, and he saw that she knew his name already.

"Where am I?"

"You're in Washington. You were hurt in Manassas."

"How long have I been here—is this a church?"

"Yes, Trinity. You've been here for over a week."

"My regiment—where is it?"

"I believe they're chasing the Rebels. Up Frederick way, I hear."

"I have to go. I have to rejoin—"

He attempted to sit up, but the pain—it felt as if something was tearing inside of him, and he lay back down, and he rested.

•   •   •

DAYS LATER, Mordechai reached beneath his cot and retrieved the pen, paper, and ink pot that Louisa had brought him the day before. He started where he had left off the previous evening, when the rose-colored sunlight streaming through the stained-glass windows became too faint for him to continue writing his letter home.

Dear Father,

So sorry I've not written for a couple weeks, but things have been quite hectic, and I've been somewhat indisposed for a while. The good news, Father, is that I'm coming home soon, just waiting for the paperwork to be finalized and such. I got hurt near the town of Manassas, Virginia, nothing that will keep me from the company, of course. I'm sure you read about it in the *Times*, a dreadful business, and not the first time we've had a spanking in that burg.

I've spent two weeks in a hospital, a church really, in Washington. They're quite short of hospital beds in this town, and the wounded are put anywhere that will take them. I've been treated quite well, like a king, and I've had a wonderful nurse who saw me through the worst of it. I'm going to be staying in a private home here in D.C. to finish my recovery. I don't have a name or address, even, but will send once I'm settled. Since the battle of South Mountain, up in Frederick, they've hundreds of new wounded to treat, and those of us from Manassas are either going back to their regiments, or going home.

And so it will be for me, Father, as soon as I'm well enough to travel. But time will tell. I will write you next

week and update you on all my adventures. Good-bye
for now,

Mordechai

The soldier put away his pen and corked his miniature ink pot.
He blew on the paper, hoping the ink would dry in the humid air
of the church, then folded the paper. He placed it in an envelope
and sealed it with a drop of honey from a small tin that Louisa
had given him for that purpose.

MORDECHAI'S FATHER HAD ARGUED vigorously against his
enlistment. "Wait for the draft," he had said, "don't rush to enlist
out of naïve patriotism." The son had said nothing, knowing that
if it came to the draft, his number would never be called, that his
father had too many prominent friends in the community. If he
pressed the issue, he suspected that his father would get him an
appointment to West Point. It wouldn't be hard; his father was in
the same Masonic Lodge as Congressman Delaplaine. A West
Point nomination could keep him out of the action well past the
end of the rebellion.

So one cold spring morning, with his father at the office and
the servants elsewhere, he had penned a brief note, packed a ruck-
sack, and headed for muster at the Battery dockyard.

That was six months ago now.

As Mordechai lay in his hospital bed, he marveled at how wonderful it felt to be dry and clean again—in spite of the pain in his
ribs. The months he had spent with his brigade had been filthy,
wet, and miserable. It was an uncomfortable existence for a young
man raised with luxuries few of his peers had enjoyed, but he was
not one to complain. He had not had a hot bath since the day he
left home, and hot meals had been a rarity, though hardly a treat.

The meat, not so bad during the cool days of spring, in summer tasted like it had been boiled with dirty socks. Despite these deprivations, the weeks of torturous training, the lousy food, and the paradoxical loneliness of a young man surrounded by thousands of his peers, he had found within himself something unexpected.

He could stand up for himself, he had discovered, although he usually came out on the losing side of the inevitable brawl that followed an insult or other provocation. He found out that he could be hit and survive the experience. And he could hit back, once knocking his opponent to the ground. After that, the name-calling, the mockery subsided, and he began to win a small measure of respect and even make some friends. He wondered what his father would have thought of that small, violent victory against the boy from Brooklyn.

Mostly, as Mordechai lay there in the cavernous Gothic church amid hundreds of other wounded soldiers, he thought about his last day in camp.

MORDECHAI HAD AWOKEN before reveille, roused by the growing daylight and muggy, still air. He climbed over his stirring mates, careful not to step on a blanket-covered limb as he moved, and untied the flaps of the A-frame tent. He remembered looking over the stillness of the camp—lines of tents that seemed to run forever across the gently rolling Maryland countryside.

He watched the sun fighting to break through the heavy cloud cover that had brought the previous night's rain. The effect was magnificent, each individual ray visible as if sent from heaven, the colors crisper and clearer than anything he had seen before. There was a word for that meteorological effect, he remembered. He tried to recall it from his schooling, as he put on his boots. The soldier was motionless now, laboring to retrieve an obscure term from his memory, unable to put one foot before the other until the word materialized. A full minute passed, and out of the corner of his eye he could see that the line was growing long at the mess wagon.

Crepuscular rays.

He smiled broadly, released now from his paralysis, and joined the others in line to receive the marching rations—coffee, hardtack, sugar, boiled beef, salt pork. They were all men from his brigade, the Tenth New York State Volunteers. His row, and the one before it and behind it, comprised Company G, "McChesney's Zouaves," as they called themselves after their commanding officer, Colonel Waters McChesney.

He was always glad to be out of that filthy, sodden tent, and was usually the first one off the canvas. Four men in that impossibly cramped space! The snoring, the smells, every possession damp and grimy.

The early-morning sunshine was overcome by dark storm clouds as they began their march. The rain fell until midafternoon. They marched and marched until Mordechai thought he would drop. And then, as it was nearing sunset, the column approached a substantial clearing, the halt flags went up, and the cavalry raced ahead to scout out the place. In the distance was a small farmhouse with a tin roof, little wisps of smoke escaping from its chimney. A few cattle grazed on the grass beside it. Mordechai could see some Union officers on horseback approaching the house, and could see a woman standing in its doorway. Mordechai imagined the conversation: *"We'll give you twenty dollars for six of your cows."* He could see the woman nodding, her hand out, well aware that the cattle would be taken whether or not she accepted the meager payment. They were in Rebel territory, and the Union foragers took what they needed to feed a hungry army.

One of Mordechai's tentmates, Al Mason, had a fire going already. The men were making coffee, always the first course of any meal in the army. Mordechai retrieved from his sack the tin can that served as his coffee cup and filled it with water from his canteen. He carefully removed the new coffee ration from his knapsack, and poured a little onto a cheesecloth square. He tied it shut with twine and plopped it into the water. The can had baling wire tied to holes in the rim, and he held the contraption above the fire with a stick for ten minutes until it resembled coffee. Now it was time to bargain.

"Who wants to trade for my salt pork?"

"Not again, Mort. Nobody wants your goddamn salt pork." This was as pleasant as Mason would be all day.

"You know I can't eat this shit. Will, I'll trade you for half the amount of your boiled beef."

"No thanks, Morty." Will Thomas was holding chunks of beef on a stick above the fire.

"How about your desiccated vegetables? You never eat them."

Will thought for a moment, and pulled a paper-wrapped package from his knapsack.

"Sure. Tastes like hay, anyhow." He tossed the dehydrated vegetables at Mordechai's feet, and he reciprocated with the half-pound package of pickled pork. Mordechai boiled the vegetable ration in an empty water-filled can over the fire and downed it as best he could. No matter what he did to it, it always retained the consistency of straw.

The fire burned low, and Mordechai took his cue from the other men. They were reluctantly eating their hardtack—thick flour crackers that formed the bulk of their rations. The soldiers had several nicknames for them, many not repeatable in the company of ladies—not that the men found themselves in such company often. The biscuits were flavorless but filling. Mordechai took two from his greatcoat pocket and was disgusted to find that something was already eating them. Maggots, worms, he did not know what. But with no idea when he might see his next ration, he was in no position to discard them, and hardtack was generally not tradable. So he made do. He plopped the crawling biscuits in the boiling hot coffee and set it aside.

"Yours too?" Mason asked, having already submerged his hardtack.

"Yeah. Army's idea of a joke, I guess," he replied. "I'll spoon 'em out when they float up. You want 'em? Like 'em boiled?"

Mason spit to his side and glowered at Mordechai. Both men had their spoons out and were scooping the motionless creatures from the surface of their coffee, then tossing them aside. The maggots, or weevils, or whatever they were, did not leave a discernable taste to the biscuits, and the coffee softened the hardtack up a bit and gave it some flavor. The men drank their coffee and ate their newly vacated hardtack with spoons.

Will Thomas had taken his hardtack and crumbled it into a tiny frying pan that already contained a chunk of hot, greasy salt pork. He held the pan over the fire until it was cooked just so. This "skillygalee" was considered the haute cuisine of U.S. Army cooking. He emptied the concoction onto his tin plate and set the frying pan aside, to be washed much, much later.

Mason spoke up. "I hear Jackson is near. We'll see fighting soon. Maybe tomorrow."

The men had nodded at this. The Tenth had seen battle already, two months prior at Gaines Mill. Eight of their men had been killed, and two officers. Forty had been wounded, but most of those men had recovered and rejoined the Volunteers. They were already veterans by then, had all been hardened in battle.

Mordechai sighed in his cot and looked up at the intricately carved ceiling. Most of them were dead now.

CHAPTER 6.

CAREY DID NOT SLEEP WELL Sunday evening. In the morning, he showered and shaved, stashed his suitcase and sleeping bag in the cellar, and set to work in his office.

Promptly at eight, he heard keys jangling at the front door. He trotted from his office and opened it. Arthur Wallace stood there, eyes wide with surprise, newspaper under one arm.

"Good morning, Captain," Carey said.

"Wasn't expecting anyone here. I mean—I forgot that you were..." He pushed past Carey and into his office. He shut the door. Carey returned to his desk.

Ten minutes later, his new employees began to arrive. Don Mullins was first, and Carey escorted him to his office and said that they would hold a meeting when the others showed up.

Norm was thoughtful enough to bring doughnuts, and at nine A.M. the four men gathered in Carey's office, dragging chairs from their own. Brian Kelsey's grimy percolator gurgled in the next room, producing an oily liquid even less potable than the stuff Carey had tasted in the army. Yet each man held a mug of its black, scalding coffee as they sat in his office.

Carey began his prepared speech. "I'd like to thank each of you for agreeing to join this project—uh, you don't have to raise your hand, Don, just talk."

"Shouldn't we invite the captain?" Mullins pointed toward Wallace's office.

"You're right, we should. Excuse me." Carey didn't want to be accused of excluding him at some later date. Nor did he think Wallace would want to participate. He stepped into the hallway, rapped lightly on Wallace's door, and pushed it open. The man was asleep, his chin pressed against his chest, arms at his sides. Carey pulled the door shut.

"He's not interested." Carey returned to his seat. "So, where was I? This project is really about buying equipment this department needs, using this federal grant you'll hear more about. Our job is to mitigate the paperwork—which is formidable—and find legitimate reasons to buy scout cars and—well, if we can think of anything else the MPD might need—buying it, too.

"I've put a mimeograph of the grant on your desks. Just get settled in, and spend the rest of the day reading the information packet. Start thinking, as you read, what kind of projects we can propose that would require radio-equipped squad cars, preferably Plymouth Furys with V-8 engines. Take notes and be prepared to discuss it tomorrow. And—until someone tells me otherwise, plain clothes are acceptable. No need to wear out your uniform sitting around here."

The men returned to their offices, some carrying extra doughnuts.

Toward lunchtime, he heard Wallace rustling about in his office, and knocked softly on his door.

"Come in."

"Hi, Captain. Just checking in."

Wallace glared, set down his newspaper, and used his foot to nudge the kerosene heater farther behind his desk.

Carey shut the door behind him. "You've been in this building for what? Two years?"

"Eighteen months. Nineteen."

"Have there been any people, derelicts maybe, who have been

sleeping here, call it home?"

"No."

"When you were in here all those months, did you ever hear the front door slam? Footsteps going up the stairs? Stuff like that?"

Wallace paused, and his pinkish eyes opened wider. "Uh, no. Nothing like that."

Carey could see that he had Wallace's attention. "Ever spend any time in the rest of the house?"

"Why all the questions? You performing an investigation, Sergeant?" His defenses had clicked on.

"No, sir. Just curious. Thanks for talking with me." Carey shut the door behind him.

AROUND ELEVEN, Carey headed out for lunch and then took a bus uptown.

The Chancery looked no different. He rode the one working elevator to the seventh floor and checked to see if anyone was in the hallway before getting out. He slid his key noiselessly into the lock, and the tumblers made tiny clicking sounds. Marie had not changed the locks.

He stepped back, wondering if there was any possibility she were home. Why would she stay home from work?

He rapped softly on the door, three times, and thought about trying to imitate the voice of the superintendent. Jimmy was a black guy, about sixty, with a raspy blues-singer's growl that Carey could not approximate. The thought was absurd, and if she had opened the door afterward, he would look like a fool. He turned the doorknob.

The apartment was spotless, as he knew it would be. He examined the living room, noted the afghan draped over the sofa, its corners aligned perfectly with the cushions. In the kitchen, every dish was clean except a butter knife in the sink. The door to the bedroom was ajar, and he entered.

The bed was neatly made, its baby-blue patchwork bedspread carefully turned under and over the pillows for the viewing pleasure of God knows who. He examined the room critically. Not a sock out of place; he expected nothing less. He entered the bathroom.

The toilet seat was up. This by itself was not alarming. He knew her to be quite neurotic about keeping the toilet clean. Indeed, the water inside still professed soapy bubbles and, when examined, the toilet brush was wet to the touch.

Carey rinsed his hands under the tap. He examined the assortment of spotless towels on the rack, arranged as if she were expecting guests at any moment. Over the shower curtain rod, he found the towel she had used after her shower a few hours earlier and dried his hands on that.

He examined the tiny, metal trash can beside the toilet. He found, among the used dental floss and razor blades, a folded square of tissue that had been placed atop a wound, and bore a tiny round blood stain.

Like a man would use to stanch the flow of blood from a shaving cut. Or, like a woman might use to do the same thing.

He placed the trash can back behind the toilet and opened the medicine cabinet. There was the usual assortment of balms and bandages, and there was a pill bottle. The department physician had prescribed him Seconal when he had started working night shift some months back; he had no trouble staying awake all night, but getting to sleep in midmorning had proved difficult. After the first few days, he had not needed them; twenty-five remained in the bottle. He put the bottle in his coat pocket and closed the cabinet.

In the bedroom, he opened the closet. The top shelf held some items that Marie had not thought to pack when she kicked him out. There was a stack of pictures from Korea in a cellophane wrapper. He opened it and flipped through the photos. There was Kim, the orphan boy who lived in his tent and did the laundry for the five soldiers bunked there, in exchange for food. A grainy shot of Keith, the guy in the next bunk, who was killed when he stepped on a mine. *One of our own mines.* A picture of Ed, another bunkmate, whose battlefield cowardice nearly got Carey killed. He placed the photos back in the cellophane and put them back on the shelf. He stretched his arm farther back and found the tiny Japanese-made camera, hidden away beyond the line of sight. He pocketed it and shut the closet door. He spent a few moments trying to decide whether the bathroom door had been closed, open, or somewhere in between. He decided on leaving it ajar, and quietly left the apartment.

CAREY WAS DETERMINED not to be spooked by his overactive imagination that evening. He would stay in Substation C until Marie took him back or, depending on how long that took, until he saved enough for a down payment on his own apartment. It was probably wrong, somehow, against the rules of conduct for an officer, and he wondered what regulation he might be breaking, but couldn't imagine such a document existed. "No police officer shall reside in his substation." He just couldn't see it.

Dinner was takeout spaghetti and meatballs from an Italian restaurant on Capitol Hill. The owner, an effusively cheerful man with distant ties to the Philly mob, would never take his money because he knew Carey was a policeman. Carey tried not to take advantage of this but patronized the joint monthly because the food was good. After dinner, he stopped by a People's Drug for film, flashbulbs, and batteries.

Back at Substation C, he sat behind his desk and stared past his open door to the stairway, dimly lit by the overhanging bulb. From his coat, he took the bag from the drugstore, the camera, and the pill bottle. He placed the pills in his desk drawer, from which a pint of bourbon beckoned, but he pushed the drawer shut. He loaded the camera with its batteries and film, and examined the flashbulb. It was actually three flashbulbs in one, mounted vertically, and with a pair of glass terminals at the bottom. He pushed the delicate terminals into the rubber aperture of the camera and brought it to his face.

Through the tiny viewfinder, the stairs appeared distant. He pushed the shutter release, and the flash discharged. From beneath the camera, he extended a tiny metal arm and advanced the film to the next frame. He took the camera and the *Washington Post* he had read during dinner and went upstairs to his new bedroom. He disrobed and put his wallet, watch, keys, camera, and service revolver on the chair. Tucked into his sleeping bag, he read a few paragraphs about the test-firing of a military atomic plant to be used for electricity production. *Why would anyone think it was a good idea to fire up one of those atomic piles over here?* He lay his head down as he remembered his week stationed in Nagasaki in 1951, a city so utterly devastated that entire families had become nothing more than shadows against a bridge siding — one moment alive, a child's arm held out against the flash...and the next minute, just this...image. They were no more. He hadn't taken that photo with his little camera.

He wondered if people still left flowers at those little shrines, the images of their ancestors, or whether the authorities had since removed the bridge edifices and subway cars that held those strange, confused, disjointed traces of those who had gone before and now had only their shadows to tell their stories. Not every such place could remain a shrine, he knew, and most of them were probably underneath new office towers now.

Thump. Carey's eyes fluttered and opened. He did not know where he was at first, a creepy sensation that he experienced each time he awoke in this room. *Thump.* He rolled over and propped himself up on his elbows. He heard a scraping sound now, as if something heavy and metallic were being dragged across the wooden stairs. He could hear movement on the stairs now, very soft, but very distinct nevertheless. The more awake he became, the softer the sounds became, until he wondered if he was hearing anything at all. He was sitting up in his sleeping bag now, the bright moonlight through the window illuminating the camera on the chair. He took it and held it in his lap.

The scraping started again, followed this time by a *thunk!* Carey shivered, his heart beating rapidly now. *Thump-thump-thump-thump-thump!* They were footsteps, running up the stairs, getting closer, then stopping at the top. Silence.

With a creak, the door opened a few inches. Carey propelled his body backward against the wall under the window, put the camera to his eye, and pressed the shutter release. The bulb popped with a high-pitched whine, a screech Ben thought may have been merely in his head, and the door stopped moving.

Carey became aware of a ringing in his ears, like a television warming up, as he stared at the doorway. His hands were trembling as he wound the little metal bar to advance the film. In the dark hallway, he thought he could see motion amidst the shadows through the crack in the door. Whispers seemed to emanate from behind it. He sat up, raised the camera, and fired again.

But that was the end of it. After a few minutes, he turned on the light and opened the door wide with his toe. He donned his shirt and trousers. The hallway was empty. In a moment, he had turned on every light in the house. At his desk downstairs, he poured himself an eye-opener of scotch. He placed the uncorked bottle next to his paperweight cannon.

No way he was going back up there tonight. He wished he had brought his sleeping bag with him downstairs. He was freezing, and he walked over to the radiator to make sure heat was coming out. There was a sharp rap at the front door, and Carey jumped a foot in the air.

He peeked through his office window to see two young officers standing at the front step, whispering to each other. He did not recognize them. He walked to the front door and opened it.

"Good evening, sir, sorry to bother you, but we saw you were awake and we were concerned." The one on the left spoke first, the shorter one.

"Why?" Carey tried to say, but the word disappeared into a hoarse cough.

"Well, sir, we were walking by on our beat. We heard a scream," the officer on the right said.

Carey stared blankly at them.

"Do you mind if we come in, sir? We're concerned for the safety of the occupants of this house."

"There are no other occupants. I'm the only one here," Carey replied, although he had already decided to let them in. They clearly had no idea it was a substation.

"Well, sir, that's not true, I saw a little boy looking out the upstairs window as we came to the front door just now. We just want to make sure he's all right. Can we come in?"

Bewildered, eyes wide, Carey stepped aside to let the men in. When the door was closed, Carey said, "Officers, I'm Sergeant Carey of the planning unit. My identification and service revolver are on a chair upstairs. In the room opposite the top of the stairs." He saluted. The men did not reciprocate.

"You left your gun in the room with a child? Are you nuts, *Sergeant* Carey?" The taller officer motioned for his partner to check out the upstairs.

"There is no child, officer. I'm here alone."

"Who did I see, then?"

"I don't know." Carey tucked in his shirt, finding something to do with his tremulous hands.

Carey and the officer began a staring contest, which lasted until the other officer returned to the base of the stairs. In his hands were Carey's badge and his departmental identification. The officers studied Carey's picture and raised their heads in unison to examine his face beneath the entranceway lamp.

"There's nobody upstairs, Jim. I'll check out the rest of the house." He disappeared down the hallway toward the bathroom. Carey and Officer Jim resumed their staring contest, and Carey noticed that Jim was starting to look distinctly uncomfortable. In a moment, the other man returned and shrugged. It was time to take control of the situation.

"Let me tell you what will happen now, officers. I know you as badge number 5991 and badge number 6025. That is because you never identified yourselves to me. That is a procedural violation." Carey was just getting started.

"I invite you in, tell you I have a gun, and you don't even perform a *cursory* pat-down. You endangered your life and your partner's."

The officers were staring at their shoes now.

"And lastly, as soon as you became aware I was a superior officer, you should have offered me a salute." Carey was bluffing here. Sergeants don't usually get saluted. But he had them where he wanted them. "Tell you what, Officer 5991 and Officer 6025. Let's just pretend this whole incident never happened. You leave it off your shift report, and I won't call Inspector Price in the morning."

The men stood there wordlessly, and the shorter one, Officer

6025, clicked his heels and saluted. Jim ignored him and walked past Carey in silence. Carey had the door open for him already. Officer 6025 returned to Carey his badge and ID, and offered a slight smile and shrug on his way out the door.

Carey sat on the front steps, his raincoat drawn over his shoulders, and tried to make sense of what had happened.

A little boy? He saw a little boy in the window?

He shivered in the cold.

IT WAS CHRISTMAS EVE and business as usual. He didn't expect much effort from his team today, and he wasn't disappointed. Wallace didn't bother to show up, not that it mattered.

Around lunchtime, his phone rang. It was Marie.

"How have you been?" she asked.

"Fine." His voice was flat, unemotional. He didn't want to give away how much he wanted to come home.

"I haven't heard from you. I was getting worried. I called the precinct house, but they gave me this number."

"You didn't want to hear from me. That was the whole point, I thought."

"No….I don't know, but—it's been four days, and I thought—"

"Thought what? You throw your husband out on the street five days before Christmas, no explanation, no nothing, and you're wondering why I haven't called? Christ."

"Don't talk to me like that, Ben," Marie said, a little defensively. "Please don't pretend that things have been fine with us. You know they haven't been for some time."

"So you couldn't talk to me about it?"

"Every time I tried," she said, "you would either get real quiet or blow up."

"I don't remember it like that…" He trailed off, knowing there

was some truth to what she was saying.

"I just needed some time alone to think, to figure out what I want," she said.

"Oh, wonderful..." Marie could hear Ben slam the palm of his hand down on his desk in frustration. "So?" he asked.

"So *what?*"

"Have you figured it out?"

"Give me some time, Ben," said Marie. His response was an exasperated sigh. "You know," she said, "I still care about you. I'm not doing this to hurt you. You do know that, don't you?"

Ben thought for a moment. "I guess."

"I think we should talk after the holidays," she said. "After we've both had a chance to be by ourselves for a while."

"Whatever you want, Marie."

"Take care of yourself, Ben." She added, "Merry Christmas."

"Yeah," he said and hung up, immediately regretting it. He wanted to tell her that he still loved her, that he wanted to make it work, or at least return the "Merry Christmas," but instead he had done exactly what she'd complained about. He'd clammed up and went silent.

He waited for the phone to ring again, but it did not.

Little was accomplished that afternoon. The men took long lunches and came back to the office bearing gift-wrapped packages. For some of them, it would be the first Christmas ever spent with their families instead of walking a beat. They were looking forward to this, Carey knew. Norm had said that last year he woke his children before his shift—when it was still dark—to open their gifts from Santa.

At five P.M. the men filed out, each wishing Carey a happy holiday with a warm smile. Norm was the last to leave, and pulled from his battered leather briefcase a gift-wrapped box.

Carey was taken aback. He had never received a gift from

another man before, except his father. "You shouldn't have, Norm. I don't have anything for you."

"I don't care. I just want you to have a merry Christmas, and I hope this helps."

He looked knowingly into Carey's eyes, shook his hand, and pulled the door shut behind him. Carey shook the box. A bottle.

With the station house again empty, Carey set off to find a restaurant open on Christmas Eve and found himself in China-town. The area had changed a great deal since he was a kid. At that time, it was mostly a Jewish neighborhood, and he remembered helping his father on his carpentry contracts there. Ben and his father had helped build two of the townhouses on H Street, and another on 6th. In the late 1930s, the Chinese who lived on Capi-tol Hill began quietly buying up the properties around 7th and H Streets NW. When the federal government announced it was asserting eminent domain and razing the neighborhood just west of the Capitol to build the U.S. Court House, it destroyed many ethnic enclaves. Little Italy, Little Athens, they all disappeared. But not the Chinese. They packed up their belongings and moved, in an automobile caravan, into their new neighborhood.

The neon OPEN sign of The Golden Dragon was the first one Carey encountered on his walk, so he went in and ordered lo mein and a Coke. Unable to eat alone without something to read, he took a Chinese-language newspaper from a vacant table and made a game of figuring out what the picture captions were say-ing. When it arrived, he ate half the food and left with the rest in a wax-paper carton ensconced in a paper bag.

On the cold, rainy walk back to the substation, Carey passed two young Chinese men, both wearing yellow slickers. The men eyed him warily, and Carey realized they were "community activists," as the civilian security force called itself. The Chinese had been policing their neighborhood like this for decades, and in his plain clothes, Carey realized he was seen as a suspicious interloper.

Sergeant Kelsey had worked this neighborhood in the early '40s, and had once told Carey a story over coffee and doughnuts. Mr. Lee, the neighborhood patriarch, had been attacked and robbed while out for a walk with his dogs. His wallet, which contained only pictures of his grandchildren, was taken, but the old man died a day later. The community was outraged. Two detectives were put on the case, and within a few days they had identified a suspect, a petty thief who lived in the neighborhood just north of Chinatown.

Shortly after, one of the detectives was visited by two elderly Chinese gentlemen, who wanted to know what the police were doing about the murder. He told them they were looking for a suspect, whose mug shot happened to be on his desk at that moment. The detective showed them the picture. The men thanked him and left. The detectives never found their suspect, as the thug was never seen again. The Chinese had been protecting their own, enforcing their own justice, and on this damp evening, Ben knew that these two fellows in the yellow raincoats were his escort out of Chinatown.

The rain was blowing harder now, and the two Chinese men had stopped and were staring in his direction. He came within a block of his substation and checked his back, and saw that the men were gone. Once inside, he opened the present from Norm.

BY MIDNIGHT, he had become convinced that Old Grand Dad was the greatest bourbon ever distilled, and considered sitting before Brian's typewriter and pounding out a thank-you note to Norm, or perhaps a complimentary letter to the distillery, but decided it would be wise to take a nap first, since he was suddenly groggy, it having been a long day.

He lay in his bag, resting his eyes, but could not sleep. He had a feeling of unease in this house, like he was being watched, and even the numbing effects of good booze could not overcome this senseless notion. He thought of the leftover Chinese food sitting in the kitchen, without benefit of refrigeration, but of course it was cold down there anyway—*have to remember to turn up the heat before I freeze to death up here, he thought—and maybe I should call Marie tomorrow. Maybe I should call her right now, see who answers the phone. Maybe I should put on my pants and go over and see for myself who keeps company with my wife nowadays.*

No, that would be dumb. Carey was not a violent drunk, just the quiet type.

His stomach was upset, and he could not imagine sleeping or taking another drink without food in his belly. In his underwear, he wandered downstairs to the kitchen, greeted by that damn gray cat who came and went as he pleased without ever needing doors opened or closed for him. From the Chinese food carton, he pulled out a small piece of chicken and threw it to the floor. The animal munched it gratefully and waited for another. Carey ate the cold noodles with his fingers, the cat staring at him all the while, and saved the last morsel of protein for the animal, who sensed the party was over after the paper sack went into the trash. The cat trotted off to the dark of the house. Carey rinsed his fingers in the sink.

Carey spent some time in his office, staring at the bottle of Old Grand Dad, wondering why the hell he did not feel tired after working a full day and drinking half a bottle of booze. His feet were cold, but his stomach was still too distressed to consider another drink, and the thought of reclining made him wonder if he might upchuck in the bag.

Carey opened his desk drawer and took out the bottle of Seconal. He read the label. *Take one or two as needed for sleep.* Well, he needed sleep, that was for sure, but with a belly full of bourbon and greasy food, he opted for a single red capsule, which he popped into his mouth. The pill bottle went back in the drawer. He occupied himself for a few minutes reading work-related items, hoping the pill would kick in before his feet froze to the metal legs of his swivel chair, and then he would be able to climb into the warmth of his sleeping bag without that damn creepy feeling of being watched, or the fear of vomiting Chinese food across the floor.

He was less than halfway through version three of a grant proposal when his vision went double. Time for bed. He stumbled his way toward his office door, suddenly needing to grab doorjambs for support, and from there he lurched toward the stairwell, the gray cat in the hallway eyeing him warily. He held the banister tightly and pulled his way up the stairs. He staggered clumsily toward his bedroom and literally fell into the sleeping bag, sure at last he would get a sound night's sleep, except he left the bedroom door open, so that cat could get in…

And there was the sound of the front door slamming.

He is in the hospital again. He tries to sit up, tries to breathe, tries to do anything but lie on that cot. He lies there helpless. Now he hears footsteps coming from the stairs below. Where am I? It hurts to breathe, as if the wind had been knocked out of him. A bearded, dirty-looking man with piercing brown eyes and an old western black hat is standing in the doorway, his hands in the pockets of his greatcoat—Why can't I sit up? Say something, damn it! The man with the dark hat grins, his mouth an assembly of filthy and rotten tooth shards, and just stares at Carey.

Carey was bolt upright now, his T-shirt completely soaked with sweat. The room was dark and cold and he was alone. He could remember bits and pieces of the dream, but they were slipping away as he wiped the sleep from his eyes. The bottle of Old Grand Dad was on the floor by his feet, and this time he dispensed with the glass and the tap water and took his drink directly from the bottle. It did not take long before he was unconscious again.

CAREY AWOKE IN THE downstairs bathroom, curled around the toilet. There was vomit on the floor, and on his shirt, and in the kitchen. A wave of nausea overcame him, and he dry-heaved into the toilet bowl.

He got to his knees, pulled a handful of toilet paper off the roll, and attempted to clean up the filth from the floor. He flushed the stinking wad, crawled out into the kitchen, and finished mopping up there. When he tried to stand, black spots surrounded him, a sea of confusion and numbness, and then the pounding started in his head, the pain almost unbearable. He stumbled back into the bathroom and stood, grasping the sink until he felt steady, pulled off his underclothes, and climbed into the tub. The shower spigot gurgled and hissed and finally emitted freezing, rusty water.

Merry Christmas, Ben Carey.

The water warmed eventually, and when it was turned off, he was convulsed with shivering. Weakness overcame him again, and he sank to his knees in the tub with his towel around his shoulders. He tried to dry himself in this position, but his shivering was unstoppable. He contemplated running a bath, but realized he had no plug for the tub. So he stood, dried his shaking body as best he could, and ran naked toward his sleeping bag, thinking what a bad idea it had been to combine barbiturates with booze. He was lucky to be alive.

An hour or so later, when his appetite returned, he crawled out of his bag, put on underwear and a T-shirt, and went downstairs to find something to eat. He had thought to buy some white bread and grape jelly, and he consumed them at his desk, knowing he wouldn't find the Waffle Shop—or anything else—open on Christmas Day. Maybe the Chinese place would be open for dinner, he thought; it was just another business day for them.

For that matter, maybe he could find a Chinese laundry open today. He was running low on clean clothes—in fact, he had just put on his last pair of clean boxers, and his last T-shirt as well. His feet were freezing, and he was on his way upstairs to find socks when he noticed that Arthur Wallace's door was ajar and his light was on.

Carey glanced at his watch—eight A.M. exactly—why would he come to work on Christmas Day? He hadn't heard Wallace come in. *He's going to see me in my underwear and know I'm living here.* He peeked through the crack in the door. The captain was sitting at his desk, in uniform, staring straight at Carey, a slight smile gracing his face. Carey pushed the door open a little more.

"Hello, Captain. Merry Christmas. I wasn't expecting you…" he looked down at his undershirt and boxers "…obviously."

Wallace did not answer, but instead his smile became wider, a grin almost, which looked odd, because it occurred to Carey that he had never seen this man smile. Wallace looked good—his skin had some color for once, and his face looked less puffy, less sickly. His uniform seemed freshly pressed. Carey wondered if he was losing weight.

"Captain, is everything all right?"

Again Wallace did not answer, but took a leisurely drag from his cigarette, tapping his fingers on the cover of his notebook. He looked up at Carey with wide, menacing eyes. "You shouldn't be here," is all he said.

Carey could hear his phone ringing.

"Um…excuse me, Cap," he stammered.

Carey walked back to his office and picked up the phone. "Carey."

"Ben." It was Marie. "Norm came over to see you. I'll put him on." He could hear the phone being handed off.

"Ben. Norm. Sorry about this, I expected you'd be home this morning when I stopped by. Didn't think you were going to work today."

"What's going on, Norm, why aren't you home with your family opening presents?"

"Kids are still asleep. Ben, I got a call from Inspector Price. Middle of the night."

"What did he want?"

"It's about Captain Wallace. He killed himself last night. Shot himself in the head. In his bathtub. The gunshot woke the neighbors in the next apartment. They called it in."

What the hell? Carey began walking toward his office door. Norm kept talking. "They wanted me to identify the body. I checked the place out. No sign of forced entry, no sign he had any help." Carey was in the hallway now, the phone cord taught. As he reached the steps, the phone slid off his desk and crashed to the floor. "What was that?" Norm asked. "Ben, are you still there?"

He stood at Wallace's office door and stared at the empty chair. He could still smell the smoke from Wallace's cigarette.

PART II

CHAPTER 7.

Baltimore and Ohio Railroad Station
Wednesday, September 17, 1862

UPON STEPPING OFF THE TRAIN, the man from New York was
struck by how much the dingy little town had changed since his
last visit some four years earlier. The population seemed to have
doubled; men in uniform were everywhere. Some of the soldiers
were purposeful in their stride; others seemed aimless and forlorn,
bedraggled, lost. Women walked about unaccompanied, into and
out of office buildings. Nevertheless, some things had not
changed. Many roads were dirt, and with the recent rains, they
were mud. Of course, he knew that the adjacent towns of Georgetown and Alexandria boasted cobblestone streets, as they had for
a hundred years.

Aaron Hilldrup didn't like Washington. He was a New York
man, born and bred, and couldn't imagine living anywhere else.
Yet he was intrigued by this visit. Unlike four years ago, the city
smelled of excitement. Having Rebel armies within a hundred
miles certainly helped, but that wasn't the whole reason. It had
the feeling of a boomtown, a town with a big future, and he was
determined, upon his return to the City, to talk to his boss about
expansion into the District. Of course it would have to wait until
the rebellion was put down, but that shouldn't take but a few more
months.

And it would have to wait until his mission was complete.

He had been given a substantial advance, and found the

temptation to patronize a first-rate hotel hard to resist. He had first inquired at the Saint Charles, on B Street, but found the rates too high for his liking. As he left the hotel, he became aware that he was being watched, and turned a complete circle on the street, without seeing anyone looking his way. Then he heard a cough, looked down at the sidewalk, his eyes running up to the side of the building, and discovered that he *was* being watched. Through a tiny grate, several black faces peered at him from almost ground level. It was a slave pen, a convenience for the guests of the hotel.

This was peculiar, for he had read in the *Times* that Lincoln had freed all slaves within the District of Columbia last April. He pondered this as he walked along Pennsylvania Avenue, his eye now searching for an eating establishment of apparent repute, a judgment to be made by the quality of the signage. He entered a place called McDoules on 4th Street, as it seemed to be doing a lively business.

The tavern was a seat-yourself affair, somewhat rough around the edges, but he could not ignore the wonderful smells that were coming from the kitchen, so he took a seat at the bar. His initial attempts to catch the eye of the barkeep were futile, and he eventually found it necessary to tug at the barkeep's sleeve as he passed by. The burly man handed over a penciled listing of the day's meal choices.

Always partial to beef, he ate his stew and the thick, dark bread and mentioned to the barkeep his experience on the street near the Saint Charles Hotel. The barkeep explained that tobacco farmers from Maryland, when visiting the District on business, stayed at the Saint Charles to take advantage of this amenity. Slavery still remained in several border states in the Union, and seeing the men locked up like animals had offended the visitor's Northern sensibilities. But he was not surprised. He was in the South now.

Hilldrup left the tavern around three P.M., a suitcase in each hand, in search of a place to bed down for the night that would meet his eminently reasonable requirements. He stopped next at the National Hotel, at 6th Street and Pennsylvania Avenue. He found the prices acceptable, but the establishment itself was clearly past its prime, and evidently devoid of customers. The barkeep had suggested this place, but hinted that it did little business since its owners were well-known Confederate sympathizers.

Willard's Hotel, at 14th and Pennsylvania, was more to his liking. In the lobby, important-looking men ambled about with cigars in hand, army officers chatted up ladies in petticoats, and the smell of roasted meat wafted throughout the first floor. Fatigued after walking several miles, he spent ten minutes waiting in line at the front desk, only to be told that no rooms were available. Not surprisingly, after slipping the clerk a folded wad of bills, a vacant room was found, and by seven P.M. he was dining on a sumptuous meal of beef, potatoes, and greens, in the bustling and elegantly appointed dining room. In all, the experience compared favorably to a well-spent evening in the City.

After his meal, he reclined in a lush, leather armchair in the parlor to smoke his meerschaum pipe, and struck up a conversation with a young lieutenant, a Washington native who proved an invaluable source of information about the town. Over several glasses of brandy, he learned that Washington had several haberdashers, and purveyors of ladies and children's clothing, and that housewares could be found in several places, but nowhere could a customer purchase all of these things under one roof. It seemed an ideal town for expansion. Upon his return to his room, he took copious notes, quite certain that Mr. Brandon would appreciate the effort.

At the tiny desk in his room, Hilldrup remembered his true mission, and it disturbed him. Strictly a business transaction, he realized, but nevertheless, it was an unsavory business, and one in which he had, fortunately, little experience. Mr. Brandon had promised him that nothing like this would ever be required of him again, and that a promotion—assistant vice president?—would surely follow the discreet resolution of this distasteful matter.

The man from New York rubbed his face with his hands and felt the anxiety well up within him. Twenty-two years he had been with the company—most of it on the sales floor—and he was not going to let one unpleasant assignment derail his ambitions. Since his mother had died (God rest her soul) the company had been his only family, and Brandon like a favorite uncle. Brandon had taken him under his wing years ago, while the other guy—the Jew—had never given him the time of day. Rumor had it that Finkel had consumption and was already half-dead. This leant a certain urgency to his mission, he knew.

His notebook lay before him, and he began to write:

> 1—Find the kid. Pretend to be a relative. Army camp?
> Who runs the hospitals?

Remembering a building he had passed on his walk through the city, he wrote:

> Sanitary Commission?
> 2—Hire someone. Where to find this person? Brothels?
> Gambling dens?

He folded his notebook, undressed, and put on his silk pajamas. On his pillow, he found Belgian chocolates. This made him smile.

From his bag, he removed the various powders and potions prescribed to him, and proceeded to stir a spoonful of each into a glass of water until it was a viscous goo. Into the mix he poured a hearty dose of Dr. Wilson's Sleeping Tonic, and gulped the entire concoction down. It tasted grainy and bitter, and he ate the chocolate to kill the taste of the laudanum. Sleep came quickly.

IN THE MORNING, Aaron Hilldrup hired a carriage. He stated his destination—the Sanitary Commission—to the driver, and the two agreed upon a price. They rode a few blocks without speaking.

"Looks like it's going to be a fine day," the passenger said, breaking the silence.

"I reckon. The skies are clear. Where ya from?" The driver's accent betrayed his Appalachian roots.

"Philadelphia." Hilldrup wasn't sure why he lied.

"Ah never been there. Hear it's nice."

"Yes, it is. Uh…let me ask you something. I'm new to this town. Where might a gentleman find a little…company for the night?"

The driver did not miss a beat. "Well, that depends, see. If you're partial to darker ladies, you'd just step out of Willard's and walk south, right down 14th Street. Block or two. Be careful, though. They call that part of town 'Murder Bay' for good reason."

"I see."

"If you like 'em lighter, go 'bout three blocks north of the train station. Lot of Irish folk over that area; people know it as 'Swampoodle.' You can find a poker game there, too. Any time of the day or night. They not likely to let you walk away a winner, though." He laughed.

The carriage stopped, and the passenger paid the driver nearly twice what had been agreed upon. Smiles were exchanged; the driver whipped his horses and was gone.

The Home Lodge of the Sanitary Commission was a cluster

of small, cottage-like buildings, with a pillared, four-story building at the southern end, all surrounded by a white picket fence. As the carriage grew distant, he could hear men talking through the open windows of the larger structure and could smell food cooking on a charcoal grill somewhere on the grounds—pork chops, he decided. He walked past a wretched old horse tied to a hitching post and into the first cottage. The tiny office looked recently occupied—the desk was covered with papers and a cup of tea that was warm to the touch—so he sat and waited, and after a moment, became aware of footsteps coming from the direction of the large building. He removed his bowler and placed it in his lap.

A woman entered, thick, gray, and somewhat startled to see a visitor. He stood, she looked him over and immediately launched into a well-rehearsed diatribe. "I'm sorry, we don't have any medicinal supplies. You'll have to—"

"I'm not here for supplies. I'm looking for my nephew."

"Oh. I'm sorry. I thought you were….Where is your nephew?" She took her seat behind the small desk.

"I was hoping you could tell me how to find him. I know only that he was injured during the last Battle of Manassas. And that he'll be going home. I've come to take him."

"Sir, we do not have patient listings for every hospital in the city. You'll have to ask the military authorities—"

"I believe he's been discharged from the hospital, and may be staying in a private home, or perhaps one of your lodges. Any assistance you could render would be greatly rewarded, I can assure you."

Her eyebrows rose at this, and he became concerned that she would take offense. He spoke again quickly. "He said in his letter that the hospital was a converted church, but he wasn't sure where. Does that help?" The Jew had let this last detail slip out during a meeting with the managers, while on another of the semi-coherent ramblings he had become prone to as his health declined.

The matronly woman was frowning now. "It's very odd that he didn't know the name of the church. All he had to do was ask a nurse. Do you have the letter with you?"

His mouth fell open while he searched for an excuse. "No, I left it with his mother. It's all she has of him..."

She took a scrap of paper and scribbled half a dozen words on it. With a weary smile, she handed the paper to him. "This is a list of the churches in the city that are being used as hospitals. This is all I can do for you. Good day."

"God bless. Thank you, madam. Good day." He tucked the paper into his vest pocket, put on his hat, and walked out.

THERE WERE SIX CHURCHES on the list, but the kind woman had not written locations for any of them. Hilldrup asked a passerby on the street where Epiphany Church was—it being the first name on the list—and the elderly gentleman told him to walk down Pennsylvania until he came to 13th Street and then turn right. He began walking, looking over his shoulder occasionally, hoping to find a cab for hire. The late-summer sun was beating down, making him feel somewhat sticky. He removed his suit coat and carried it over his arm. His empty stomach rumbled.

By the time he reached the church, his collar was unbuttoned and his shirt damp with sweat. He stood before the church, dabbing at his face and neck with a kerchief. Epiphany was an imposing structure, with a square belfry that seemed to rise six stories or more. Parked outside was an ambulance, its horses searching for grass to eat on the barren dirt of G Street. An army supply carriage, guarded by one sleepy-looking private, was behind the ambulance.

He ascended the steps and walked through the open doors. Once inside he hesitated, unsure of what he was seeing. Then he understood. The pews were hidden under a wooden deck. Wounded soldiers were placed on this planking, which raised them to waist level, where they could be cared for by nurses who didn't have to kneel. The nurses, many of them black women, walked along the aisles carrying food, blankets, and medicine to their charges.

The man from New York removed his hat and pressed himself against the wall, trying to look inconspicuous. Then he noticed that several soldiers were receiving visitors, and decided that he didn't look out of place after all. Although he knew his quarry wasn't in the room, he couldn't help examining the faces of the wounded soldiers as he walked past. One man, a deathly gray color, was mumbling to himself, his eyes squeezed tightly shut. The soldier in the next berth was lying on his side, playing solitaire. "Hey, mister. Game of poker?" But the visitor just smiled and walked on.

The only light came through the stained glass windows, filtered through the stagnant dusty air. Every window and door was open—he knew this was to prevent hospital poisons from accumulating—but there was no wind to speak of this day. He walked past a very sick looking man, whose armless torso was swaddled in bandages, and was nearly overcome by the stench. The man's infections oozed from beneath the bandages.

"There's nothing left to amputate, I'm afraid. He's not long." Beside him was an older woman, dressed like the other nurses but holding papers instead of food trays. She was thin and tall, and the inflection of her voice told of a Southern upbringing. Her narrow face was aged by the pain of a thousand strangers.

"Pardon…madam…I'm searching for my nephew."

"His name?" She led him toward an office in the antechamber.

"Mordechai Finkel. He was discharged within the last week. But I'm not sure what hospital." He fingered his hat nervously.

She walked to a table and picked up a folder. He could see the word "DISCHARGE" written on it. She thumbed through one set of papers, and then another, and with a resigned sigh, put the folder back on the table. "I'm sorry. No Finkels have been through here."

"I appreciate the effort, madam, and if I may impose just once more, could you tell me where I might find..." he looked at the second name on his list "...Trinity Episcopal?"

"Yes. Trinity is at 3rd and C Streets. Northwest."

Hilldrup walked toward a bustling hotel and had lunch in its restaurant. Outside, he had little trouble hiring a cab, and arrived at the church shortly after noon. This neighborhood, about a block north of the Saint Charles Hotel, was somewhat run-down, contrasting greatly with the vibrant area surrounding Epiphany. In the distance, he could see the U.S. Capitol building, surrounded by scaffolding, its incomplete dome sprouting a bird-like crane from its axis. He looked around. Whole city blocks were nothing more than dirt. The church itself, a brownstone monstrosity with twin steeples, shared its block with a wooden shack (its sign read simply "GROCERY STORE") and little else.

There was some evidence of civic planning, however, because birch saplings had been planted at evenly spaced increments, their tender trunks protected by tiny circular fences of green-painted wooden slats. Across the street were a few modest federal-style homes, and across from the grocery store, a lovely, turreted Victorian with a wraparound porch.

Remembering how Epiphany had been laid out, he decided to go around to the back of the church, hoping to walk right into the office space and avoid laying eyes on the dreadfully wounded men. He walked along the southern wall as the sun disappeared behind dark, swollen clouds. A warm blustery wind caught his hat, and he pressed it to his head; he marveled at how quickly the weather was changing. At the rear of the church, he could see a pile of dirt, a shovel stuck into it, and then a hole — not a grave, because the hole was round, not coffin-shaped. He could not help but stop at the edge and examine its contents; it looked to be a pile of bloody rags.

An orderly emerged from a rear door, his apron smeared with blood, and gave the visitor a sidelong glance as he threw another bundle of bloody rags into the hole. Without a word, the orderly turned on his heels and rushed back to his work. The visitor looked into the hole again. A hand was sticking out of the latest bundle, and nearby he could see a bloody foot. He turned, his bile rising, and walked away from the hole and past the door from which the orderly emerged. He stood there, breathing deeply and steadily, eyes closed, and composed himself before continuing.

He walked along the back wall of the church, found another door, and pushed it open. A black woman, chopping vegetables in the church kitchen, gave him a sullen look as he walked wordlessly past her and into a vestibule. He came upon a man seated at a desk in a closet-sized office with room for a desk and a chair and nothing else. The man, bald on top with gray muttonchops and wire-rimmed glasses, was staring at him with a raised eyebrow.

"Good day, sir. Might you help me? I'm trying to locate my nephew. He was wounded at Manassas. Can you tell me if he was cared for here?"

"Name?"

"Finkel. Mordechai Finkel." There was a silence of perhaps thirty seconds as the man leafed through the piles of paper before him.

"Ah, yes. Here we go. Mordechai Finkel. Admitted August 30, discharged September 14. There you have it."

"Discharged where? He's not arrived home. His mother and I are very worried—"

"You might try the Sanitary Commission. They often help discharged soldiers find their way home."

"They've no record of him. They sent me here."

The man sighed, and folded his arms. After a moment, he said, "There are some private citizens who take discharged soldiers into their homes until they are well enough to travel. There's the Murphys, over on 13th Street. And of course, Senator Morrison and his family, God bless them. His daughter volunteers as a nurse's aide here. I would check there first. They're right across the street."

"Across the street?"

"Yes, the big house on the corner. The Senator is a generous soul. A man of his standing, yet he takes the wounded into his home. He doesn't have to do that, you know."

Something was going on in the street. Both men turned toward the sound of horse-drawn carriages, shouting, and people running about. "You'll have to excuse me. We've been expecting more wounded. There was a terrible battle yesterday, in Sharpsburg. The first batch arrived before dawn. We were told there would be more."

"I will take my leave then. Thank you—" But the hospital administrator was already on his feet and headed toward the commotion, leaving the visitor standing before an empty office. He departed the same way he had arrived, through the kitchen. The cook was gone, perhaps to help unload the ambulances, and he picked up a piece of carrot from her cutting board and popped it into his mouth as he left the church.

He walked around the north side of the church, but a fence restricted access to the street, so it became necessary to walk behind the grocery store. He ended up on C Street. Walking back toward Third, he could see that the street before the church was entirely blocked now by a dozen ambulances. The commotion, people running about carrying stretchers, shouting, men crying in pain, all made him quite anxious.

The elegant mansion's door was open, and a lovely dark-haired woman held the knob, looking not at Hilldrup but at the procession of ambulances. She pulled the door shut behind her and ran down the wrought-iron steps past him and toward Trinity Church. In a moment he could no longer hear her footsteps amid the cacophony of wagon wheels, crying men, and commands shouted at unseen orderlies.

The man from New York climbed the four steps to the porch slowly, admiring the wicker rocking chairs and the brass spittoon on the porch and the other touches that denoted a family of some wealth. Each of the double doors sported a large brass knocker. Hilldrup knocked twice and waited. A door opened, and a young black woman stood before him, a domestic.

"Good afternoon, madam."

She stared.

"I'm with the Sanitary Commission, and we understand that some soldiers are staying with the Senator and his family. In order to assist families who are searching—"

"The Senator's not home, he's on business. Back in Jersey."

Hilldrup exhaled heavily. "Very well, but I needn't his assistance, I need only a list of the soldiers who are staying with you. The commission would be grateful—"

"Lady of the house just left, sir." Her eyes were drawn to the ruckus across the street.

"I just need the names of the men. Could you ask each of them what their name is and tell me?"

She considered this for a moment, and then began to close the door in his face. "Just a moment."

He waited patiently, two minutes, three, and then began backing down the steps, hand on the railing, eyes searching the second-floor windows.

And then Aaron Hilldrup had his answer.

Mordechai Finkel was leaning out the open window of the second-floor turret, gazing toward his wounded comrades being carried into the church. No doubt about it—that was him, and Hilldrup quickly rounded the corner and proceeded down C Street toward 4th, lest he be seen. Would Finkel recognize him from the store? Probably not, but best not to tempt fate. At 6th Street he hailed a cab, and returned to the Willard to plan his next step.

HILLDRUP WAS CONSUMED by fear and anxiety at the prospect of carrying out his mission. Two glasses of port, taken at the hotel bar, failed to deliver any courage. He beckoned the bartender and requested a serving of brandy, which he swallowed in two gulps. He rose, unsteadily, deposited one dollar upon the bar, and stumbled toward the entrance, where the concierge eyed him contemptuously as he walked past.

The night air was cool, and he hesitated before proceeding, wondering if he could just forget the whole deal and change his name and start a new life in Washington, with a clear conscience. Or he could turn the tables on Brandon—go to the papers! The tabloids would love a story like this. And pay handsomely for it. He could imagine the headline: DEPARTMENT STORE MAGNATE ACCUSED OF MURDER-FOR-HIRE.

Instead, he began walking south. He made a bargain with himself. *You don't necessarily have to do anything tonight. Just get the feel for this Murder Bay neighborhood, see what it's like, maybe stop in a gambling parlor or two, and come back tomorrow night and try again*. Hilldrup was suddenly struck by how naïve he was, how closeted for a man of forty-five years. He had never married, never come close, and although at one time he believed he wanted a wife, lately he had become content in his solitude. Being alone no doubt contributed to his frequent melancholy, but as his fortieth birthday became distant, he stopped believing he was even capable of living with another person, of accommodating, of compromising.

Hilldrup's thoughts were interrupted by the hooting and howling of drunken men. They were soldiers, four of them, in a tiny one-horse cart, waving bottles and shouting obscenities at passersby, specifically him. In a moment they were gone, but Hilldrup had become aware that the quiet gentility of the area around the Willard had given way to something coarser as he walked along 14th Street. The street was much more crowded now, and the men who passed — there were few women — were mostly soldiers, unkempt, some with dirt on their faces or in their hair, as if they had come from the battlefield just hours before.

Perhaps most startling was the presence of Negro men wandering about, in this otherwise tightly segregated city. Some wore rags, but others wore the uniforms of factory workers, butlers, and cooks. One man walked with dignity, carrying his groceries home after a hard day's work; another staggered and stumbled along the gaslit streets, oblivious to all that surrounded him.

Hilldrup had just crossed the street to avoid a particularly sinister-looking fellow when he heard a woman's voice from above — "Hey there, stranger" — and he looked up to see a women hanging half-out a second floor window. She winked at him — and pulled open her blouse to reveal her breasts, making sure he got a good look, then slamming the door shut again. Too startled to speak, he walked on, still staring up, and stumbled into a soldier, who took him by the shoulders and threw him to the ground.

"Watch where you're going, old man." A sharper insult Hilldrup could not imagine. The soldier went on his way, and Hilldrup picked himself up. He looked up toward the window again, but the woman was busy teasing some other man now, a portly, well-dressed gent who did not hesitate to climb the stairs of the row house and ring the bell. Hilldrup read the hand-painted sign above the door: THE BLUE GOOSE. A moment later the woman disappeared and then reappeared to shut the window and pull the curtains closed.

He turned his back to the bordello and continued down 14th Street. Here came a woman in her bloomers, swaying slightly to the piano music coming from a nearby establishment, her face painted in gaudy shades of purple and red. On the other side of the street, saloon doors swung open and two men spilled into the sidewalk, fists flying, while several men holding tin mugs emerged to cheer on their favorite.

Walking past a darkened alleyway moments later, Hilldrup could hear grunts and scuffling sounds but kept walking, not wanting to know what was happening there. He was sobering up now, an intolerable situation in this neighborhood, and resolved to enter the next saloon he passed that didn't frighten him with its appearance from the street. *How low my standards have fallen*, he thought.

After a few more blocks he gave up trying to find a decent establishment and entered a bar called The West End. This place, at least, had a name, unlike the dozens of anonymous pits he had passed on his walking tour. Inside, men played poker and smoked cigars at tables of five and six. The bar was tended by a mulatto woman who was quite attractive, if you went for that sort of thing. There were about twenty people in the place, and although there were some unoccupied tables, Hilldrup opted for a seat at the bar and asked the woman for a brandy.

She looked quizzically at him. "We don't have that."

"A glass of wine?" She shook her head.

"We have gin. Eight cents. Beer. Five cents. What will it be?" She was mechanically wiping the counter with a filthy rag.

"Gin, then, please."

She stared at him, arms folded now, and he came to understand that she wanted eight cents.

The gin was awful, a soapy, cloudy concoction, and the glass was dirty, but he expected nothing less, in fact prayed only that he didn't go blind from drinking it. *Enough of this*, Hilldrup thought. *Back to the Willard, as soon as the bottom of this glass reappears.*

The man who sat down next to him stank like he had not bathed in weeks. Hilldrup gagged on his drink, glanced involuntarily to his left, and met the gaze of a bearded, crazy-looking man of about thirty. Hilldrup didn't speak, and neither did the man, who motioned toward the bartender. His right index finger tapped the bar three times: *put gin here*.

Hilldrup could hardly keep from staring at the man, who was now gazing into his own cloudy glass of gin. His western hat, caked with dirt, hid much of his face. But when the man turned to meet Hilldrup's gaze a second time, Hilldrup could see the gaunt expression, eyes impossibly wide and unblinking. The taut flesh of his cheeks seemed to disappear into his beard.

"What're you looking at?"

"So sorry, I thought I knew you from somewhere."

"What the hell are you?"

"Pardon?"

"What are you? Provost marshal? City cop?" He turned toward Hilldrup on the bar stool, pulling back his grimy greatcoat to reveal the hilt of a large bowie knife. His hand hovered above it.

Things were going downhill fast. Hilldrup stammered. "I— just—"

"Relax, Ronald, he ain't no law. Look at him. I think he's one 'them Nancy boys. Could be he's just taken a shine to you." The mulatto woman was smiling, one arm on the bar, the other under it. "Cut him some slack." She poured Ronald Eddy another glass of gin with her free hand. The other stayed hidden.

Eddy's intense gaze remained on Hilldrup for another ten seconds, an eternity in a room in which all talk, all motion ceased, everyone staring at the spectacle, waiting to see if a crazed derelict would cut the throat of an unarmed haberdasher. Now, both the bartender's hands were under the bar. She started to speak again: "This ain't that kind of saloon, fella—"

Hilldrup saw the fist coming, perhaps could even have dodged it, were he not afraid to anger this lunatic further. Instead he was hit on the side of the face and knocked off his barstool. He fell to the floor like a bowling pin. He opened his eyes after a moment to see two black boots, crusty with mud, inches from his face. Hilldrup looked up into the darkness beneath the hat. "Let me buy you a drink," he croaked, and the room erupted in laughter.

CHAPTER 8.

Wednesday, December 25, 1957

WALKING ALONG PENNSYLVANIA Avenue on a blustery, overcast Christmas Day, Ben Carey was no longer convinced of his sanity. He felt pretty sane out here, in the world. Inside of 301 C Street, he was nuts.

Could I have been dreaming I saw Wallace when Marie called? he thought. I had to have been, he concluded.

Or the place was haunted.

Haunted. The word sounded absurd to him, suitable only for fiction, like the cheesy movies they showed on Saturday nights in Korea during the periodic truces. He remembered one, *The Canterville Ghost*. Robert Young was an army man in wartime England, bunking in a castle, and Charles Laughton was a double-exposed ghost...

Had he seen Wallace's ghost? Carey didn't believe in ghosts. It had looked and sounded like Wallace, but it was definitely not Wallace. Other than being Not Wallace, though, he had no idea what it was. He tried to rule out the crazy explanation.

But there were other nagging things about that house. The policeman who saw a boy in the second-floor window. How to explain that? The other noises, the man whom the painter saw upstairs. The hysterical cleaning woman. A few too many weird happenings for it to be coincidental, but not enough evidence to draw any conclusions.

Carey had always been a skeptic. He was a cop and had a cop's predilection for believing in the simplest explanation. *It's a creepy, run-down old house. It creaks when the wind blows. Its hot-water boiler is ancient. Its pipes are old and rusty. It would be full of strange noises.* There was the cat. And people imagined things. He knew from experience that witnesses to crimes were unreliable. They see what they want to see. Or what they're afraid of seeing. He didn't have to explain the strange behavior of the others. Who knows what they did or didn't see?

It was a little more difficult to explain what he himself had seen...and heard. Looking at it objectively, he had to admit that he'd been under a great strain recently. Plus, he'd been drunk a good deal of the time. If someone had told him his story—seeing a dead man sitting in his office on Christmas Day, after having downed a bottle of scotch and a sleeping pill—he would have drawn only one conclusion: the man was hallucinating. Still, it wasn't someone else's story, it was his. He knew what he'd seen, even if he couldn't believe it.

Either there was a simple explanation for all this, or a supernatural one. Either way, Carey decided, he needed to get to the bottom of it. *I'm a cop, for chrissakes. It's my job.*

He started to replay the events in his mind. What things did he actually witness? What couldn't he explain? There was Not Wallace, sitting in his chair. Full uniform. Smiling. Cigarette. Tapping his fingers on that notebook.

Was the notebook still on his desk? Had he taken it home? Had he imagined it? Something to check into.

Then there were the footsteps he had heard. The big gray cat? Probably a combination of the cat and the booze. But he had taken pictures. He should develop the roll of film and see if it held any answers. *Now we're getting somewhere*, he thought.

He stopped and realized how foolish he sounded in his own head. But, no, it made sense. He had to do this, if for no other reason than to regain his marbles. Prove to himself he wasn't going insane.

Carey turned back toward the house now and quickened his pace. If Wallace's notebook was still there, maybe something in it would shed some light. If it's not in his office, it might be at his home. He could ask to see it. Police business.

Carey arrived at 301 C Street and ascended the rusty cast-iron steps to the porch. He stopped before the front door, afraid suddenly to go in, afraid of what new surprises might be in store for him. Feeling lightheaded with a lingering hangover and fear, he pushed open the unlocked door.

Wallace's office no longer smelled of smoke, and his desk was clear except for a fresh layer of dust and an ashtray overflowing with cigarette butts. The notebook was not on Wallace's desk. *That's all right,* he thought. *If Wallace wasn't real, why would the notebook be? Better search the desk.* Carey walked cautiously around the desk and seated himself on the worn vinyl chair, its upholstery scuffed and cracked in places, its armrests completely devoid of covering, nothing but cold, metal bars. Monday's newspaper was folded and tucked between the desk and the wall. He chucked it in the trash can and emptied the ashtray.

The first desk drawer, the shallow, wide one, held matches, reading glasses, pens and pencils, and a half pack of Winstons. He thought about saving them for Kelsey, who smoked that brand, but thought better of it. Nobody wants a dead man's cigarettes. They went in the trash.

He opened another drawer. Big surprise here. A bottle of gin, good stuff, Beefeater, about half full. It went in the trash. Another drawer, a pint of whiskey, trash. There was something else in the drawer: an address book. Carey thumbed through it. It was almost empty, and most of the female names had been crossed out. He looked under W. No family in his address book. He put the book back in the drawer and pushed it shut. Wallace's next-of-kin might turn up and want his personal belongings. Had to have something to give them.

Pulling open the last drawer, he discovered the black hard-cover notebook. A shiver went up his spine as he opened it. What he saw surprised him. It wasn't a notebook, after all, but a sketchbook. Pencil drawings filled the unlined, cream-colored pages. The first few pages showed drawings of the house—its façade, details of the porch, the turret, interiors of different rooms in the house. Carey knew nothing about art, but he could see that Wallace was skilled. There were few erasure marks, and the drawings looked realistic, the shading giving the images light and depth. Carey immediately recognized the various rooms of the house in the pages. Some of the drawings showed the rooms as they appeared now—mostly empty, a desk and chair here or there. But other drawings showed the same rooms with furniture—a dining room table, a bed and nightstand, an old-fashioned sofa—how the house must have looked when people lived here.

Then Carey came upon the first face. The drawing was rougher than the others. Perhaps Wallace didn't draw people. Not surprising. The face staring back at him had long sideburns, arching toward a dimpled chin, deep-set, intense eyes, unkempt, light-colored hair, and a large, hooked nose. It was a handsome face, but troubled. There were more faces on the following pages. And the quality of the sketches improved. There were more of the man with the sideburns. And a young woman, eighteen or nineteen, with long dark hair, dressed in period costume. She had an idealized, angelic face. A fantasy. Some drawings showed her with a young boy, four or five years of age, who could have been her son. The face that disturbed Carey, though, was the one of the man in the dark western hat and long greatcoat. He had wide, glazed eyes, a dirty beard, dirty face, and dirty hands. Carey had seen the type a thousand times—a lowlife, a predator, a criminal.

He didn't know why, but Carey recognized the man with the beard. Where had he seen him before? He could have been a perp brought down to the station for booking. He could have seen him there; Captain Wallace could have, too. But he had never seen Wallace at his old precinct. Wallace certainly hadn't arrested the man. As Carey flipped through more pages, he saw more drawings of the bearded man, always half in shadows, menacing, watching. Maybe Wallace had hallucinated the faces he drew. Carey certainly knew what an alcoholic haze could do to your senses. Perhaps he simply invented them.

He turned the page. It was blank. The rest of the pad was untouched. He took the sketchbook and walked to his office. He put it in his bottom drawer. Wallace's sketchbook only raised more questions for Carey. Instead of pointing toward a simple explanation, it only deepened the mystery. He'd have to have some other pieces of the puzzle before he could guess what significance those drawings had.

Carey walked back to Wallace's office, took the cigarettes and the two half-empty bottles from the trash and put them in the paper sack his Chinese food had come in. He left Substation C and walked north, in a light snow, until he encountered a bum in an alleyway.

"Merry Christmas, fella. Hope this keeps you warm tonight." He handed the bag over.

"Thanks. God bless."

Carey nodded and went on his way, feeling like some kind of perverse Santa Claus.

THAT AFTERNOON, Carey thought to call his mother. She was glad to hear from him, but clearly upset. "I worry about you, Ben, that's all," said Charlotte Carey to her son. "I'm still your mother, after all."

"I know, Mom, but you don't have to," he said. "Things will work out, or they won't. It's really up to Marie at this point." There was silence on the other end, and Carey could tell that his mother was crying.

"Where are you staying?" she asked.

"I found a nice, inexpensive hotel not far from the office," he lied.

"Why don't I drive in and see you?" she offered. Carey and Marie usually spent Christmas Day with her parents in Alexandria. "It's Christmas, and I don't want you to be alone. We could go see the tree at the White House and find someplace to have a hot meal."

"Okay, Mom. Just come to my office. It's on 3rd and C Northwest."

His mother arrived at the house just as it was getting dark. From his desk, Carey could see her peering into the window as she stood on the front porch, unsure if this was indeed the place. He walked into the foyer and opened the front door. "This is the place," he said, seeing her startled face. "Merry Christmas, Mom."

"Ben," his mother said and reached up to give him a hug.

Carey showed her into the foyer. "This is where I'm working now," he said. "The department's owned this building for years, and my unit's stationed here. It must have been a nice house at one time." His mother looked around a little uneasily. "It's got a lot of character, doesn't it?"

"I guess," she said. "So you're working on Christmas?"

"I'm just catching up on some reading. It's all right, I'm going to get my own apartment when I can afford it." She frowned at that. "Look, Mom, I just need to grab a few things and get my coat, and then we can go."

She was gazing up at the old plaster walls of the foyer, and her eyes settled on the stairway. "I'll just wait outside, honey," she said. "I could use the fresh air."

Carey took his mother to Chinatown, and they had a nice but quiet dinner at The Golden Dragon. After he walked his mother to her car, he waited until she was out of sight and walked up the steps to the front porch of Substation C, preparing himself for another night in the old house.

A FUNERAL IS ALWAYS a solemn affair, and a cop's funeral is often a national event. When an officer dies in the line of duty, police departments around the country send representatives to the funeral, and they usually send motorcycle officers. It makes for a dramatic scene: hundreds of motorcycles following the hearse to the graveyard. When an officer dies of natural causes, the man's coworkers and family still attend, and it is still a solemn event, if not without the national import.

When a drunken cop blows his brains out in his bathtub, he can expect a little less attention.

Carey was there, in a cold drizzle, at Congressional Cemetery in Southeast. Inspector Price was there, as were Crawford, Kelsey, and Mullins. They and a chaplain watched the body lowered into the grave.

THE MOOD WAS SOMBER in Substation C. Crawford had taken leave the rest of the week, and the rest of the guys sat around much of the morning sipping coffee, eating pastries, and talking in hushed tones about Arthur Wallace. Around eleven, they began discussing the grant paperwork, and broke for lunch at noon. Carey stopped at his favorite deli and headed back to the office.

He had taken the first bite of a roast beef sandwich when his phone rang.

"Carey."

"Hi." It was Marie. Ben couldn't tell if she sounded happy or just nervous.

"Hello." His voice was cold. He missed her, but he was used to it.

"I was sorry to hear about Captain Wallace," she said. "Um...can we get together sometime to talk?"

He paused, caught off guard. "Tonight, after work," he said. "I'm free." He was free every night, and Marie knew it.

"Uh, tonight?" She paused, considering. "Mmm, okay. How about, say, six-thirty at the apartment?"

"Sure." *The apartment?* What used to be just *home* was now *the apartment*, as if it were neutral territory.

BEN SANK DOWN on the overstuffed couch in the living room of "the apartment," while Marie fixed him a cup of coffee in the kitchen. This wasn't going to be dinner. *Not a good sign*, he thought.

Marie brought over the cup of black coffee on a saucer and set it down in front of him on the coffee table. She sat down in the chair next to him, her hands folded in her lap.

"Ben," she began, "I'm glad we could get together to—"

"Can I ask you a question before you get started?" he asked. Marie pursed her lips and nodded. "Are you seeing someone?" he said.

Marie shot Ben a wounded look and shook her head. "No," she said.

Ben stared at her as an interrogator would, waiting for her to crack. Several seconds passed, but no beads of sweat appeared on her upper lip, no twitching eyelid. "Fine," he said finally.

"I've had some time to think about things while we've been apart," she said, clearing her throat. "I think we should try a trial separation for a few months."

"Jesus." Carey looked away, shaking his head.

"Ben, I've been unhappy for a long time." It hurt him to have to hear that. "I'm not blaming you, I just don't think we want the same things out of life."

"What is it you think you want that I can't give you?"

"Come on, Ben, I'm talking about more than something you can go out and get for me. We were so young when we got married, so young and foolish."

"Speak for yourself," he said, getting up from the couch. "I may have been young, but I knew that I loved you. No matter what happened, I thought I always would. That was, until you kicked me out of the house with no warning."

"I'm sorry I hurt you, Ben."

At least she said it, he thought.

"But," she said, standing to meet his eyes, "the fact that you think there was 'no warning' kind of makes my point, doesn't it?"

"Tell me there's still a chance," he said and walked closer to her. "Or tell me to get out now. I just want to know if there's still a chance for us."

She looked at him and tried to gather her thoughts. But seeing him, the way he looked at that moment, all she could think of was the longing she had for him as a nineteen-year-old. "There's always a chance," she said.

He kissed her, and though she knew it was a bad idea, she couldn't help drawing him closer and returning his kiss.

•   •   •

WHEN MARIE ASKED HIM to leave shortly after he got dressed, Ben began wondering just what had transpired between them. Was it simply a moment of weakness on her part? Had nothing changed? Or was it just foolish to expect that anything had? That night, he lay awake on the floor of his room for hours before falling asleep.

He is climbing the stairs to his makeshift bedroom. Except the stairs are like new. A yellow Persian runner lines the steps. There is fresh paint on the walls and molding, and the banister is stained dark with a shiny coat of varnish. The second floor comes into view, and it is new like the rest of the house. He approaches the turret bedroom, his room, and he can see that the door is ajar. It is day-time, and light is streaming in through the open windows. He can make out the shape of a woman sitting in a spindle-back chair next to a bed on which a man is lying. It is Marie, but she is dressed in an odd, old-fashioned dress.

Marie turns, sees Carey standing in the door, rises, and walks over to him. She brushes past him through the doorway, and he grabs her arm. She says nothing. She looks at him imploringly for a moment, pulls her arm from his hand, and slips away into the darkness of the corridor.

Carey looks over at the man on the bed. Is this the man? he wonders. But he doesn't feel angry, he feels sorry for the man. He walks closer to the man now and realizes he is not lying on a bed but a cot, and he is dressed in ragged clothes. The room looks lived in, a dresser against the wall, curtains on the windows, an ornate red Turkish carpet on the floor. Out the windows, it is late summer instead of late December. To the left, he sees the Gothic steeples of a huge Catholic church standing in the empty lot across the street. Where the hell did that come from? To the right, above the trees, he sees the Capitol dome in the distance, which would not be unusual, except that the top third of the dome is unfinished, a crane sticking up out of the center, its skeleton exposed.

Carey is transfixed by what he is seeing. Things so familiar yet unfamiliar. Suddenly, he hears the man coughing. The man has blond hair with long sideburns and wears suspenders over an old-fashioned, button-up undershirt. Carey recognizes the man now. He is coughing and holding his left side. His eyes turn to Carey, beseeching him, and he holds his bloody hands out to him now, mouthing words that he cannot hear. Carey looks down and sees that the man has a gaping wound on his left side. It is bleeding, and the blood is flowing over the man's shirt and onto the sheet under him.

Carey awoke with a start. The room was dark now, and unfinished as it was when he fell asleep. He got up and looked out of the windows. No church, just an empty lot. To the right, the Capitol dome was back to normal, no longer under construction. *That man! I know that man.* Carey ran out of the room and bounded down the stairs. He hurried to the desk in his office and opened the bottom drawer. He grabbed Wallace's sketchbook, flipped on his light, and started turning the pages. He stopped when he got to the light-haired man with the sideburns and the crutch.

That's the man!

Carey studied the other drawings of the man. It was him. Of course, he'd been looking at the drawings quite a bit. It was possible the faces in Wallace's sketchbook were popping up in his dreams simply because he'd been thinking about them so much. Marie was in the dream, too. But none of the drawings showed a church or the Capitol building. He'd never seen that church before, and he couldn't remember ever seeing a picture of the Capitol dome being built. He didn't even know if any such picture existed.

If Carey was ever going to make sense of any of this, he needed to start writing things down. He turned to the back of the sketchbook where there were some blank pages and began to write:

—Things I dreamt: Marie in house. House new. Blond-haired man with sideburns. Young, 20–25. Same as man in W's drawings. Soldier—Civil War? Injured in gut, dying. Church across the street. Was there ever a church on Third and C? Unfinished Capitol dome. When built?

—Things I saw or heard: Someone opening the door, climbing the stairs—the cat? W sitting in his chair, smoking. "You shouldn't be here." Was I awake? The scraping on the stairs, then running up and opening the door. Check photos.

—Things others saw or heard: Billy (the painter) saw a blond "kid" with sideburns upstairs—I saw no man. The cleaning lady saw something frightening—no idea what. 2 cops saw a boy in the window, heard a scream—I saw no boy, heard no scream.

Looking over the list, Carey suppressed a shiver. It was good to get these things down, he told himself. There seemed to be some reason this young blond man with the sideburns kept showing up. He wasn't sure how to follow that lead. But he could answer the questions about the church and the Capitol dome with a little research. Perhaps he would look into the history of this house, as well. And he would take his film to be developed the next day.

He tucked Wallace's sketchbook under one arm and turned out the lamp. For a moment, he stood there in the pitch black of his office. With no other light on in the house, he was suddenly five years old again and terrified of the dark. He quickly turned his lamp back on and scanned the shadowy corners of the room for any commotion. He made his way out and ascended the rotting old staircase to his empty room illuminated by nothing but the dim light coming from his office door.

CHAPTER 9.

Monday, September 22, 1862. Four A.M.

SHE SLEPT LIGHTLY, and woke easily, alert to the every moan, cough, or sneeze of her four charges. Often, after she soothed a frightened soldier's nightmares or eased his pain with a spoonful of laudanum, she would find herself unable to resume her sleep, and she would attend to chores neglected during daylight hours.

On this early morning, she turned her oil lamp high and began writing a letter:

> September 22nd, 1862
> Mr. Horace Brown
> 458 Porter Street
> Boston, Massachusetts
>
> Dear Mr. Brown.
>
> Your son, Joseph, has been recuperating in our home as our guest for three weeks. His spirits are high, and he has been asking to go home. With the approval of his doctor, we feel he is ready to travel and ask that you come to Washington to escort him. His honorable discharge from the U.S. Army is complete.
>
> I understand that he has written you of his injuries, which he sustained at South Mountain some weeks ago, so you should be prepared for them. He has lost the use of his left leg, at the thigh, and was also injured

in the face, which is healing nicely. Two of the fingers on his right hand have been injured, as well.

Take the Baltimore and Ohio railroad to the Washington station. My home is nearby, at 3rd and C Streets Northwest. I look forward to our meeting. Joseph has told us much about you.

I am very respectfully yours,

Louisa Morrison

She felt drowsy again, snuffed her lamp, and crawled back under her warm covers. Louisa cared for these men as she would her own children, though, at eighteen, most of the injured soldiers were older than her by a year or two. Her care for them, not to mention her tender tone and clear beauty, had generated proposals from many of the men who came through the house, though Louisa took none of them seriously. It was her goal in working at Trinity and in keeping her house running as a sanctuary to get them back on their feet—or at least back among the living—so that they could rejoin society, not so she could find a husband.

Given that much of her time was spent either at the makeshift hospital or at home tending to the wounded, not surprisingly there was a dearth of suitors calling on her, and those who did were met with a stony glare and a single question: *"Why aren't you out defending our union instead of standing in my doorway holding flowers?"* This exact scenario had played itself out once already with her childhood friend, Harrison Rogers, the son of her godfather, Tyler Rogers, the assistant secretary of the Navy. Harrison, who was four years her senior, was considered one of Washington society's most eligible bachelors, and had already set up a law practice in town. Growing up, he had been smitten with Louisa, but she had always felt he lacked seriousness. Like scores of wealthy young Washington men, he had bought his way out of the draft, hiring a substitute whose flesh would be menaced by hot lead for eighty dollars, plus a private's pay. It was all perfectly legal, of course. "I can't very well provide for you if I'm killed on some battlefield in Virginia," he protested.

"It's hard for me to see how anyone can shirk their duty to their country," she said. "What are you going to do if Lee's army marches into Washington? Sue them?" And she showed him to the door.

Harrison, however, was not easily dissuaded. As far back as he could remember, the Rogerses and the Morrisons referred to their children as a couple. Of course, when they were children, the idea of their union was discussed as a distant prospect. But as Harrison grew older, marrying Louisa became part of his life's plan. Now, twenty-two and successful, he was ready to move on to the next stage—one with a beautiful, loving wife who would raise his children and further propel him into high society.

That Louisa rebuked his advances only served to heighten his urgency to make her his wife. In fact, he had already purchased a ring—emerald, the purest and most brilliant he could find—for that purpose. On the nights when sleep eluded him, he'd walk past her house, twirling the ring around his own finger, and imagine the look in her eyes when he'd present it to her. Sometimes the Morrison house would be dark, and he'd stand under the elm tree in the front yard, watching the curtains in Louisa's bedroom window flutter in and out. On other nights, he'd see lights on and figures moving past the windows. Then, he could watch Louisa tending to those in her care, on quiet nights he could even hear her voice. While he didn't understand her need to help them so directly—he helped in his own way by funding medical supplies for the hospitals—he did admire her warmth.

She would, someday, make a good wife for him.

• • •

EDNA MADE BREAKFAST in bed for four, griddlecakes and maple syrup, and Louisa brought back a melon from the Center Market, for which she paid a small fortune. There was no meat for this meal, although the men seemed enormously grateful for it, anyway. As she helped Edna with the breakfast dishes, a new batch of wounded arrived across the street, mercifully few this time. She was back home by eleven A.M.

For lunch Louisa prepared beef, courtesy of her cousin in Silver Spring, who had slaughtered one of his cows just two days earlier. It was tough (a brisket cut) but flavorful, and she stirred up a thick gravy from the bottom of the pan, into which she sliced an onion. Boiled potatoes accompanied the meat and gravy.

All of the men made it to the table. Joseph Brown, still able to smile despite his heavily bandaged face, was the first to seat himself, stowing his crutches on the coat rack placed near the table for that purpose. Mordechai Finkel sat next to him, looking hale and handsome, and hung his single crutch on the rack. His glance met hers, and they exchanged a secret smile, her eyes quickly returning to the steaming bowl of gravy she was stirring with a wooden spoon. Robert LaChance came to the table, a quiet man whose right hand now consisted solely of a thumb. Oscar O'Brien, the most seriously injured man in her care, was pushed to the table by Louisa, who set the lock on the wheelchair before taking her seat at the end of the table. The senator's daughter cleared her throat, and talking ceased as all hands attempted to join for the saying of Grace.

"Our heavenly father, we thank you for this day, our daily bread." She paused for a moment, and continued in a quieter vein. "We are grateful for the health and safety of the brave men at this table, and ask that you bless their journeys homeward, and allow no more evil to befall them the remainder of their days on this earth, oh Lord, for they have known enough evil, and have made enough sacrifices for God and country. Amen."

"Amen," the table replied, and their hands separated and reached for the serving spoons.

"Robert, have you begun reading the book I gave you yesterday?" Louisa asked as she served herself a tiny portion of meat.

"Yes, ma'am, although I reckon I don't understand much of it."

"What part are you reading?"

"I'm reading the part where he's bragging about how little his house cost to build. Twenty-eight dollars and twelve cents, if I recall. Don't know how anyone could build a house for that sum."

"He proved it could be done. His point was that in a country where you can build your own home, and eat what you can grow and gather, then nobody need be poor," she said.

"But he was living on borrowed land. Emerson's, I believe," Mordechai said softly. "And he even borrowed the axe he used to fell someone else's trees. Maybe not a model for us all. Someone has to buy the land."

"Mr. Finkel. You've read *Walden*?"

"Yes," he said, nodding as he helped himself to more gravy. "Thoreau seems quite the revolutionary."

"An abolitionist before his time. More brisket, Oscar?" Louisa heaped a spoonful of meat onto Oscar's plate.

O'Brien looked confused. "Who's Thoreau?"

Louisa, wanting to include the other men in the conversation, cut in. "Joseph, I understand you'll be going back home soon. Have you thought about what you will do back in Boston?"

"No, ma'am—um, miss, I mean—I don't know what I'll be able to do, what with....You see, I was hoping to go into the family business." Brown pushed the beef around his plate with a fork.

"What kind of enterprise is that?"

"Jewelers. My father is a jeweler, his father before that....But I don't see so well, since...and my fingers....So I don't know what I'll be doing."

They ate in silence. In a few minutes, Edna began clearing away the dishes, and the men produced cigars and pipes and began to fill the room with smoke amid subdued conversation. As Louisa rose to help Edna with the dishes, the front door bell chimed. Edna quickly wiped her hands on her apron and started toward the door, when Louisa stopped her. "That's all right, Edna. I can get it."

Mordechai and the other men looked on with interest as Louisa answered the door and spoke with an excited young man in a vest and tie, wearing oval spectacles and holding a black stovepipe hat in his hands. Whatever news he had come to deliver, Louisa was clearly bowled over by it. He gave her an envelope with a printed handbill inside. The men were all leaning forward in their seats when Louisa bid farewell to this messenger and headed back to the dining room, reading the paper in her hand.

"That was my father's secretary," she said breathlessly. "You'll never believe what I've just been told."

Edna came into the room just then, retying an apron around her thin waist. She looked at the young men all turned toward the senator's daughter in expectation, and then back at Louisa. "Believe what?" she said.

"Mr. Lincoln," said Louisa, holding up the piece of paper, "has freed the slaves."

"THIS PROCLAMATION of Lincoln's," said Mordechai, looking over the copy Louisa had shared with them, "while it may be a bold statement, won't free one slave."

Mordechai, Louisa, and the other soldiers were still gathered in the dining room, abuzz and in heated discussion over Lincoln's Emancipation Proclamation. Mordechai continued playing devil's advocate. "First of all, it won't go into effect until the first of the year. And then it will only free slaves in those territories held by the Rebels. And even then only if they persist in their rebellion."

To Louisa's way of thinking, Lincoln's act was nothing short of a miracle. A momentous pronouncement to the world and a transformation of the United States's justification for going to war — from preserving the Union to ending slavery. Not all of the others agreed.

"This war has always been, and will always be, about slavery," she said.

"The South may have seceded over their fear that the federals would interfere in the institution," said Mordechai, "but Lincoln did not make war on the South over slavery. If they had stayed in the Union, there would be no war, and we would still have slavery. At any rate, I'm not yet convinced slavery will be abolished even if we win the war."

"How can you say that now, after what the president has done?" she said, a little defensively.

"But all he's done, Louisa," he replied, "is to promise to free the slaves in territory he doesn't control. And only if the Rebels continue fighting."

Robert LaChance nodded his head. "It was mighty clever of Mr. Lincoln," he said and took a puff from his pipe. "Slaves in the South'll rebel against their masters, or run away north. It doesn't say anything about slaves in Maryland or Missouri or Kentucky."

"Or Delaware," pointed out Joseph.

"The most 'portant thing is that England and France won't help them Rebs now," said Oscar. "They wouldn't dare."

"But don't you see?" said Louisa. "The practical concerns of war and politics are unimportant when compared to the righteous cause of ending this immoral and evil institution."

Mordechai cleared his throat, taking care with his words. "You speak of righteous causes and morality as if everyone knew that these trumped material things. But that has always been the struggle throughout history—the war between those who strive to serve a higher calling, and those who strive only to serve themselves."

"I quite agree with you in that," she said, "but I do prefer to believe our wars are fought—and our brave soldiers are dying—for higher causes than profit."

Mordechai chuckled, and Louisa turned a perturbed eye on him. "I'm sorry, Louisa," he said. "I'm not laughing at you at all. I just think it'd be nice if the politicians felt that way."

Louisa glanced at the portrait of her father hanging above the sideboard and then met Mordechai's gaze. She smiled. "Not all politicians think the same, Mr. Finkel. Perhaps you'd benefit by a conversation with my father when he returns home. I think you'd find his mind to be far more open than you'd expect."

LOUISA MADE HER NIGHTLY ROUNDS, checking on each man to see if he needed anything before she turned in. She visited Mordechai last, as was her routine, and the two talked in hushed tones. She sat on his cot in front of the open window, the curtains opened to let the night breezes in. The two were alone in the room. The house was quiet, save for the sounds of far-off horses plodding down the street and footsteps outside from a passerby on a late-night stroll.

"Stay with me. Talk with me." Mordechai was propped up on one elbow.

"No, not tonight, not with my father due back in the morning."

"I've really enjoyed his trip to New Jersey."

"So have I." She smiled and ran her fingers through his hair.

"Have you thought any more about what we—"

"Mordechai, I can't leave Washington. I can't leave my father all alone. The hospital, they need me here, too."

"But the war won't last forever. Will you marry me after the war is over?"

She smiled. "If you still want me. Who knows when that will be?"

"I want to talk with your father tomorrow. I want to ask him for your hand in marriage." He looked at her, holding her hand and stroking her arm with the back of his fingers. "I don't care if we have to wait to be married. But I won't wait any longer to declare my intentions. I love you, Louisa, and I always will."

"I love you," she said and kissed him gently on the lips.

Back in her room, lying in her bed, sleep did not come easily, and she stared out the window at the nearly full moon hanging in the cloudless sky above the unfinished Capitol dome. It bathed the room with soft light, as it had lit up Mordechai's room the night before.

It hadn't been their first kiss. That had happened several days ago, when they had been left alone in the parlor. It had been adolescent horseplay, really. Mordechai had moved his crutch so that Louisa would trip over it, and she fell into his lap where he sat on the French loveseat. He tickled her and she laughed, and he bussed her on the cheek. She pretended not to notice and sat in his arms until Edna happened to walk in. They detached themselves in response to her raised eyebrow.

That night, the first night her father had been out of town, Edna built a roaring fire in the parlor, and Louisa and Mordechai sat before it talking until well after midnight. She learned that his mother was dead, like hers, and that his father ran a shop in New York City. They talked about their shared loss, and Louisa realized after a while that she had never discussed her mother with anyone, even her father. It felt good to talk to someone else who understood what is was like to lose a parent.

They talked of the future. Her experiences as a nurse's aide left little doubt in her mind as to her chosen vocation. She already had sent letters to two nursing schools in the Washington area, and another in Baltimore, asking for admission, but hadn't heard back from them yet. Her father was supportive, perhaps sensing that she was far too energetic to be satisfied by the leisurely life normally accorded a young woman of her social standing. But she had never coveted the status brought by her father's position. She had, in fact, scorned her peers with their debutante cotillions and juvenile gossip.

Louisa had stopped going to school when the wounded started to arrive (although she had been assured she would be invited to take the graduation examinations) and had lost contact with her friends. Her peers—she really did not consider them her friends anymore—were content to continue their privileged lives as if nothing untoward were happening. She could not ignore what was happening across the street, and volunteered as a nurse's aide first with the Army Medical Department, which insisted it needed no help from civilians. The army, quite frankly, seemed to have little interest or ability in helping the battlefield wounded. So she applied to the Sanitary Commission, a Christian group that took on the tasks that rightfully should have been handled by the U.S. Army.

Before she was assigned to work at Trinity, she was tested for fitness in several ways. First, she was made to observe the amputation of an injured man's leg. Every one of the prospective volunteers who was in the room passed out—except her. Next, she was instructed to change the diaper on an unconscious two-hundred-pound man. She had little trouble turning the man on his side, but began having second thoughts as the task became more distasteful. As she wiped the feces from the man's backside, she reminded herself that he was God's creature, and that it could just as easily be her on the bed needing to be cleaned up by a stranger. She passed all her tests, and began caring for wounded men just as her former friends were beginning their school year.

A coach rumbled by beneath Louisa's window, and she was brought out of her reverie. She turned on her right side, her arm folded beneath the pillow. What had happened last night? She knew about sex, having seen the relevant parts up close on innumerable occasions and, not content with that, having visited the Library of Congress to examine discreetly an anatomy textbook, some months back. It all seemed very mechanical in the book, rather coarse, and not something she particularly aspired to.

However it had come about last night, it had been her idea. Mordechai had acted with restraint, with honor, right up until the moment her hand found its mark beneath the coarse woolen blanket. The scent of his body, distasteful only moments before, became delicious to her, and she found herself kissing his neck and chest. Then she was on top of him, pulling the blanket over her shoulders against the cool night air, her clothes in a rumpled pile beside the cot.

His eyes were wide, knowing yet not knowing what was happening, shocked by her forwardness, unaccustomed to a woman's touch. He lay there, hardly breathing, while she moved above him, and when she collapsed in a torrent of hot breaths, he had only to move forward and back a few times before he, too, had found his way. She laid her head beside his, her right hand examining the bandage on his left side, below his rib cage, searching for moisture, or stickiness, or other signs that she may have opened his wound. But the bandage was dry.

She didn't remember falling asleep, but woke up some hours later in his arms. He was awake, watching her, and gently kissed her forehead. She responded with a somewhat more substantial kiss on the lips. It was still dark and chilly.

Mordechai had proposed to Louisa right then and there. They talked in whispered tones of war and the hospital and her father. She had longed to spend the night beside him but could not risk discovery, even if only by Edna. She donned her blouse and skirt, left him with a final kiss, then tiptoed to her room and pushed her door shut silently.

Then, as now, sleep did not revisit Louisa, and then, as now, she lay there and thought of Mordechai.

Through a crack in her own bedroom door, Edna had watched Louisa return to her room that night, moments before the sun would make its appearance above the marshy wetlands of southeast Washington.

LOUISA READ THE CABLE her father had sent that morning. He had to remain in New Jersey longer and wouldn't return to Washington until Saturday:

> ...KNOW YOU WILL MANAGE WITHOUT ME FOR ANOTHER
> FEW DAYS. UNAVOIDABLE BUSINESS IN TRENTON. WISH I
> COULD BE WITH YOU TO REJOICE IN LINCOLN'S PROCLA-
> MATION. SECY CHASE HAS INVITED OUR FAMILY AND SOL-
> DIERS TO HIS HOME FOR CELEBRATION AND THANKS-
> GIVING. PLEASE ATTEND ON MY BEHALF AND SEND MY
> APOLOGIES. MISS YOU VERY MUCH. LOVE, FATHER.

Louisa detested the clipped language of the telegraph—that damnable invention—and she missed her father. More important, she wanted him there so that she and Mordechai could share their good news. She knew that Mordechai would be disappointed in having to wait longer.

Later that morning, as Louisa and the boys were enjoying breakfast, Edna received a visitor on the front porch, an army corporal with papers for Mordechai. "You'll see that he gets these?" he said.

"Yes, sir," Edna assured him, realizing what they were. She shut the door and rushed into the dining room, heading toward Mordechai. He looked up at her, and she handed his discharge papers to him with a wide, toothy smile. "You're going home, Mr. Finkel!"

Louisa and Mordechai exchanged glances. "That's wonderful news," said Mordechai, forcing a smile. "Thank you."

That afternoon, Mordechai complained of pain on his left side. The doctor, who was there to check in on the other fellows, warned Louisa and Edna that Mordechai's injury might be taking longer to heal than he had thought, and that too much activity could reopen the wound. He ordered bed rest, and Mordechai complied.

At about four in the afternoon, Louisa and Edna gathered up the soldiers into a carriage and headed over to Salmon P. Chase's mansion on McPherson Square, near 15th and H Streets, just a few blocks north of the Treasury building and the executive mansion. Chase, Lincoln's secretary of the Treasury, had been a vehement abolitionist and a lawyer on behalf of runaway slaves before the war. A two-time senator and former governor of Ohio, he was one of the founders of the new Republican Party. In 1861, he returned to Washington to serve once again as senator and renewed his friendship with Louisa's father, Eugene Morrison. Like Chase, Eugene was a Republican and a fervent abolitionist. Chase served only two days in the Senate when President Lincoln tapped him to head the Treasury, a vital cabinet role with the nation on the verge of civil war. Chase now had the daunting responsible of financing the Union's war against the Confederacy.

Unlike Senator Morrison, Chase lived in the toniest part of town on H Street, home to senators, cabinet members, and prominent businessmen. Chase lived down the street from the celebrated and reviled General George B. McClellan, whom he regarded as, at best, inept and, at worst, a traitor.

It was a warm, breezy day, and the carriage carrying Louisa, Edna, the three soldiers, and one wheelchair slowed as it approached Pennsylvania Avenue. A military parade was going on, a common occurrence these days, but considerably fewer citizens had turned out to watch the green soldiers march and the cavalry act dashing than would have been expected six months earlier. The city welcomed this fresh batch of warriors from lands up north, but they did little to cheer the populace. Since First Manassas, they had felt under siege; Lincoln had ordered these troops to man the forts around the city. Nevertheless, Washingtonians felt themselves the capital of a country located elsewhere, unsure whether Jeff Davis might not be residing in the White House come spring, unsure whether neighboring Maryland might be organizing Rebel militias, as the rumors insisted. But Antietam had at least given them hope. For once, Lee's army had been stopped, even if McClellan had let them go; even if it had cost the North twelve thousand dead and wounded. Louisa knew what that meant. A new batch of boys, bloody and broken, missing arms and legs and eyes and ears, already laid shoulder-to-shoulder and head-to-foot at Trinity Church, would soon arrive to fill the rooms of her father's house.

The terrible price the soldiers had paid at Antietam had paved the way for the president's proclamation. It ensured that Britain and France would never recognize or aid the Confederacy. And it satisfied the hearts of those opposed to slavery anywhere — it righted the wrong in words even if it could not yet in deeds.

When Louisa and the soldiers arrived at Chase's grand home, the doors spilled open to reveal a festive display, with more than forty other guests reveling in the victory of Lincoln's proclamation. Chase, one of the most powerful men in Washington, beamed while he and his two daughters received guests at the entrance to the great hall.

Louisa knew the Chase daughters, Kate and Nettie, and greeted them with a kiss. Salmon Chase took her hand in his. "God bless you and your father, my dear," he said. "I know he wanted to be here on this day." His eyes moved down to Oscar in his wheelchair, and to Robert and Joseph, who stood behind him. "And God bless you for the sacrifices you have made." The fuss he and his daughters made over the injured soldiers made them turn red and sheepishly stammer their thank-yous. It was for each of them the fanciest party they were ever likely to attend.

Edna, who had not asked nor been invited to join the party, walked down H Street toward 14th and then south of Pennsylvania Avenue into the slums of Murder Bay. She dropped in on her cousin, who was a barmaid at one of the neighborhood bars, and celebrated the proclamation with a mug of dark, cloudy beer.

WALKING EAST ON C Street, Edna could see the façade and the twin Gothic steeples of Trinity Church grow larger as she approached the senator's house. Laden with two heavy bags filled with bacon, bread, eggs, and lard, her breaths came in heavy bursts as she adjusted her load. On the road she passed a bearded man wearing a dark western hat and greatcoat, whose wide eyes caught hers before she quickly looked away. His face and clothes were caked in dirt. There were many soldiers who had come back from battle looking as dirty, but none as menacing. She wondered where it was he was going, or where it was he had been.

Edna arrived with the house dark and empty but for Mordechai. After lighting the lamps downstairs and putting the food away in the larder and bread box, she climbed the stairs to the turret room to check on the sleeping soldier. Mordechai was lying in the same cot he had been when she left. She knew how much he meant to Louisa and wondered if he weren't malingering to stay longer with her.

The turret room was dark, lit only by the candle Edna held in her hand. But as she drew closer to the sleeping Mordechai, she smelled blood. It was dripping from his cot onto the floor and had gathered in a pool beneath him. Some of it flowed in a meandering stream across the floor toward the half-open window in the turret. His bedclothes and sheets were soaked red. Edna put her hand to her mouth and gasped. She bolted from the room and bounded down the stairs. Frantically pulling the front door open, she ran onto the porch and was met by Louisa and Robert, who had just arrived with the other soldiers still in the carriage.

"Miss Louisa!" she cried. "Mordechai!"

Louisa's eyes widened with horror. She ran past Edna up the stairs and into the house. By the time Edna reached Louisa, it was too late to shield her from the sight of Mordechai's body. Louisa sat on the floor next to his cot, clutching his hand in hers and whispering in a rushed, terrified voice. Edna tried to pull her friend away, but Louisa only drew herself closer to Mordechai so that the brilliant blue gown she so flatteringly wore during the party just moments before now was soaked red with blood.

THE POLICE WERE GATHERED in the soldier's room, talking to Robert LaChance and the surgeon who had been summoned from Trinity along with two orderlies. One of the officers said to Robert, "So he had been complaining of pain on his left side, where he had been wounded?"

"Yes, sir," said Robert. "I didn't think it was that bad, but I guess we were wrong."

The surgeon, an older man, patted Robert on the back. "There's nothing you could have done. His wound simply opened up. He bled to death. Unfortunately, it happens every day." The doctor wore a bloody white smock and carried paperwork of some sort. Two young orderlies were binding Finkel's arms and legs in preparation for the removal of the body from the house. A stretcher had been placed nearby.

The doctor returned his attention to his charges.

Removed to the parlor, Louisa sat on the loveseat now, sobbing with Edna beside her, arm around her mistress, crying too. Oscar and Joseph sat across from them, shocked and subdued after an evening of gaiety.

The two policemen entered the parlor, one wearing the uniform of a District of Columbia police detective, and the other the tin badge of a provost marshal. Both wore prominent side arms. Robert and the surgeon followed them into the room.

The detective bent down to Louisa and spoke. "Miss, any reason to think this was anything but his battle wounds?"

Louisa looked up and hesitated. She alone knew that Mordechai had not been in pain that afternoon, that he was feigning illness to have a reason to stay in the house until the weekend. But she did not want to admit this to them, and she could not think of anyone who would want to do him harm. She shook her head, unable to speak and cringing in pain as if she were the one who was wounded.

Robert spoke up. "He'd been fine. Till this afternoon, anyway. Got sick then, pain on his side and weakness." There was a creaking from the stairway as the two orderlies descended the stairs with the stretcher bearing Mordechai's body.

Louisa turned from Edna and collapsed into the arm of the sofa.

The detective and marshal spoke with the surgeon for a few moments, thanked him, and let him go. Convinced the death had been a result of wounds received in battle, the two officers bid the lady of the house and the other soldiers good evening. Edna slid her arm from underneath Louisa's shaking body and showed them to the door.

"Sir?" Edna implored the young provost marshal as he stepped onto the porch.

"What?" he asked. The detective was already walking down the front steps ahead of him.

"I was the one who sent for the police."

"All right, so?" he said. His eyes traveling the length of her young frame.

"I don't think that boy was sickly. He was getting better every day," Edna said.

"You heard the doc, didn't you?"

"But the thing is, sir, I saw a man on the road near the house just before I found him like that. He looked outta place."

"You get a good look at the guy?"

"Not a good look. He was wearing a Union coat, I think, but it was so dirty, see, it coulda been black instead of blue. Big old hat, hid his face. Long beard. I passed him on the road. He could have been coming from the house. I could almost smell him from a block away."

The marshal scratched his stubbly chin. "Why would someone want to kill a recovering soldier?"

"Don't rightly know, sir."

"Well, ma'am, I'll keep all that in mind." He turned to leave, and stopped at the doorway. He turned toward Edna, her red-rimmed eyes looking down at her shoes.

"You and the Morrisons do good work here, woman. God bless you. Good day." He turned and left.

CHAPTER 10.

Monday, January 6, 1958

NORM CRAWFORD WALKED silently into Carey's office and sat down in the wooden chair in front of his desk. Carey was poring over the pages of a black notebook, oblivious to Crawford's presence. He cleared his throat, startling Carey.

"Jesus, Norm," he said, as Crawford suppressed a laugh. Carey closed his notebook, pushed it into a desk drawer, and set his gaze on his friend.

"Hey, Ben," he said, "how you been?"

Carey shrugged. "All right, I guess."

"Look, I know you and Marie have been having problems. She's asked me where you're staying. I told her I didn't know."

Carey stared at him blankly.

"The thing is, I think I do know. You're living *here*, aren't you?" Carey looked away as if the idea were ridiculous. "Ben, you're the first one here every morning and you stay later than anyone else at night. I passed by the office the other night around eleven, and a light was on in the second-floor window. Are you really working that hard? Because you don't really seem all that interested in the work we're doing anymore. It seems like you're in your own little world. I mean, marital problems will do that to a man, but…" He trailed off, afraid he'd gone too far.

"But what? If you don't like the way I'm doing my job, you can take it up with Price, okay?"

"That's not what I meant and you know it," said Crawford, a

little annoyed. "I'm trying to…Ben, what I want to know is if there's anything I can do to help. You're welcome to stay with me and Mary, you know." Crawford was looking him in the eye now, and Carey shifted uneasily in his chair.

Carey sighed, the thought of sleeping on Norm's couch with their little monsters running around briefly crossed his mind. He leaned forward in his chair. "Norm, this is going to sound like an odd question, but….You're going to night school. You do research papers?"

"Well, most of my classes are math and accounting. But, yeah, I've done some research papers. Why?"

"If I wanted to look into the history of a neighborhood—what buildings existed, when they were built, who lived in them, what people did there—where would I go?"

Crawford was silent for a moment. "How much do you know already?" he asked.

Carey thought about it and said, "Well, the time period probably would have been around the Civil War. There was a church, which is no longer there, and a house…." He paused. "It's in D.C. The Capitol was still under construction."

Crawford stared at Carey for a moment, his eyes magnified behind his spectacles. They both knew what "neighborhood" Carey was talking about. "It's lunchtime," Crawford said. "Walk to the Library of Congress. First try the folio section and look for maps and photos from that time period. That should give you the name of the church. Next go to the periodicals room. Start with the Journals of the Columbia Historical Society. They should be indexed. Look for your church there."

Carey nodded.

"Since we're talking Civil War, you might look up U.S. Army official histories. Red Cross records. Or whatever they called themselves back then." Crawford was still staring at the ceiling.

"Another possibility is the D.C. Government. Land deeds, tax assessments, building permits, that sort of thing. Try the Office of Vital Records. It's on North Capitol."

Carey was scribbling now, on scrap paper. "Thanks."

Crawford smiled. "If you want to talk about anything else, I'll be happy to listen."

"Thanks, Norm, I know what I'm doing."

"If you say so."

Crawford pulled the door shut silently behind him.

CAREY'S FIRST EXPERIENCE at the Library of Congress did little except make him feel ignorant. Card catalogs, the Dewey Decimal System, and endless rows of dusty books all intimidated him. But the librarians were efficient and helpful, and soon he was leafing through huge binders of ancient maps covered with cellophane. It was frustrating work. Many maps had symbols for "church" but no names. Others had elegant calligraphy denoting other, more famous churches, but not his.

Finally, he discovered a map from 1866 that had numbers beside all the major landmarks. The U.S. Capitol building had an ornate "1." The legend was in tiny script at the bottom of the page. Number two was a long-gone structure called the "Old Capitol Prison." His finger searched the map for 3rd and C.

Bingo. A church symbol. A number 17.

17. Trinity Episcopal Church

That was the easy part. For the next forty minutes Carey flipped through military records and historical journals, not finding anything remotely useful. His lunch hour long since gone, he trudged back to the office, numb with disappointment.

•   •   •

ON TUESDAY AT NOON Carey paid a visit to the D.C. Office of Vital Records. The clerk did not seem anxious to help until Carey, dressed in his street clothes, produced his badge. The implication was clear that this was police business, even if Carey had no idea what kind of business it really was. Carey was invited into a restricted archive area to browse at his leisure. He spent twenty minutes just walking among the rows of dusty binders, occasionally stopping to pull one from a shelf and flip mindlessly through it.

The Land Deeds section was listed chronologically and started in the middle of the 1840s. There was one binder per year throughout that decade, then two per year, and by the 1890s there was one binder per month. Carey decided he had no way of knowing when the wartime occupants of the house might have bought it or sold it. So on a hunch he took the three 1865 binders from the shelf and lugged them to the table where his legal pad and ballpoint awaited.

An hour later, he asked the clerk if he could leave the binders at the table so that he could continue his research tomorrow. The clerk, a short, balding, bored-looking man of about fifty, shrugged and returned his attention to his magazine, *True Crime*.

Friday evening found Ben Carey in his office before another plate of chop suey, a warm bottle of Coke, and a legal pad. Written at the top, and underlined twice, were the words KNOWN SO FAR.

1. Senator Eugene Morrison of New Jersey, first elected 1852, builds house at 301 C Street. House completed in September 1853. Morrison moves in with wife, Emily, and daughter, Louisa, born January 1844.

2. Wife Emily dies in childbirth, 1857; baby dies as well. Morrison reelected 1858.
3. Morrison dies 1863. Leaves estate to Louisa Rogers (married name?), who dies in 1933. Sold to F Street Builders. They hold onto it until 1955 when the feds buy it; they've been leasing the house to MPD since then.
4. Trinity Episcopal Church built 1835, used as hospital early in the Civil War, 1862–1863, demolished 1901.

Carey began a new heading: UNKNOWNS.

1. Who is the blond man? Was he a wounded soldier?
2. Is there a connection between Trinity and the senator's house?
3. What was the soldier doing in this house? Did he die here? What was his name?
4. Who is the woman in Wallace's sketchbook?—The senator's wife? Daughter? Is the boy her son?
5. Who is the bearded man?

The National Archives building sat on Pennsylvania Avenue halfway between the Capitol and the White House, about four blocks from Substation C. It was a short walk, but a long way from the office in which Carey worked. Neither the fifty-foot-high, six-foot-thick Corinthian columns nor the half-naked Greeks cavorting on the pediment above the north entrance put Carey at ease.

Carey had decided to spend his Saturday following a hunch. The Archives had a massive collection of Civil War records—

including the names of countless Union and Confederate soldiers, where they were from, where they fought, if they were killed
or wounded, and where they went afterward. Carey knew it would
be an uphill battle without a name. But he thought if he could
find a list of wounded men who had come through Trinity Episcopal Church, that would be a start.

It wasn't easy. He took the elevator to the fourth floor, walked
down the hall, and pulled open the large wooden door to Room
400. With the help of the woman behind the counter, Carey
found plenty of lists of infantry units; names of men killed,
wounded, and missing; names of pension applicants; and other
military records indexed by name. After three hours of searching
through scores of indexes, box after box of CMSRs (compiled military service records) and other yellowed, tattered paper forms, he
felt completely defeated. He hefted the most recent cardboard file
box up onto the counter. The archivist, a short, sandy-haired
woman of about fifty, who had been pulling records for him most
of the day, looked at Carey and smiled.

"Any luck this time?" she asked.

"I'm afraid not," said Carey, scratching his cheek. "I don't
know if I'll ever find what I'm looking for this way."

"Well, what is it you're trying to find?" she said.

Carey explained that he was looking for information about a
man, a Union soldier, who may have been wounded near Washington and who might have been treated at Trinity Church when
it served as a hospital. The man may have also had a connection
to Senator Eugene Morrison, who lived in an old house on 3rd
and C.

"Are you a descendant of the senator's?" she asked.

"No."

"Oh, so are you related to this soldier somehow?"

"Not exactly, no."

She decided to leave it alone. They all had their reasons. Carey seemed so determined, and there was something kind and a little sad in his face that touched the older woman. "There's a very knowledgeable old gentleman who uses this archive room quite often," she offered. "His name is Charles Hinton. He used to be a history professor at UVA before he retired. He's written a number of books on the war, and still writes. He might be able to help you or at least point you in the right direction."

"Really?" said Carey. "How would I get in touch with this gentleman?"

"Well, you could go up and introduce yourself," she said. Carey looked puzzled. She pointed to a man hunched over a stack of papers at a table in the far corner. "That's him right over there."

Charles Hinton sat like a question mark in his hardback wooden chair, staring at the papers he shuffled with his left hand, while his right lifted and lowered bifocals onto his nose. He wore a van dyke, with bushy eyebrows and a full head of close-cropped white hair. His face and hands were as wrinkled as his gray suit, and he looked to Carey as though he may have been old enough to have fought in the Civil War.

"Excuse me, Professor Hinton?"

Hinton looked up as if an insect had just buzzed by his ear. He saw Ben standing there. "Yes?"

"Hello, my name is Ben Carey," he stuck out his hand, and Hinton just looked at it. "I'm sorry to bother you, sir, but I was told you were an expert on the Civil War, and I'm trying to find some information in the archives, only I seemed to have hit a dead end. I was hoping you might be able to help me."

"I might," said Hinton. "What are you trying to find?"

"Well, I'm looking for a man whose name I don't know."

Hinton tossed his glasses down on the table and leaned back

in his chair, studying the young man before him. "How do you know who the man is without his name?"

"I've seen the man's picture," Carey said, measuring his words. "I know where he was for part of the war. He was a Union soldier, wounded near Washington. He was treated at Trinity Episcopal Church, I think....He may have stayed at a house owned by a Senator Morrison from New Jersey."

"That all?" Hinton asked.

"I'm afraid so."

"Hmm." Hinton rubbed his eyes with his thumb and forefinger for a what seemed a long time. "You think he was treated at Trinity for his wounds, eh?" Carey nodded. "You know there were almost no hospitals in Washington at the start of the war?" Carey shook his head and took a seat across from Hinton. "Churches were often put to use as makeshift hospitals," Hinton continued. "Later on, they built massive, airy hospitals all over town. But through '63, most of the medical care was administered in those churches. Of course, they were overburdened, so many private homes volunteered to act as halfway houses where the wounded soldiers could convalesce before being shipped back to the front...or sent home."

"So Senator Morrison's home could have been one of these halfway houses?" Carey asked.

"It's possible," Hinton nodded. "But if I were you, I wouldn't bother searching these archives." Carey frowned. "There's a book on medical care in the Civil War which was written by an old colleague of mine, Avery Pritchett. Unfortunately, he passed away several years ago. But it might give you some information on the churches and homes that were once used to treat soldiers. I forget the title, but just look it up under 'Pritchett.' The public library ought to have it."

. . .

CAREY WEIGHED THE FADED, blue, clothbound book in his hands as he sat behind his desk. *Blood on the Battlefield: Medical Care of Wounded Soldiers in the Civil War* by Avery M. Pritchett was a thick text heavily illustrated with black-and-white photos. Carey began reading the introduction. It described the primitive medical technology of the day and the treatment the wounded soldiers received, which consisted mainly of amputating limbs. Scanning the table of contents, Carey saw chapters on army surgeons, the introduction of women nurses, the ambulance system, field tactics, sanitation and hygiene, and finally a chapter on the general hospitals and the cities in which they were built to treat the wounded—the most prominent of which was Washington, D.C.

According to Pritchett, the army had at first not been well prepared enough to care for all the wounded soldiers who came back from the front lines. This hardly surprised Carey. Ambulance systems had been developed during the Civil War to help save many of the wounded who, in some cases, waited for days while their wounds festered or they bled to death on the battlefield. Pritchett described the network of private organizations that provided medical attention to the soldiers—the Christian Commission, the Sisters of Charity, and the Sanitary Commission. The Sanitary Commission had been responsible for coordinating much of the medical care of the wounded during the war, establishing hospitals, keeping records of soldiers who had been wounded, training many of the first female nurses, and working with many individuals who offered their homes to recuperating Union soldiers.

When Carey came to the page, the image struck him immediately. The photograph was obviously very old, but all of the details were crystal clear. Looking down from the north and west, Trinity Church stood tall in the foreground, with its western façade brightly lit by the afternoon sun. Its twin Gothic steeples, topped with open arches rising to a single spire, towered over the neighborhood a hundred feet above the ground. A hexagonal baptistery rose above the southeast corner of the church, half as high as the towers. All of the windows were ornately decorated with stone tracery and stained glass. It was hard to imagine that the church would be demolished less than forty years later; the building had the feel of a medieval castle, timeless, permanent. And yet today there was no trace of it.

Most of the surrounding area in the photo consisted of empty lots and newly planted trees, with a few low buildings huddled beside the church, including a grocery store with a pen in back, probably for pigs and chickens. What struck Carey immediately, however, was the sight of the Capitol building in the background, its half-finished dome clearly visible, a giant crane protruding from the middle, exactly as he had seen it in his dream.

As Carey examined the photograph more closely, he noticed the corner of a house peeking out of the lower right-hand corner of the frame. It was blurry, but it was obvious to Carey that it was a part of the turret room in which he now slept.

The caption read: "When the wounded started pouring into Washington in the spring of 1862, any available building was put to use as a hospital, as was this church—Trinity Episcopal at Third and C Streets NW."

Carey began to read the text from the beginning of the section on Washington:

> When the sick and wounded from General McClellan's divisions started arriving in Washington by the shipload in the spring of 1862, the authorities had no choice but to commandeer churches, fraternal halls, hotels, schools, and colleges....Even the Capitol build-

ing became a hospital after the thousands of wounded soldiers from Second Manassas showed up on Washington's doorstep in late August.

He read on:

> By October 1862, there were close to sixty hospitals in Washington, up from only one dispensary in May 1861....Trinity Episcopal Church saw more than two thousand wounded soldiers come and go through its doors from 1861 till 1863, when new, larger, pavilion-style hospitals were built....
>
> In order to lessen the burden shouldered by the many makeshift hospitals in Washington, many private homes were opened to soldiers with less severe wounds, or who were recuperating from injuries treated in hospital....Senator Eugene Morrison (Rep.-N.J.), a leading abolitionist, was one of the most prominent members of Washington society to open his doors to these recovering soldiers....

Aha. Carey's instincts were right, he was sure of it now. However, he was still no closer to discovering a name. He felt like he was on the brink of finding the man, he was just out of reach. *This book must hold the key*, he thought.

He started flipping through the pages randomly, searching for something, anything. He got to the back of the book, glanced through the acknowledgments, a note on the sources, an appendix, and the index; he turned back to the author's sources. Carey read through a dense and detailed description of the secondary sources Pritchett had used, some that he recommended, and others he did not—*A Medical and Surgical History of the War of the*

Rebellion; *The History of the United States Sanitary Commission*; *The Boys in White: The Experience of a Hospital Agent in and around Washington*; and so on. After eight pages of this, Carey came to the last paragraph, describing the author's primary sources. "Some of the most important manuscripts," Pritchett wrote, "are held in the archives of the United States Sanitary Commission…" Carey's eyes lit up. "Comprising 1,200 boxes of papers, this collection was housed in New York's Lenox Library shortly after the Civil War. When the Lenox Library was absorbed by the New York Public Library, the Sanitary Commission archive was moved to the Library of Congress in Washington, D.C., where it now resides in a subbasement of the Library building."

Son of a bitch. Carey knew where he would be spending his Sunday.

Carey arrived at the Library of Congress shortly after it opened at ten A.M. He located the subbasement room in which the Sanitary Commission's boxed archives were kept. Pritchett had specifically mentioned two subsections that contained the most pertinent documents: The Papers of the Army of the Potomac and The Papers of the Washington Office. With the help of the librarian, he began to wade through the boxes of papers of the Washington Office at around 10:30.

It took over an hour of leafing through the crumbling records, but just before noon, he found what he was looking for: discharge records by date, sorted by hospital—including the names of soldiers discharged to the care of private homes for recovery. On a few dozen sheets of faded vellum paper were the handwritten reports for all of the soldiers discharged from Trinity Church Hospital for the years 1861 to 1863. Next to each neatly written name was a short description of the soldier's destination, such as "rejoined unit," "discharged from service," or, in some cases, the name of the private home to which the soldier was sent to recuperate—

"Gibson," "Case," "O'Sullivan," "Morrison,"...

Carey started in 1861 and began to copy into his notebook the names of each soldier who was released into the care of Senator Morrison. By the time he reached the end of 1862, he had transcribed the names of nineteen men. He scanned the list of names from the beginning:

> Geo. Goodale
> Peter Corbett
> Wm. McKean
> John Dunleavy
> Walter Lee
> Nicholas Hensen
> Lucius Andrus
> J. M. Lewis
> Robert LaChance
> Jos. Brown
> Mordechai Finkel
> Oscar O'Brien
> Samuel Crowley
> ...

None of the names meant anything to Carey. Though he felt certain the name he was looking for was on this list, he had no idea which one it could be. He returned the papers to their box, closed his notebook, and headed back to the office.

MARIE CLIMBED THE STAIRS and stood on the front porch of the old Victorian house, not at all sure that this was the right place. It was the right address—301 C Street—but it sure didn't have the look of a police building. Above the old-fashioned mail slot next to the door was a typewritten note duct-taped to the wood siding that read:

METROPOLITAN POLICE DEPT.

SUBSTATION C

SUPERVISING OFFICER: SGT. BENJAMIN CAREY

So this was the place. She rang the ancient doorbell but didn't hear a sound from inside. She knocked on the door, gently at first, then firmly, the way cops do, she thought to herself.

No one answered. Marie felt a little silly standing on the front porch of Ben's workplace on a Sunday afternoon. What did she expect? But she had an inkling—Ben was not staying with anyone they knew, and she knew he didn't have enough money to be staying at a hotel. She suspected that maybe Ben had been sleeping at the office. Now that she saw the place, it started to make more sense to her. She debated whether or not she should wait to see if anyone showed up when she looked up to see Ben walking up 3rd Street, a hopeful expression on his face as his eyes met hers.

"Marie?"

"Hello, Ben," she said. "I just came by, hoping to find you." She looked around the place as he climbed the porch steps. "I wanted to apologize for the other night."

"No need to be sorry," he said, a trace of a smile on his face. "You could have called, though. I'd hate for you to think I'm easy."

"It wasn't fair of me to lead you on like that," she said.

"Oh." He tensed his jaw, not liking the direction in which the conversation was headed.

"I'm not sure what to say," he said softly, his eyes searching her expression.

She grew more tense standing there, and said, "I still have feelings for you, Ben—"

"But…" he added.

"You'd asked me if there was anyone else, and there wasn't—"

"*Wasn't?*" he repeated.

"Isn't, I mean…." she stammered and paused, trying to choose her words carefully. "We haven't done anything." There was the *we* Ben had been dreading, confirming his worst fears. "But I've developed feelings for someone else, and…I don't know what to say. I never intended for this to happen."

Ben turned away and sighed, shaking his head. "God," he said, closing his eyes and letting the truth of it sink in for the first time. "I've been such a goddamned fool."

"No, you haven't," she said.

"Why?" he said, trying to look her in the eye but not wanting to. "Can you just tell me *why?*"

Marie looked down but said nothing.

Ben stared across the street at the empty lot that once held the cathedral. He wished he could be angrier, that he had the will to break something—anything to alleviate the pain and make him feel better. But what he felt most of all was sad and desperate. There was no way to fix this kind of hurt, and he wished he could leave his body and forego the suffering. The longer he stood there and thought about it, the more he hated himself for being so naïve, for not being able to see this coming.

"You know," he said, as much to himself as to her, "the first thing I learned about police work is that the simplest explanation is usually the right one. Somehow, I just couldn't bring myself to accept that." He gripped the porch railing with both hands, as if to steady himself, and stared at her, wishing she were unable to hurt him so easily. "So who is it?" he asked finally. "Anyone I know?" Then, homing in on the more likely suspect: "Someone from work?"

Marie turned away, drawing a handkerchief from her bag and

dabbing at her eyes.

"Never mind," he said. "I don't want to know."

"You deserve better than this, Ben, I know," she said. "I'm sorry."

Somehow her apology meant very little to him this time.

CAREY SAT DOWN behind his desk. He had spent hours in the Library's subbasement earlier in the day poring over documents. By the time he had found what he was looking for, his vision was so blurry he could barely make out the words on the page. He never realized how exhausting that kind of mental exercise could be.

Then Marie showed up. Part of him was relieved—the stress of wondering if there was "still a chance" had ended, along with any hope of reconciliation. But mostly he wavered between helpless anger and self-pity, and he wondered when it was going to stop hurting so much. He looked at his notebook lying on the desk, rolled his eyes, and threw Wallace's old sketchbook into the drawer.

Out of the same drawer he retrieved a short glass along with the bottle of scotch he'd been keeping there. He'd felt guilty about going off the wagon after Christmas, but he didn't give a damn now. He poured himself a generous eye-opener. He threw the drink back in one gulp. Still sad and angry, but the scotch did take the edge off. He poured himself another drink, trying to stop the thoughts racing through his head, wanting only to sleep...

He is lying on the cot alone in the room again. Out of the window he can see the Capitol dome, still unfinished, as if frozen in this condition. He tries to move his legs but cannot. He turns his head around to see someone looking down on him. Her face comes into the light, and he can see that it is Marie. She is crying but won't

*look him in the eye. She starts to back away from him. She is hold-
ing a knife and it is covered in blood, as are his hands. He reaches
out to her but cannot touch her before she is gone. He hears the
door shut and looks down to see the wound in his belly, oozing
blood, soaking his clothes and sheets.*

*Everything is foggy now. He looks back to the door and sees the
man again. The hat is pulled down to his wide, staring eyes. A dark
beard and caked-on dirt conceal the rest of his face. The bearded
man stands there, holding something shiny and round in his hand.
But he does not approach the man on the cot. He keeps looking at
the dying man and backs out of the room with a malevolent smirk
on his face.*

*He closes his eyes and all is black. He hears a banging, soft at
first, then growing louder, more insistent—*

Carey sat bolt upright, his sleeping bag damp with sweat. The
banging continued. The heat was kicking on and the rhythmic
clanging had returned, only this time behind every hollow *clang*
was a sharp *knock*, alternating in a strange syncopation, spreading
through the walls. The hairs on the back of his neck stood on end.
As the clanging began to die down, the knocking grew louder. It
was coming from downstairs.

Rising to his knees and cocking his head, Carey concentrated
on the sound.

Clanng…

Thump.

(clanng…)

Thump!

Carey pulled on his pants and headed to the top of the stairs.
As he listened from the top step, he could hear it clearly now, and
it was coming from the wall by the basement door. The clanging
had stopped, only the strange knocking continued.

Thump!
Thump!

He rushed down the stairs, his bare feet blue from the cold. By the time he reached the basement door, the sound had moved. It was now coming from the wall in the basement. He opened the door and started down the darkened stairwell. Carey had left a claw hammer on the ledge behind the door earlier, and he grabbed it now, not really sure why, but it made him feel a little safer.

The knocking led him down the stairs and into complete darkness. Probing the blackness with his free hand, Carey felt for the light-bulb chain, finding it at last. He grasped the chain firmly in his hand and held his breath. He pulled the chain, throwing the corner of the room into stark brightness, shadows bouncing along the walls as the bulb danced on its cord. Carey's eyes had trouble adjusting to the bright light, but he soon fixed on the source of the knocking. It was coming from inside one of the interior walls a few feet above the floor. The sound only grew louder, and Carey could see the whitewashed wooden boards of the wall shake with the force of each knock.

THUMP!

Was something trapped inside? His first thought was an animal, but he immediately doubted that. What then? Something unknowable, which scared Carey more, but compelled him to find out at the same time. It was madness, he knew. His whole body was trembling when the knock came again—

THUMP!

Dust billowed out from the wall, illuminated by the bare bulb above. Carey thought he was losing his mind. "*Goddamnit!*" he shouted. "*What the hell do you want from me?*"

There were several seconds of silence before a low rumbling began within the wall, building to a torrent of staccato knocks, maniac drum beats shaking everything around him and echoing through his skull.

Carey dropped to one knee, drew the claw of his hammer back, and drove it into a crack between two of the boards. Splinters flew up, but Carey just kept tearing at the wall, pulling back shards of rotten wood, until there was a hole in the wall the size of his head. In his frenzy, Carey hadn't realized that the knocking had stopped. He stared at the hole for a moment and then reached his hand in. Bits of paper insulation, a wall stud, more debris on the floor inside the wall...nothing.

Now the silence confronted him. He was alone in the basement, in front of a hole in the wall he'd just put there, lit by a single bulb. Kneeling on the floor, trying to catch his breath, he heard the first footfall at the top of the stairs. The stair creaked, and Carey looked up, but the stairs were in shadow. A second footstep, as of someone descending the basement stairs. Carey gripped the hammer tightly in his right hand and quickly rose up, but he did not see the five-inch cast-iron drain pipe three feet above his head.

The back of his skull slammed into the pipe, knocking him unconscious.

CAREY AWOKE a few hours later in a heap on the floor of the basement, his head throbbing from its encounter with the drain pipe, as well as the scotch. This insult was added to the injury of Marie's infidelity and what he hoped were his hallucinatory imaginings.

He pressed on the large lump on the back of his head and winced in pain. It seemed as fitting a manifestation as any of the wound his wife had delivered earlier in the day. Focusing on one misery at a time, he tried not to think about the house anymore, or any of its mysteries. He drank himself to sleep that night and trudged around in a stupor the next day. The next two days were a haze.

Wednesday night, Norm insisted Ben join him for dinner at his house. Though it didn't exactly make him forget his troubles, between his first home-cooked meal in over three weeks and the company of Norm's wife and kids, it made for a welcome distraction. He stayed long after their boys went to bed and talked with Norm and Mary late into the night, beginning to feel like a normal person once again.

Ben bid them good night and caught a streetcar back to the office. Climbing the stairs to his temporary asylum, Ben felt less of the dread he thought he would. In the light of his sobriety, the house seemed less malevolent to him than it had, less sinister. It was just a house, after all.

The next day Ben began to climb out of his hole.

He decided to make the best of his situation. He could save for a new apartment and have enough to move out by the end of the month. In the meantime, he could pick up a few things to make his stay in the house easier. He made shopping plans for lunch.

While rearranging papers on his desk, a slip of paper fell out from Wallace's black notebook. It was the claim slip for the film he'd dropped off two weeks ago. He had forgotten all about it. Ben decided to do some shopping at Finkel's over lunch, and then stop by People's Drug to collect his prints on the way back from the department store.

IN THE PAST, Finkel's department store had been a grand destination in downtown D.C., especially during the holidays, when families stood in line to eat at its fine restaurant and children waited for hours for a chance to sit on Santa's lap. Its flagship store in New York had once even rivaled Macy's. The first big department store to expand to other cities, Finkel's other East Coast branches had become local landmarks. But recently they had had to close some of their stores.

In a town with its own venerable department stores, Finkel's had made its mark in D.C. when it opened its first store in the 1880s. Taking up almost an entire city block at F and 6th Streets, the eight-story Finkel's building was an impressive monument to conspicuous consumption. During the 1950s, Finkel's competition had begun to cater to higher-end customers—Macy's and Bloomingdales in New York, Wanamaker's in Philadelphia, and Woodward & Lothrop and Hecht's in Washington—which squeezed Finkel's into the unaccustomed position of trying to appeal to price-sensitive consumers while keeping its toney image. It wasn't quite working; although for most, like Carey, Finkel's was still a good, solid place to find most anything. Plus, it was a short walk from the office.

Carey had been living at Substation C for close to three weeks now and needed some of the comforts of home. A toaster, a new coffee pot, a pillow, some towels, and a new shower curtain and bath mat would be a start. As Carey wandered through the housewares section, trying to locate a coffee percolator, he brushed past a display of shiny aluminum saucepans and knocked the neatly stacked pyramid off its table and onto the floor. He quickly dropped to a knee and began picking up pots with both hands. A pretty young saleswoman bent down and began helping Carey put them back on the table.

"Thanks," he said. "I don't know how I managed to do that."

"Don't worry about it," she said. "I think this display gets someone just about every day." They both stood up as she placed the last saucepan on the table.

"Thanks for saying that," he said. "I think I'm just a little off today. Never had my morning coffee. Which I guess is why I'm here."

She smiled at Carey. "You did look a little lost," she said. "My name's Ruth. Is there anything I could help you find?"

"Ben," Carey said and extended his hand to Ruth. "I think that might be a good idea."

Ruth led Carey around the department, helping him to find what he was looking for. He was flattered that someone as young and attractive as Ruth had noticed him—*before* he knocked over the display. Carey realized that, for the first time since he had proposed to Marie, he was noticing another woman.

CAREY WOUND UP buying more than he had intended to and couldn't carry everything he bought with him. He didn't think it would look good to be carting a load of kitchen and bath items into the office, anyway, so he arranged to have it all delivered on Saturday. On the way back to the office, Carey picked up his photos at People's Drug and shoved them into the pocket of his trenchcoat. He would look at them after work.

It turned out to be a good day. After lunch, Carey received a letter from the Justice Department informing him that their grant proposal for twelve new air-conditioned cruisers had been partially approved. They had allocated money for six new cars. Carey called Crawford, Don Mullins, and Brian Kelsey into his office to make the announcement. Carey knew that his group had been a little down, and that it had been his fault. He could see that this first small success gave them a sense of accomplishment and purpose in their jobs.

"We need to start thinking now," Carey said, "about how we can use the implementation of these new cruisers to justify the purchase of additional vehicles."

"Good idea," agreed Mullins.

"We should hear back from Justice about the two-way radios any day," said Crawford. "Based on this, I'm fairly optimistic."

Carey spoke to his men for a few minutes and tried to encourage them. "You have to be patient," he told them. "It takes a while for everybody to see results from this. But this is a good start." He felt guilty about his leadership of the unit so far. Work had been the last thing on his mind since breaking up with Marie. But despite everything, he still cared about his job. He told his men how important the planning unit was, that it would end up making their fellow officers' jobs less dangerous and could even save lives. And he believed it.

That evening, Carey left the office with his fellow officers at around 5:30. At six, he returned with a burger and a Coke. He set the burger and the soda bottle down on his desk and dug the pack of photos out of his coat pocket. He tossed it onto the desk and hung up his coat. Sitting down, it occurred to him that this was the first night in a long time that he didn't feel like having a drink.

Carey felt at times as though he were straddling two worlds. There was the real world, with its problems and heartaches, but a world of sanity, reason, a place where you could count on certain things. Then there was this house—a place harboring dark secrets, unexplained sights and sounds, and strange, frightening dreams.

He preferred the real world. But something wouldn't let him let go of this mystery, in spite of his own troubles. He was drawn to it, as he always had been drawn to the things that scared him. Familiarity was his way of dealing with the unknown. And, unlike his own life, he was naïve enough to think it was something he could fix. So he opened the packet of photos to find out what was there.

There were only two photos Carey was interested in: the ones he had taken the night the officers came in looking for a young boy. The rest of the roll he had filled up with photos of the house and street. After flipping through some of these, he came to the first photo of the upstairs doorway. The door of the turret room was slightly ajar, and the flash had lit up the inside of the room, leaving the hall in darkness. He couldn't make out anything meaningful in the first photo. The second photo was from a slightly different angle, but more or less the same, it seemed: a brightly lit door and walls, dark shadows thrown from the fireplace into the corner of the room, a sliver of wood floor, and a darkened hallway with nebulous gray shapes where the light from the flash met the shadows.

But Carey looked closer. On the floor of the hallway, he could make out what looked like a small wheel, about two or three inches tall. *What the...?* Carey's eyes gazed across his desk and rested upon the toy cannon he had found in the basement, which he was now using as a paperweight. The wheels were identical. *What was the toy cannon doing in the hallway?*

ON FRIDAY'S LUNCH BREAK, Carey returned to the Office of Vital Records. Being his second visit, he was more comfortable searching through their records and knew where to look for certain kinds of information, such as marriages, deaths, and births. By the time his lunch hour was over, he had discovered some interesting facts. Louisa Morrison married a man named Harrison Rogers on October 26, 1862. When her father died in September 1863, she inherited the house, her name then being "Louisa Rogers." What's more, Louisa and Harrison had had a son, James, who was born on June 24, 1863. *They didn't waste any time*, Carey thought to himself.

The Rogers family lived in the old house after the senator's passing, and as far as Carey could tell, they never had any more children. Were the drawings Wallace had made of a young woman and a little boy Louisa and James Rogers? If so, where was Harrison?

It raised other questions. What did these people have to do with the blond-haired soldier or the bearded man? Or what did *they* have to do with the Rogerses?

Carey wrote down more notes and underlined his questions. He felt that he was making progress, but it was slow-going and frustrating.

ON SATURDAY MORNING, Carey set about the task of fixing the basement wall. He wasn't really sure why he felt the need to fix it. After all, the house was going to be demolished in less than a year to make room for more federal buildings. But it did give him something to do. He was feeling stuck with his extracurricular investigation, and he would just be thinking about Marie otherwise.

He tore out all the old boards with the hammer, cleaning and preparing the space between the studs for new one-by-eights. As he removed the last broken board at the top of the hole, he saw the corner of a bright white piece of paper sticking out from under the old board above it. Carey reached his hand in and felt the paper, thick and stiff and smooth. It was flat against the inside of the wall, the top corner stuck in between two other boards. His fingers felt along the back of the paper until he was able to move it slightly downward and grab the bottom corner. He pulled gently, but it wouldn't come loose. He pulled down harder until he heard a muffled rip, and it came free.

He brushed away the dust and debris and turned it over in his hands beneath the light. The piece of paper was a photograph. Though one corner had ripped when he pulled it out, it was intact. Ben could see that it was a family portrait—a young woman, her husband, and their young son.

He carried the photograph up the stairs, went into his office, laid it down on his desk, and looked at it under the light. It was plain that the photo was very old. The image was worn from moisture and debris, and the family's formal dress, stiff poses, and stern expressions were a telltale remnant of the era.

Carey had seen a lot of old photographs. Aside from the prints at the Library of Congress, he remembered from his childhood many of the late-nineteenth-century family portraits that his grandmother had held onto. The unusual thing about this photograph was that the image had crisp, dark lines and shadows. Light faded photographs over time. It must have been inside the basement wall for a very long time.

The woman in the photograph was young, in her twenties, and very pretty, while the boy was about five or six years old. He strongly resembled his mother. The father appeared somewhat older, with black, slicked-back hair and a pencil-thin mustache and goatee.

He turned to the sketches Wallace had made of the woman and child and looked at the notes from his research. *Was the mother Louisa Rogers?* The poses and expressions were different, but the likeness was readily apparent. It made as much sense as anything that this was the same woman. *What was the boy's name?* Carey flipped back through his notes. *James.*

He wondered, *Could the toy cannon have belonged to the boy in the photo?* And then a disturbing thought occurred to him. *Was he the same boy the officers saw that night, looking out of the window? Had he been playing with his cannon when I took the pictures?*

If the woman was Louisa and the boy, her son, James, then the man must have been Harrison Rogers, the boy's father. Carey slipped the photograph in between the pages of the notebook, then scribbled down this note: *Old family photograph — of Harrison, Louisa, and James Rogers(?)*

The old photo had to be of Harrison, Louisa, and James. There was no other explanation Ben could think of. But would it bring him any closer to discovering the identities of the blond-haired soldier and the sinister-looking, bearded man? Ben couldn't figure out how, but he thought there must be a connection.

AFTER A LUNCH OF COLD CUTS, he returned to repairing the wall in the basement. He primed the new section of one-by-eights and waited for it to dry. While he waited, he thought to rig up a hook and chain so that he could turn the basement light off and on from the top of the stairs.

That afternoon, the delivery truck from Finkel's arrived. A new coffee pot, an automatic toaster, some plates and cups, a new shower curtain, and bath towels were among the creature comforts Carey had picked out, with Ruth's help. He thought of her again and smiled.

It took Carey until after dark to finish cleaning up in the basement. The two-by-three-foot area looked like new, in sharp contrast to the hundred-year-old wall surrounding it.

Carey climbed the stairs and pulled the ball at the end of the chain beside the basement door, turning out the light. He opened the box of bath items and carried the towels and shower curtain into the bathroom, along with his shaving kit, which he kept in his office. After he tossed out the ragged, moldy old shower curtain and put up the new one, he stripped down to his boxers and turned the hot-water handle on full in the shower. The cold bathroom immediately began to fill up with steam. Carey wiped his hand across the mirror over the sink and lathered his face with the brush. He filled the sink with water, took out the ivory-handled straight razor that his father had given him on his eighteenth birthday, and again wiped the mirror with his hand.

He dragged the blade down his right cheek and dunked the

razor into the water. As he moved on to his neck, the fluorescent light above the mirror began to flicker off and on. Carey flicked the plastic casing around the bulb with his finger, and it stopped. He dunked the razor in the water and raised it to the other side of his neck. As he did so, the light again flickered off and on, and off. It stayed off this time, even after Carey flicked it. In the darkness, he felt for the side of the sink with his hand and put the razor down on the rim. This time he held the light casing with his left hand and whacked it hard with his right. The light flickered back on.

Carey reached for his razor, but it wasn't there. He looked on the floor under the sink, figuring it had fallen down there, but couldn't see it. Confused, he looked up into the fog-covered mirror and saw a pair of eyes staring back at him. All he could see were the eyes, and before Carey could turn to face whoever was standing behind him, a glint of steel flashed in front of his face and came toward him. As quickly as he could, he blocked the razor with his right hand, the blade slicing into his palm.

Carey screamed in pain as he stumbled backward, and the assailant forced the razor closer to his neck, trying to cut his throat. It was all Carey could do to reach behind him and grab the back of the man's head. With all his weight, Carey forced the man backward into the shower curtain, and they both fell hard into the tub, the water from the shower head spraying down on them.

Carey's head ached, having hit the rim of the far side of the tub. He wheeled around to see who it was who had attacked him, but no one was there. There was nobody else in the bathroom. As the hot water trickled down his face, he stared in disbelief at the straight razor he gripped in his bloody right hand.

CHAPTER 11.

Wednesday, September 24, 1862

OF THE NINETEEN SOLDIERS who had been guests in Senator Morrison's home, Mordechai Finkel was the only one who had left in a shroud. The other eighteen had recuperated enough to return home—some of them wrote to Louisa and the senator from time to time, two of the families sadly related the deaths of their soldiers after they returned. While such news came as a blow to the house, it wasn't shocking. Mordechai, however, was different.

Louisa did not send Mordechai straight to the cemetery along with the numerous other casualties of the war that day but to the undertaker's shop. She paid the $10 for his body to be cleaned and returned to her house for mourning. By the time Mordechai's body returned to the parlor, Edna had draped black fabric on the windows of the house and had collected a sufficient number of candles and garden flowers to keep the house smelling decent, at least throughout the vigil.

Edna insisted that Louisa not stay in the parlor more than usual, but the girl didn't move from the chair she had pulled to the center of the room. Instead, Louisa sat perfectly straight in a starched black dress while tears rolled freely down her face and splattered on the fabric of her skirts with a steady *pat-pat-pat*. Late September heat crawled through the drapery and curled around the room. The small tray of biscuits Edna had prepared for Louisa sat on the floor, untouched. Louisa's only motion all day was a slight swaying she was not even aware of.

With the exception of Edna and the three remaining soldiers still under her care, Louisa mourned alone. She had wired Mordechai's father about his son's death, trying to appear caring but detached. As far as Louisa knew, Mordechai hadn't mentioned her to anyone in his inner circle, let alone his father, and so she felt it was not her place to interfere in their lives. A grief-stricken Samuel Finkel replied to her wire with another, this one saying he was too ill to travel to attend his son's ceremony but he would send money along to her for whatever service Louisa saw fit. Expediency, he said, was of utmost importance to him over his ability to be present at the burial. Though brief, the telegram broke Louisa's heart. Mordechai often spoke of the close relationship he and his father shared, and she guessed that Samuel was the one other person on Earth who was just as devastated as she. Louisa kept the telegram as a physical link to Mordechai and placed it inside the back cover of her family's bible.

The next morning, Mordechai's closest acquaintance in the house, Robert LaChance, stood in the doorway to the parlor, facing the rest of the household and the simple wooden casket. He spoke in a slow drawl.

"I'm not a pastor or anything, but Miss Louisa asked me to say a few words about the passing of one of us. Our brother and soldier Mordechai didn't believe the same things we did, in a religious way, I mean. But he never said a bad word about anyone, and he always helped out here when he could. Even with his injury," Robert looked to the ground, to his own two capable feet, "he helped the best he could. He served with us and, in every way I can think of, then, he served God."

Robert sneaked a glance at Louisa, who remained rigid in her seat. The dark-haired man who stood next to her had arrived at the house early that morning, and immediately was able to calm Louisa from her agitated state. He and Louisa had grown up together, Edna had explained over breakfast, and he was to be treated in the highest regard. Harrison Rogers was, after all, the son of Senator Morrison's close ally, and it wasn't difficult for anyone within sight of the two of them to notice the paternal affinity the senator had for Rogers—clasping the younger man on the shoulder, offering up his personal study for Rogers to use, and, so it seemed to the rest of the household, making sure Rogers stayed at Louisa's side.

Robert could see that Rogers obviously had the means and the manner of privilege. His muslin shirt was pressed and sat beneath a silk vest that perfectly matched the black silk lining of his wool frock coat that was exposed whenever he leaned over to whisper something to Louisa. From his slicked back hair to the clean laces on his shoes, everything about Rogers was in its place. And though a damp heat hung in the house, Rogers looked refreshed, as if, Robert thought, the man was even able to control his own sweat glands. Still, Rogers appeared to be truly hurting for Louisa, and he rested his hand on her shoulder in a most familiar way. Robert was grateful to him for this.

He continued, holding up a small leather book. "This man Thoreau seemed to believe that God is 'the Artist who made the world,' and I think that's true. That makes Mordechai a special creation, no matter what he believed. Furthermore, as it says in this book, 'Walden was dead and is alive again.' That's my favorite line here. It reminds me of my own religion and the Spirit everlasting. I know in my heart that Mordechai is dead, but his spirit will live on."

Just as he finished speaking, two gravediggers from the local cemetery approached the steps outside. Robert crossed the room, placed his hand on the lid to the makeshift casket, and closed it silently.

"Good-bye, my brother," he whispered.

Everyone in the room began following Robert in prayer except Louisa. For her, everything already had gone dark.

AS ARRANGED, they met in The West End, at a table in the back of the room. Aaron Hilldrup arrived on time, ninety minutes before Eddy showed up. It had grown dark while he waited. Hilldrup's heart began racing when Eddy entered the noisy, crowded establishment, and as the gaunt assassin took the wooden chair across from him, Hilldrup wondered why any man would arrive ninety minutes late to get paid.

After all, I didn't have to show up for this, Hilldrup thought. *I could have caught the next train back to Manhattan and the deserter would be out $400.* Hilldrup had put down $100, and that should have been enough for any job, he believed, and by being here, he only cemented the connection between Eddy and himself. And yet Eddy had spooked him somehow. Hilldrup intended to make good on his debt.

"Deed's done." Eddy looked toward the bar, beckoning the mulatto woman. She brought him a half-full glass of cloudy liquid.

Hilldrup waited for the woman to walk away. "I assume you have some proof," he whispered.

The outlaw turned his glare toward Hilldrup, his mouth twisted around the stump of an unlit cigar. "Like what, his ear?" But as he said this, he open his clenched fist and dangled a pocket-watch in front of Hilldrup's face, its chain held tight between Eddy's thumb and forefinger. Hilldrup tried to read the initials engraved onto the back of the watch, but it swayed back and forth only twice before Eddy snatched it away.

"I took it off of him after," said Eddy. "He won't be needing it anymore."

"Jesus," said Hilldrup, a man not used to swearing. The reality of what he had set in motion was beginning to sink in.

"I found him in the turret room. 301 C Street, right? Long side-burns, blond hair. Man was in that room. Missing a foot. Soldier, I reckon. Was wounded in the gut, too." Eddy gulped his drink, returning an empty glass to the table.

With shaking hands, Hilldrup pulled a bulging envelope from his pocket. He peeled twenty bills from a thick wad and tossed them to the table. "I, of course, thank you for your discretion in this matter." He stood and stuffed his wallet back into his vest, and headed for the door.

Eddy watched him leave, and stared at the swinging tavern doors until they were motionless. Then he stood up, folded the bills into his pocket, and followed Hilldrup into the empty street.

CHAPTER 12.

Monday, January 20, 1958

DON MULLINS WALKED down the hall on his way to Norm Craw-ford's office. As he was about to pass his sergeant's door, Carey opened it and emerged from his office, nearly running into Mullins.

"Oh, hey, Ben," Mullins said, "'morning."

"Hey, Don."

Mullins saw the large bandage wrapped around Carey's right hand. "Ooh, what happened to your hand there?"

"Oh, that." Carey paused. "I…um, caught my hand on a nail over the weekend. Tore my palm up."

"Ouch."

"Yeah," Carey said, shaking his head.

Mullins was unconsciously staring at Carey's face, which was red and raw, with dark stubble sprouting from patches on his neck and chin. "You growin' a beard or something, Ben?"

Carey gave Mullins a confused look before remembering why he would ask him that. "No, no. Regulations wouldn't allow it, anyway. I've just switched to one of those new electric razors."

"Oh.…If I were you, I'd switch back."

"Well, I'm thinking about it," said Carey, getting tired of the conversation. He moved aside and nodded his head toward the kitchen. "I was just going for some coffee."

"Oh, sorry, don't let me stop you."

Mullins walked across to Crawford's office and knocked before pushing the door open. "Hey, Norm, I got those reports you wanted."

"Thanks, Don," said Crawford. "Just put 'em on that pile." He pointed to a corner of his desk a foot deep in paper. Crawford was reading through a new equipment request he'd been working on.

"Say, Norm?" Mullins said, hanging around in his doorway.

"Yeah, Don?"

"You and Ben go back a long ways, don't ya? I mean, you served together in Korea, right?"

"Yeah. It seems like a long time ago now," Crawford said, taking off his glasses and rubbing the bridge of his nose. "You serve?"

"In the navy, yeah. I was too young for the war, though." Mullins took the question as an invitation and closed the door, sitting down in the wooden chair across from Crawford's desk. "The reason I ask is, I like Ben a lot, I mean, we used to be partners and all, but…"

"But what?"

"Seem to you like he's been acting a little strange lately?"

Crawford sighed. "Don, Ben's a very private man. I'm not sure he'd want me telling you his business." Mullins nodded and looked down at the floor. "On the other hand, I'd rather you weren't drawing your own conclusions. You married, Don?" Mullins shook his head. "Well, it looks like Ben and his wife are going to split up. Get a divorce. And he's pretty shook up about it. He's just in a funk right now, but he's going to be all right in time."

"Jeez," said Mullins. "I had no idea." Mullins looked around Crawford's office. It had been Wallace's office, but after he died, Crawford needed the extra space. Now it had files and paperwork stacked everywhere, the look of a busy, productive workplace.

"Don," said Crawford. "You mind if I ask you a question?"

"Sure. Shoot."

"I know these old houses tend to have all sorts of odd creaks and noises, but have you heard or seen anything funny since you've been here?"

"Funny?" said Mullins. "Well, like what?"

"I don't know…just, funny. You know, anything out of the ordinary."

"Not that I can think of," said Mullins, trying to think of something. "It gets a lot of drafts, though, this house." Crawford raised an eyebrow. "I mean, it's usually plenty warm. But every once in a while, if I walk over to a certain spot on the floor, I'll feel a chill. But I can never seem to see where the draft is coming from."

"Just wondering," said Crawford. "Thanks, Don. I'll get back to you on those reports."

Mullins took that as his cue to head out. "Thanks, Norm."

CAREY SAT IN HIS OFFICE, nursing his morning coffee and tapping the tip of his pencil on the vinyl pad of his desktop. He was embarrassed by the huge bandage on his hand. He'd had to visit the emergency room Saturday night, and he couldn't even remember the story he'd made up for them. And that damn Coronet electric shaver he bought on Sunday wasn't worth a nickel. It just ate up his face every time he tried to use it. But Carey wasn't sure if he was even ready for a safety razor at this point. What was really bugging him, however, were not the nicks on his face, nor the pain in his hand.

Someone or something had tried to kill him.

Of all the things Carey couldn't figure out, this seemed the most pressing. *Why had something led me to the old photo, as if it needed me to find it? And then later try to cut my throat—why?*

Carey shook his head but could not shake the feeling. *Something.* He was talking about a ghost, wasn't he? The house was haunted, even a cop would have to admit it after all that he'd experienced. *Was it trying to get me to help, or did it just want me out of here? What had Not Wallace said? "You shouldn't be here." No kidding.*

And yet his dreams, and Wallace's sketches—someone was trying to give him clues to something, trying to get Carey to uncover something. But what? A crime? A murder?

More than one spirit must be inhabiting this old dump. One of them didn't want Carey sticking around. *The hell with it,* Carey thought. He was going to figure this thing out if it took him until the wrecking ball came and razed the house to the ground. These spirits existed, he was sure, but they weren't *really* real, and they couldn't hurt him. Nothing was going to scare him away.

Of course, that didn't mean he had to keep living in the house beyond the end of the month. Carey opened the paper and turned to the apartment listings section. He found the listings for one-bedroom apartments, took out a red pen, and began circling ones he could afford. As he flipped the page, his door creaked open halfway. It had been latched, and any of the guys always knocked before opening his door. Carey laid the paper down on his desk, open to the page he was reading. The same gray cat that seemed to come and go at will silently rounded the corner of his desk and rubbed its back against his right calf.

Carey sipped his coffee and eyed the cat suspiciously. He put his coffee down next to the paper, got up, and moved toward the door. He was readier to accept that a ghost could open a latched door than believe a cat could.

He poked his head out the door. "Don?" he said. "Norm?"

Footsteps. Going up the stairs. Uneven steps, as if someone were using a cane or a crutch. Carey saw a shadow moving on the wall of the stairwell. He rounded the corner to the bottom of the stairs and looked up to see a man standing on the landing, leaning against a crutch and staring back at him. It was the blond-haired soldier. Carey saw him now for the first time—the Union Army uniform, the left foot cut off at the ankle, the pained, imploring expression. The man turned to ascend the second flight of stairs, and Carey started after him.

"Sarge?"

Carey halted on the step and let out a breath, realizing it was just Brian Kelsey. Carey looked up, and the man was gone. He turned around to face Kelsey. "Hey, Brian."

Kelsey, a middle-aged, barrel-chested man with a round face topped with red hair, gave Carey a look of concern. "How you doing, Sarge?"

"I'm all right….How are you?" Carey said, shifting his feet awkwardly, his face flush as if caught in the act.

"I'm doing great, thanks." Kelsey noticed Carey's bandage. "Say, what happened there? That looks serious."

"Oh, it's no big deal. Caught it on a nail. It looks worse than it feels."

"I guess it must be tough to shave with your hand all wrapped up like that."

"It can be, yeah," Carey sighed.

"Well, I just wanted to let you know," Kelsey said, "if you ever need anything, let me know."

"Um…I sure will, thanks."

"Great," Kelsey said and walked back to his office.

What was that all about?

Carey returned to his desk and was about to get out his notebook when he noticed his coffee cup sitting on top of his paper. He had put it down next to the paper. And he had left the paper open to the apartment listings section. It was now open to the local news, toward the front of the paper. The mug was resting on top of an ad for Finkel's department store. Winter coats, scarves, gloves, and hats were all on sale. Carey picked up the coffee cup.

A ring of coffee stained the page, circling the Finkel's logo, under which it read: SINCE 1840.

Finkel's? *Finkel? Why does that name sound familiar?* Carey thought about it for a moment and threw open the bottom drawer. He opened the black notebook and turned to the page on which he had copied the names of the soldiers: *Goodale…Corbett… McKean…Dunleavy…Lee…Hensen…Andrus…Lewis… LaChance…Brown…Finkel.*

Mordechai Finkel. *Who the hell was Mordechai Finkel?*

IT WAS JUST BEFORE seven o'clock when Ben Carey made his way through the men's department and arrived in housewares. It was the third day in a row that he had come to Finkel's after work, looking for Ruth. If she wasn't here today, he would just have to ask someone else. He saw no sign of her once again, so he made his way to the back of the store. He followed a dimly lit hallway past the public restrooms and came across a glass door marked EMPLOYEES ONLY. He pulled on the handle. The door was locked, the offices dark.

"Can I help you?" The man walking toward him was tall, bony, mostly bald. He held a handful of keys, and pushed one into the metal frame of the door.

"I just have a few questions…" Carey didn't know what he was going to say.

"Please come in." The man was walking toward an office, flipping on lights as he went. He led Carey to a desk and sat behind it. "Have a seat. Now, what can I do for you, Mister…?"

"Carey. Ben Carey." The men shook hands.

"Edgar Pulaski, assistant manager. What can I do for you, Mr. Carey?"

"What can you tell me about the founders of the store?"

Pulaski looked startled. Carey noticed that the man was fingering a mimeographed form. "I was expecting you to ask for an employment application. We are hiring, you know. Ladies' shoes, and in appliances."

"Thank you, no, I have a job. I'm doing some research on your company. What can you tell me about its founders?"

Pulaski was silent for a moment. "Not much. We have some portraits in our hallway. I run a damp cloth over them every week. That's about all I can tell you. Mr. Carey, we'll be closing in a few moments…"

"Can I see them?"

"You walked past them on the way in here. Help yourself. Good evening."

Pulaski had turned his back toward Carey and was now shuffling papers on a credenza. Carey stood, decided against thanking the rather brusque man, and walked into the hallway.

The first portrait was of Henry Brandon, identified by a brass inscription as the president from 1869 to 1881. Brandon was a rotund man with something between a scowl and a smile on his face. Carey decided he looked a bit like Winston Churchill. He took a small notepad from his pocket and jotted down: *Henry Brandon, Finkel's president 1869–1881.*

On the opposite wall was a portrait of the founder, Samuel Finkel. The face was lined and old. The hair was long and a bit wild for the nineteenth century, and the eyes, deeply recessed against the prominent nose, seemed alive in the portrait. Was this Mordechai's father? There were no dates on the inscription, just his name, and Carey wrote in his pad: *Samuel Finkel, founder of Finkel's.*

There were six other portraits, most of them from the twentieth century, and he methodically copied down their names, titles, and other information. A voice came over the public address system saying that the store was closing and thank you for shopping at Finkel's.

On his way out, Carey saw her. She was clearing out her register in housewares, and he walked up to her counter. "Hi there. It's Ruth, right?" Carey said, feigning ignorance. She nodded, her eyes lighting up. "Nice to see you again."

"Thanks. Nice to see you, too," said Ruth. "How did the delivery work out? They get everything you ordered?"

"Yep, everything worked out great," Carey said, glancing down at her left hand (no ring). "I wanted to thank you again for helping me last week. You were a big help."

"Oh, it was my pleasure, Ben…" Ruth said, looking up at him. "It *is* Ben, right?"

"Yes. You remembered."

"So you doing some more shopping? We're just about to close, you know."

"Actually, I came in because I was trying to find out some information about your company's history."

"Really? What for?"

"Just a history buff, I guess," he said, not sure if that made him sound like an egghead. "I spoke to a Mr. Pulaski, but he wasn't much help."

"Edgar?" Ruth chuckled and leaned over to Carey, conspiratorially. "He really isn't, is he?" Carey laughed, charmed by her easy sense of humor. "What were you trying to find out?"

"Well, I was interested in Samuel Finkel's family history, that sort of thing."

"You should contact our corporate office in New York," she said. "I would think that someone in public relations might be able to help you. They love talking about the company's glorious history," she added facetiously. She pulled a small brochure from under the counter and handed it to Carey. The back of it listed all of Finkel's locations. She pointed out the phone number of Finkel's corporate headquarters at the bottom. "This flyer has their New York number if you want to try that."

"Well, thanks. That's a good idea." Carey pocketed the flyer and smiled. He paused, rocking on his heels. "I was wondering—I hope I'm not being too forward—but I wonder if you'd be interested in having lunch sometime. I work not that far from here and—"

"I'd love to."

"Um, great," Carey smiled.

"So where do you work?"

"My office is over on Third and C. It's a substation for the Metropolitan Police. I'm a sergeant. I run a planning unit there."

"Oh, a policeman…" Ruth arched an eyebrow. Carey wasn't sure if that was a good thing or not, but she still seemed to be interested. They made plans to have lunch the following Wednesday, and Carey left. On the long, chilly walk back to Substation C, Carey felt himself climbing up out of his hole and back into the real world. He looked up at the glowing sky and smiled as a light sprinkling of snow fell on his face.

AT 5:10 A.M. Monday morning, Carey was waiting on the platform of Track 16 at Union Station for the North East Express service to New York City. He was dressed in his gray suit and black London Fog raincoat, and blended in well with the businessmen on the train. Once aboard, he read the *Washington Post*, stopping to watch the endless columns of row houses whip past as the train passed by Philadelphia. After three hours, he had read everything in the *Post* except the classifieds. He opened his briefcase and pulled out a map of Manhattan.

Carey had never been to New York before and found himself

somewhat anxious at the prospect. He had taken a personal day and planned to do what he needed to during the day and return to D.C. the same evening. He had the address of Finkel's corporate headquarters on West 52nd Street as well as the names of several officers of the company in his black notebook. At the top of his list was its public relations director, Mr. Bogart, whom he had spoken to over the phone on the previous Thursday. He had spent about fifteen minutes on hold before he finally came to the phone.

"What can you tell me about Mr. Finkel, the founder of the company?" Carey had asked.

"Are you a reporter?" Mr. Bogart sounded wary.

"No, I'm…working on a book. A history of New York City. Late nineteenth century."

"Well, I know he died in 1869, and the store was taken over by his partner, Henry Brandon. Beyond that…"

"Did Finkel have any children?"

"I beg your pardon?" The man sounded distracted.

"Did Samuel Finkel have any children?"

"Not that I'm aware of. He had no heirs, as far as I know."

Carey was disappointed but undeterred. "How could I find out for sure? Is there a company library, or archives, anything like that?"

"Well, Mr. Carey, we do have boxes of old documents in the basement. We don't generally allow the public access to them…"

"I'd be most grateful if I could, Mr. Bogart. A book like mine would be very good PR for Finkel's, I think. And you'd be mentioned in the acknowledgments, of course." Carey's eyes had been tightly shut.

"I suppose you've got a point," said Bogart, thinking about it. "You know, I'm something of a writer myself. I've been working on a novel about the hectic life of a New York City PR man. I'm still looking for a publisher for this—"

"So could you arrange for me to have a couple hours with the materials, if I came up, say, next Monday?"

"I think I could arrange it. Be here early. Say, nine o'clock. We're at 52nd Street and Ninth Avenue. Go to the twenty-fifth floor and ask the receptionist to page me. Good day, Mr. Carey."

Carey depressed the receiver with his hand, got a new dial tone, and dialed MPD.

"Inspector Price. Sergeant Carey."

"What can I do for you, Ben?"

"I've got a personal issue that I need to resolve. I'll have to go out of town for a day."

"Sure, I understand. Take all the time you—"

"I'll be back Tuesday…Wednesday, at the latest."

"Very well, I hope everything works out all right."

"I hope so, too. Thank you, sir."

THE TRAIN PULLED INTO Pennsylvania Station at around 8:30 and disgorged its passengers onto the bustling concourse. The bright winter rays of early morning light could be seen through the glass-paneled roof, and Carey followed the crowd through a set of doors, up a flight of stairs, and into one of the most beautiful spaces he had ever seen. The waiting room was vast, and the vaulted ceiling seemed to float hundreds of feet above the shiny pink marble floors. He stood in the middle, stunned, and turned in a complete circle, noticing as he did that the room had inspired an identical reaction in at least two or three other travelers.

Again he followed the crowd, this time down a wide passageway lined with shops and boutiques. Flower vendors and shoeshine artists called out to him. He stopped long enough to switch his briefcase to his left hand (his right hand was bothering him) and made for the front doors.

Outside was the longest taxi line he had ever seen, thirty perhaps, and he decided that this was going to be a day for superla-
tives. He got in the first cab and told the driver to go to 52nd and
Ninth. "Please take Eighth Avenue," he told the driver, hoping to
avoid one of the trips though Brooklyn he had heard so much
about, and glad he had studied his Manhattan map on the train.

Twenty minutes later, he was standing in front of the massive
Finkel Tower on 52nd Street, arriving just a few minutes before
nine. The Finkel Tower was a brown art deco skyscraper, built in
the 1920s, and stood out from the unremarkable glass-and-steel
monoliths that surrounded it. Carey went inside, walked across
the green marbled lobby, and took a jam-packed elevator to the
twenty-fifth floor. He thanked the elevator operator, who smiled
and pulled the gate shut behind him.

Carey walked toward a wall-mounted brass logo that read THE
FINKEL COMPANIES and through a set of glass doors. The receptionist was talking to a tall, well-dressed man in his forties, and
both fell silent as Carey approached.

"Are you Mr. Carey?" Ben nodded as the man stepped toward
him and extended his hand. "Elias Bogart."

"Ben Carey." Carey shook his hand and grimaced in pain.

"Oh, I'm sorry. What happened to your hand?"

"Darned can opener," Carey lied. "Thank you for agreeing to
meet with me."

"Of course. Please. Right this way." Bogart led him through
the stylish suite to a spacious office lined with bookshelves and
knickknacks. Through the window was an impressive view of mid-
town. "Have a seat." Carey sat in a luscious brown leather chair,
which smelled as delicious as it felt. "I trust you had no trouble
finding us. Your first time in New York?" Bogart was standing
behind his desk.

Carey shook his head. "Yes, it is. Impressive town." There was a brief silence.

"So tell me about your book," Bogart said as he sat and folded his hands on his desk.

Carey hesitated, feeling tongue-tied. "Well, it's…historical." The secretary entered and handed him a cup of coffee. She pulled the door shut behind her.

"Yes." Bogart lit a cigarette.

"I'm detailing the lives of nineteenth-century New York entrepreneurs. Not the robber barons, you understand. Rather the ordinary men who made this city what it is today."

"Interesting," Bogart exhaled a puff of smoke. "And who else have you researched?"

Carey searched his mind for anything useful. He remembered an article he had read in a magazine some weeks back. "Rowland Macy. He opened his store here in 1857. First day sales were $11.06."

"And did you ask the Macy's people about Rowland's family?"

"Not yet, but I'm planning to, yes." Bogart seemed satisfied by this.

"So who's your publisher?" Bogart asked.

Carey's blank expression did little to mask the machinations of his mind groping for the name of a publisher—any publisher. "Harper," he managed to say, a little too tentatively to be believable, he thought.

"Oh," Bogart said, seemingly impressed. "Here in town?"

"Yes."

"Well, your project does seem interesting," said Bogart, "if of limited appeal." Carey wasn't sure what he meant by that. "But I do have some news for you."

"Oh, really? What?"

"You'd asked whether or not Mr. Finkel had had any children.

Well, it turns out he did. A son."

Carey scooted forward in his seat. "What was his name?"

"Mordechai. He died during the Civil War. In Washington, as a matter of fact." Carey leaned back into the plush leather and stared wide-eyed at a point over Bogart's shoulder. "Interesting, no?"

"Very."

"I'm not sure how much help our 'archives' will be, but you're welcome to search through them as long as you like. Let me know if you need a Photostat of anything, and I'll have my secretary take care of it."

Elias Bogart led Carey to the elevator, and they rode down to the ground-floor lobby, where they walked across to a stairwell. The men descended two flights, where Bogart unlocked a door marked STORAGE and reached for a light switch inside.

"It's quite a mess. Nobody comes down here much, and there's been a lot of water damage over the years." Bogart led him past rows of shelves, some stacked with boxes, others holding bits of broken furniture and other detritus. "I started here with this box, and went through those two as well. Over there, you'll find boxes with some of Finkel's personal effects, those that couldn't be sold at auctions and estate sales. That furniture was his, too. Couldn't sell broken stuff, even in 1869."

DUST ROSE in grimy clouds from every box Carey opened, and within twenty minutes his eyes were itching and watering. He blew his nose into a handkerchief between convulsive sneezing attacks. He was finding little beyond what Bogart had told him.

Carey had not fully recovered from confirming the identity of his blond-haired house guest. True, it wasn't based on a shred of hard evidence. But he hardly could believe what he'd heard. And he knew this was only the beginning. Now that he knew who the blond-haired soldier was, he hoped to find the evidence to prove it. And then, maybe, he would discover *why* Mordechai Finkel was haunting the old place.

He first examined the items Bogart had given him. An investor's prospectus, dated April 1909, gave a brief history of the company, including this passage about Samuel Finkel:

> Samuel Finkel died February 5, 1869, just seven years after his only child, Mordechai, lost his life defending the Union at the second battle of Bull Run. Samuel's wife, Marta Finkel, died in 1857.

But Mordechai hadn't died at Bull Run. He had been brought to Trinity Hospital in Washington and recovered from his wounds enough to be discharged to the care of the Morrisons. Still, it provided Carey a date for Mordechai's stay in D.C. — 1862. *When was Second Bull Run? Late August. Mordechai must have died sometime in September. Did he die in the old house? A relapse, maybe?* An undated newspaper clipping, brittle and yellow with age, was headlined "Business Notes":

> Judge John Yeoman of the First Judicial District Surrogate's Court ruled today that the will of Finkel's department store founder Samuel Finkel is valid and that his former partner Henry Brandon has no legal basis for a challenge.
>
> Observers regard this as a defeat for Mr. Brandon, who became president of the 11-store chain upon Mr. Finkel's death and has waged a three-year legal battle to reverse his former partner's will. Mr. Finkel died without heirs. Mr. Brandon has maintained that the last

will is invalid because Mr. Finkel was not of sound
mind in the final months of his life.

What was in Finkel's will? Carey wondered. He set the prospectus and newspaper clipping aside to be copied and proceeded on .
to the rest of the documents. His first priority was the boxes that
Bogart had said contained Finkel's personal effects. He ripped
open the first with his pocketknife and found a smoking jacket,
some moldy shirts and ties, an assortment of bowlers and top hats.
The next box held a collection of pipes, each in its own wood and
felt case, and a leather pouch of rotted, gray tobacco. There were
a pair of suspenders and a couple of belts.

Before long Carey had examined nine more boxes of invoices,
bills of lading, contracts, memoranda, and other business papers
that spanned nearly a century. Toward noon, he grew hungry but
stifled his growling belly. He wasn't sure he would be able to
return to the storage room if he left; he had heard the door lock
behind him. But he was getting frustrated at not finding any
answers in the boxes. He stood from his crouch and brushed the
dust from his suit, and felt a pin-prick sensation as the blood began
to flow back into his feet.

He left the dozen open boxes on the floor and walked among
the rows of shelving, trying to get a feel for which of the hundreds
of sealed boxes he should examine, when a thought pushed its
way uninvited into his mind: *Maybe the answer is not in a box.*

Carey looked around. The half-dozen low-wattage bulbs hanging from the ceiling illuminated mostly the dust hanging in the
air, but as he looked toward the door he could see the broken furniture that greeted him upon entering the cavernous room: a
chair leg, a desk with a broken back, an end table with missing
drawers. He knelt again to examine the desk. It was not business
furniture, but smallish, the sort one might put in a child's room.

Its writing surface was splintered, shredded almost, as if the desk had been picked up and twisted by a giant.

Carey pulled the tiny desk from out of the chicken-wire storage bin and set it in the aisle. He pulled open the three drawers, one by one, and found each empty, and pushed each one shut in turn. Straightening up now, he rubbed his chin, remembering that he had not shaved that morning.

A minute later he was still staring at the ancient, shattered desk. He bent over, pulled open the top drawer again, this time pulling it all the way out and setting it upon the shelf beside him. The second drawer was stickier, and he had to wiggle it back and forth to get it out of the desk. It went on top of the first drawer.

The bottom drawer slid out easily. In the dim light Carey could see some items in the hollow space beneath it, things that may once have been in the drawers but had fallen when the desk had been moved or jostled. He reached into the darkness, his hand fumbling with folded squares of paper, a pen, a key, some crumbs of God knows what. When he had extracted every last bit from the opening, he moved directly under a light bulb and examined what he had found.

The key was perhaps two inches long, rusty and without any markings. Carey set it aside on the desktop. The fountain pen was black marble and engraved with the name of its manufacturer, A.T. Cross. It looked like it might be worth something to a collector.

Carey unfolded one of the papers. It was an invoice, dated March 25, 1861, from Tinsell & Guthrie, apparently a law firm, to Samuel Finkel. The letterhead was typeset, but the services were inked by hand: 25 hours, Finkel v. Giulotti, $179; 15 hours, Finkel v. Barnes, plus expenses, $127.

Carey reasoned that a company executive was subject to many lawsuits from former employees, business partners, and customers, even in 1861. Why didn't the company cover his legal expenses? Perhaps they reimbursed him. What mattered is that Samuel Finkel engaged the services of a law firm called Tinsell & Guthrie, and that this law firm may have also prepared his will.

Carey unfolded the last piece of paper, which was separating at its creases, and began to read what appeared to be the second half of a letter:

> ...gathered to cheer us on, although frankly, we've done nothing yet to deserve such hurrahs. The 10th New York arrived here just this morning. We marched our victory parade, and now we have to go out and fight the Rebels.
>
> July 17th. We marched for seven hours straight. My legs are very sore, and there's quite a lot of grumbling, even though we're only about halfway there. Can't tell you where we're heading. Expect to be there tomorrow however.
>
> After we set up camp, I went berry picking and found some lovely wild strawberries and blackberries. If only I had some cream.
>
> July 18th. Before dawn, my brigade and several others were sent forward into the enemy. Shots were fired, and we were withdrawn. Father, I don't know why, we were on top of the situation. Our officers heard gunshots and decided we were under strength. I cannot imagine how large the Confederate force must have been.
>
> July 19th. Morgan, who bunked beside me, was killed this morning. He was on picket duty, and a sniper got him near the creek. Tonight, I'm going to write his mother a note.

His commanding officer normally does this, but I volunteered. I think I knew him better.

Good night, Father.

Mordechai

The handwriting was angular but elegant, and as he read Mordechai's letter, Carey felt he could hear the man's voice, in spite of the hundred years that separated them. Unfortunately, the old desk held nothing else of interest. Carey scanned the rest of the boxes of documents — mostly financial records, some old promotional materials, but nothing significant.

Carey left the storage room and headed for the stairway, emerging moments later in the lobby. Returning to the twenty-fifth floor, he saw Bogart's secretary, who took the papers he had gathered to be duplicated. Carey sat down and waited in the reception area, satisfied that he'd made good progress. Yet he still felt there was more to learn here.

Bogart opened his door. He was escorting another man out of the office. The man was wearing an almost identical gray suit, carrying a large portfolio, and smiling. The two men shook hands, and Bogart turned to check the messages on his secretary's desk.

"Mr. Bogart?" said Carey, standing.

"Ah, yes, Mr. Carey, find everything you were looking for?" Bogart said, backing away from Carey and looking around for someone in the empty room.

"A good deal of it, yes. I was wondering, though, if I might trouble you for a few more minutes."

"I'd love to help you, but I'm afraid I've got meetings scheduled all afternoon."

"I see," said Carey, sensing the man's discomfort.

"You've got my number, though," Bogart said, smiling. "Give me a call anytime."

Right, thought Carey.

CAREY WALKED DOWN the street to a diner and ordered a grilled cheese sandwich and a Coke. As he sat in his booth, picking at his french fries, he looked through the documents Bogart's secretary had copied for him. While Mordechai's letter was the most interesting thing he'd found, it didn't tell Carey much except that Mordechai was a devoted son and a good soldier. The will, though. That piqued his interest. He wanted to know more about that. *What was the name of the law firm?* He found the page— Tinsell & Guthrie.

Carey pulled open the door to the phone booth in the diner. It had a bench to sit on and a ledge where Carey set his papers. He picked up the phone book and began flipping through it. There was no Tinsell & Guthrie, and nobody named Tinsell in the whole city. There was a company called Guthrie, which sold and serviced typewriters, and a dozen persons named Guthrie.

Carey closed the phone book. What next? How many hours of research in a library would it take to find out what had happened to Tinsell & Guthrie? Did they go out of business, get bought out, merge? Who knew?

He opened the phone book again, this time to the yellow pages, and looked under "Lawyers." There were more than twenty pages of listings, many large display ads for personal injury lawyers and other shysters. Carey read through the simple, one-line listings, figuring Finkel's law firm wouldn't be the type to advertise. There it was, on the third page: BRADLEY, WILLIAMS, TINSELL & GUTHRIE. *Thank God it wasn't "Williams, Bradley,"* thought Carey. He picked up the receiver and dialed.

Bradley, Williams was headquartered in an imposing, modern skyscraper on Fifth Avenue, with its offices occupying the forty-first through forty-third floors. After a jarringly fast elevator ride that left his stomach in his throat, Carey entered a wood-paneled reception area, checked in with the receptionist, and waited on a stuffed leather sofa until she called him back.

"Mr. Roseman will see you now." She held the door open with her left hand and waved him into the corridor with her right, as if she were a school crossing guard and he were a first grader.

"Mr. Carey here to see you, Mr. Roseman." She pulled the door shut, and Carey and Roseman were alone. Roseman motioned toward a chair.

"Please."

"Thank you. And thank you for agreeing to see me on such short notice." Carey waved away the proffered cigarette.

"Quite all right." Roseman lit the cigarette and shook the match out. "Now, what can I do for you, Mr. Carey?"

"Well, as I said, I'm researching the life of Samuel Finkel for a book I'm working on."

"Oh, yes, you told me. I guess, as you know, our firm represents the Finkel's corporation. We've had a long relationship with that company."

"According to my research," said Carey, trying to sound authorial, "you've worked for them in some capacity since the 1860s, when your firm was simply Tinsell & Guthrie. Isn't that correct?"

"You've certainly done your homework, Mr. Carey. Samuel Finkel retained Tinsell & Guthrie to represent the corporation back in the late 1850s. We've been their law firm ever since. They're our oldest client."

"What I'm interested in is Samuel Finkel's will—" Carey noticed that Roseman raised an eyebrow at that. "It seems there was some controversy surrounding how he left things."

"Tinsell & Guthrie represented Finkel's, Mr. Carey. But as far as his will, he would have had his personal lawyer draw that up."

"Yes, but didn't Finkel's junior partner—Henry Brandon, I believe—didn't he contest the will? Wouldn't your firm have been involved in his lawsuit?"

"It's been almost ninety years since all this transpired, Mr. Carey. We don't have any files that go back that far, even if we were involved somehow. I'm afraid I'm not going to be able to help you with this." Roseman had turned suddenly very curt.

"Is there anyone else at your firm who might be able to—"

"I speak for the firm, Mr. Carey," said Roseman with an air of finality.

Carey gave Roseman a look of startled bemusement.

Roseman was not smiling.

CAREY WALKED DOWN Fifth Avenue in the cold, trying to make sense of what he'd learned since morning. He'd been sure since last Wednesday that Mordechai Finkel was the name of the blond-haired man, and that he was somehow connected to the Finkel company. He'd come to New York because he was certain of this. Now he'd had his hunch confirmed. But there seemed to be more there. Was Roseman covering something up? And if so, why? As he had said, the controversy had erupted almost ninety years ago. What was left to hide at this point?

Carey stepped into a drugstore and found a pay phone. He dropped in a dime and dialed Bogart's direct line.

"Bogart? Hello, it's Ben Carey. I know you said you were swamped this afternoon, but I'm still in town and was hoping we could talk."

A few moments of silence followed on the other end. "I thought you'd gone back to D.C.," Bogart said finally. "You're persistent, all right. Can you meet me after work?"

"No problem."

"Let's say 5:15. There's a hotel around the corner from our office, The Hudson. They have a bar off the lobby. I'll meet you there."

Carey arrived early, ordered a beer, and waited for Bogart to show. From his table in the corner, he could see the entrance. Bogart wandered in around 5:20, and Carey caught his eye. Bogart waved and stopped at the bar to order a drink. Carrying a gin and tonic in one hand and his black leather briefcase in the other, Bogart sat down across from Carey.

"So, Carey," he said, "you wanted to talk. Were the boxes in our vault much help?"

"I was able to find a few interesting things, but I wanted to ask you some follow-up questions. Perhaps get a more informal company history."

"Oh, I see," Bogart said, smiling. "Can I ask you something, Carey?"

"Sure."

"You're not really writing a book, are you?"

Carey was caught off guard by that. *Is my lack of sophistication that obvious?* he thought to himself and sighed. He looked Bogart in the eye and said simply, "No."

"Then who are you, really?"

"I'm a cop," Carey said and flipped open his billfold, displaying his badge and MPD identification. "Sergeant Ben Carey of the D.C. Metro Police."

Bogart straightened and coughed into his fist, setting his gin and tonic down on the glass table. "Uh...you're a little out of your jurisdiction, aren't you?"

"Don't worry," Carey said, returning his wallet to his breast pocket. "This isn't exactly police business."

"What kind of business is it, exactly?"

"It's a long story, Bogart. The gist is I work in a very old building, a substation the department owns in D.C. As a matter of fact, it used to be someone's home. And I have reason to believe it was the house in which Samuel Finkel's son died."

"Wait a second," said Bogart. "Before this morning, you didn't even know that Samuel Finkel had a son—not until I told you."

"As I said, it's a long story."

"Uh-huh," Bogart sipped his cocktail, the wheels in his head spinning. "Isn't it a little late to be investigating a murder that took place a hundred years ago?"

"I never said anything about a murder."

"No, but you *are* a cop..."

Carey was trying to see this from Bogart's point of view, but it wasn't the first time the idea of murder had occurred to him. "Well, first of all...technically, there is no statute of limitations on murder. Realistically, though, if it was a homicide, the killer is long dead, so it doesn't make any difference. But from what you told me, it seemed like he died from his battle wounds."

"That's the company line. He died at the Second Battle of Bull Run....I always assumed he died on the battlefield. But you say he died in somebody's house."

"It was a home for recovering soldiers. I imagine some of them didn't make it."

Bogart nodded and stirred his drink with the swizzle stick.

"I shouldn't have lied to you," said Carey. "But my interest in this case is purely personal."

"So you're saying I won't be in the acknowledgments?"

"I'm afraid not," Carey said, amused. "I found something in your vault, but I couldn't make any sense of it. It has to do with Finkel's will."

"Ahh," Bogart said and smiled. "That."

"I know that Finkel's former partner, Henry Brandon, contested the will. But when I spoke to Mr. Roseman at your law firm, he wasn't eager to talk to me about it."

DAVID R. HORWITZ

"You *have* been busy today."

"Are you going to fill me in? Otherwise, I've got a train to catch."

"Don't worry, Carey, you can catch the next one," Bogart said, pulling a cigarette from his case and lighting it with a Zippo. He blew a stream of smoke out the side of his mouth, snapped his lighter shut, and continued. "When Samuel Finkel passed away, he had no heirs, so he left most of his fortune to Jewish charities. But not all of it. His shares of the company remain in limbo."

Carey cleared his throat. "Limbo?"

"Yes. His shares made up a controlling interest in the company. Fifty-one percent. Henry Brandon was his junior partner."

"So what happened to the shares?"

"They're still out there. Finkel used a legal tool called an *inter vivos* trust. That's where a person surrenders control of a financial asset—in this case, the majority shares—to a third party, who manages the asset until the circumstances prescribed by the trust are manifest."

Carey stared at Bogart for a moment. "Could you say that again in English?"

"Let's say you have an asset you want to protect after your death. You hand the asset over to an executor—a bank, or a law firm, usually—with instructions on its dispersal. For instance, you might stipulate that if the Yankees win the pennant, then the asset is to go to Mickey Mantle."

"And if the Yanks never win the pennant?"

"Unlikely. But in that case, the asset would remain in the trust."

"Indefinitely?"

"Yes."

"Okay," Carey was getting it. "Back to Finkel, though. Who is his Mickey Mantle?"

"He doesn't exist," said Bogart.

180

"Come again?"

"Finkel stipulated that the shares could only be released to a direct descendant. Since his only son, Mordechai, died as a young man, before his father passed, and before he could marry, there were no direct descendants, and never will be."

"Strange," said Carey, trying to figure out why anyone would do this.

"Finkel was a very old man when he died," Bogart said, taking another pull from his cigarette. "He may have been a little senile when he made out his last will—which is what Brandon thought and why he contested it."

"But with a controlling interest in limbo, who owns the company?"

"Well, the missing shares never exercised their proxy votes. Brandon became the de facto controlling officer of the company, up until his death in 1881. The stock has split several times. But so have the outstanding shares. The money is out there, sitting in some bank. But if someone were able to possess the missing shares legally, he would own a controlling interest in the company."

"I imagine that would cause quite a stir," said Carey.

"That," said Bogart, "would be putting it mildly."

Bogart flipped the latches on his briefcase, which he had set down on the chair next to him, and produced a thick manila file folder held together with a rubber band.

"What's this?" Carey asked.

"As Finkel's PR director, this is exactly the kind of information I'm supposed to be keeping from people like you," said Bogart, sliding the folder across the table to Carey.

Carey slid the rubber band off the folder and opened the file, staring wide-eyed at its contents. "You mean to tell me I spent four hours in your basement, and you had the most useful information stowed away in your briefcase the whole time?"

Bogart shrugged. "If you were really doing a book on Finkel, this wouldn't make for very good PR. Finkel and Brandon had been feuding with each other for years before Finkel died. If our board knew these documents existed, they'd have them burned. I certainly couldn't release them to a writer. The police, on the other hand…well, no one would blame me for turning them over to you."

Carey looked Bogart in the eye. "Why help me now?"

"Mr. Carey, this company is past its prime. We're being destroyed by the competition — Saks, Macy's, the discount houses. Management here is lazy and unimaginative, and working here is getting to be really depressing. I have no idea what your real interest in this is or what you might uncover. But, quite frankly, this company could use a shake-up."

THE TRAFFIC WAS THICK and slow moving on 52nd Street, and Carey wondered if he was going to miss his train. But a cab soon appeared, and within fifteen minutes he was hurrying through the pink marbled halls of Penn Station.

It stormed all the way to Delaware, where the lightning and rain ceased but the skies remained bleak and threatening. Carey had the file folder open on his lap, a cup of coffee and a tuna sandwich on the arm of his chair. He had been reading through Bogart's hand-picked documents since the train left the station at 7:20 P.M. If nothing else, Carey was getting a clear picture of what kind of man Henry Brandon was. In one letter, Brandon urged his fellow stockholders to pressure Finkel into selling out his majority shares so that the company would have a "majority Christian interest" and that as the company grew, it wouldn't carry the "stain of Jewish-controlled ownership."

In Bogart's file were several letters from Brandon — some

addressed to other stockholders or board members, a few to Finkel himself. From them Carey learned that Brandon had joined Finkel's in the early 1840s as a manager. Brandon's financial expertise had made him indispensable to Finkel in those early days. Along the way, Brandon started buying up shares of the company until he was the biggest shareholder next to Finkel. By 1860, Brandon was itching to take over the reins from Finkel, who was still presiding over the day-to-day operations, despite approaching his seventieth birthday. In a letter dated March 12, 1861, Brandon wrote to Finkel, saying that he'd earned the right to run the company, that Finkel had "done remarkably well for someone of your education and upbringing. But now that you are so near the end of your long life, don't you think it's time for another, someone of talent, with youth and energy, to take this organization to the next plateau?"

Don't sugarcoat it, Brandon, what are you really trying to say?

The next letter was addressed to Brandon from Finkel. It made crystal clear to Brandon and anyone else when Finkel would be stepping down and who would be taking the organization to the next plateau:

> …I don't know if I've misled you these past years, my dear Henry, but what you ask I cannot give. No doubt your contributions to this company over the past nearly 20 years have been irreplaceable—and no doubt your ownership in some shares has been a boon to you and yours. However, as to the future leadership of this company, there is only one talented young man who can fill my shoes, and that is my beloved son, Mordechai.…

Under Finkel's letter was a page from a legal document dated 1870. It was part of Brandon's lawsuit contesting Finkel's will.

Tinsell & Guthrie had indeed represented Brandon, as Finkel's president, against Finkel. It made sense. Finkel's will had left the company's future up in the air. It was certainly bad business for the remaining stockholders. Roseman had to have known about the firm's involvement. He had lied to Carey. And, undoubtedly, the firm had records Carey would love to see.

Brandon and his lawyers had alleged that Finkel was not in his right mind when he drafted his final will. They cited the fact that Finkel had had his son's remains relocated in 1866 from a private cemetery in Washington to Arlington National Cemetery.

Carey had been to Arlington once as a child. He wondered now if Mordechai Finkel's grave would be there among the thousands of white marble markers dotting the rolling hills of the northern Virginia estate. Why move Mordechai's body? Had Samuel Finkel become demented in his old age? Had his son's death driven him over the edge? Carey didn't think so. Apart from this, Brandon couldn't really show evidence of unstable behavior. His other allegations had little supporting evidence. He'd claimed that Finkel had been inconsistent and exhibited odd behavior in the presence of several employees, whose names and affidavits were referenced, but which Carey could not find.

Carey did, however, find something more interesting.

Several pieces of paper, which had been torn out of an old ledger, seemed to record payments made from a special discretionary account that Brandon had set up in 1861. In it were a number of payments made to individuals—some of whom were the same employees who'd sworn affidavits in support of Brandon's lawsuit. Most were between $50 and $100 payments and were described in the margins usually as a "bonus" or for "services rendered." A few names kept reappearing over several years, and Carey wondered if Brandon had hired a private investigator to spy on Finkel.

One payment from September 15, 1862, jumped out at

Carey—$800 made out to "A. Hilldrup" for "misc. expenses & bonus." Carey looked back through the other entries and realized that Hilldrup's name had not appeared in any of the other documents. He was identified as a Finkel's floor manager, but for someone who had earned such an enormous bonus—no doubt the equivalent of a manager's yearly salary in 1862—Hilldrup never received any other bonuses from Brandon. In fact, he disappeared from the ledger altogether.

Carey looked at the date again, and one word leaped to the front of his mind: *murder*. Maybe Bogart had been on to something.

If Brandon were paying $50 or $100 for employees to spy or swear false affidavits, what would $800 buy him? Could Brandon have paid Hilldrup to do away with Finkel's only son and heir? This would put Brandon in a better position to pressure Finkel into relinquishing the controlling shares. Or so Brandon must have thought. Suddenly, Carey realized, he now knew the *why* as well as the *who*. He was starting to build his case.

THE TRAIN PULLED INTO Union Station shortly before eleven o'clock. Clouds blanketed the night sky, making it darker and more foreboding than usual, and Carey walked the six blocks to Substation C in a light drizzle.

He walked across 3rd Street toward Senator Morrison's former home, the house in which Mordechai Finkel had been murdered almost a century ago, and stopped. He raised his eyes from the front steps to the windows of the turret room on the second floor and tried to muster the nerve to take the first step up.

PART III

CHAPTER 13.

Monday, October 6, 1862

SHORTLY AFTER MORDECHAI'S funeral, Robert LaChance and Joseph Brown, now fully recovered from their wounds, left the Morrison home. Only Oscar O'Brien remained in the house, eagerly awaiting news that his family had successfully made the journey from Minnesota to collect him.

On a clear, breezy Monday morning, Senator Morrison sat behind his large mahogany desk in the first-floor study. Louisa sat near to him, oscillating between mending a split in one of her petticoats and staring out the window. The senator looked up from his work to see his daughter kneading her hands and lost in thought, again.

"Is there something more interesting outside than the work you have in here?" he asked, more out of concern than aggravation.

"No, Father," Louisa replied and quickly picked up her sewing. She struggled to thread her needle with a shaking hand. "I was just thinking how empty the house feels now that Mr. O'Brien is our only boarder."

"It is quieter," he said.

"It's been several weeks since we took on any recovering soldiers," she said.

"It's been nearly five since we took in that poor soul, Private Finkel."

"Five weeks," Louisa repeated aloud, calculating the passage of time in her head.

"It broke my heart to see you so affected by the death of one of our young men. You'll see that in time death and everlasting life are a great privilege to the suffering. That young man was sick, my dear. He's better off where he is now."

Louisa sat with her teeth clenched. Her fingers twitched in order, as if she were calculating a mathematical puzzle in her head. "Five weeks," she repeated.

"Yes, five weeks," he said. The senator's heavy gray eyebrows winced in pain and then lifted. "I think it's due time for you to start focusing on the living instead of the dead. We've done a great service to God and the Union by caring for our soldiers, but the new hospitals are opening. I hear that even Trinity will be back to normal by the spring. I think it best to take our address off the recovery list after Mr. O'Brien is released from us. Without the men to care for, you can care for your future."

"My future…" Louisa's shoulders sank while she nodded her agreement. "Father," she said, regaining her composure, "I've decided to apply for nursing school. That's where I can best serve. I've already looked into some of the schools and—"

The senator shook his head with a sigh. "My sweet girl, I believe you can serve more appropriately as a lady of society. You've done well in your service to Trinity, but you are beautiful, supportive, and clever. You deserve to be cared for, to be given the best. I'd say any young, prosperous man would be blessed to have you as his bride."

"A bride? I can't—"

"I've noticed young Mr. Rogers has come by to see you nearly every day of late. He's very fond of you, you know. He's a fine young man, Louisa. I wish you'd give him a chance."

The thought of being attached romantically to anyone but Mordechai caused Louisa to shudder with a sudden feeling of nausea. While Harrison had always been kind to her, she couldn't bring herself to think of him in that way. There was something in his manner that evoked a feeling of brotherly kinship, not of desire. His tone with her was gentle, as if he were addressing a child, not someone who craved higher conversation. He had no concept of how strongly she felt about the issues of the day, and seemingly no opinion of such issues himself. She wanted a man with strength, intellect, and passion. She wanted Mordechai.

She had rebuffed Harrison's advances numerous times before, and he would act forlorn, leave her company for several weeks, and return for the next rejection. Now, however, he stayed by her side constantly, accompanying her to church services, dinners, galas, once even across the street to the makeshift hospital at Trinity, though he remained in the doorway while she disappeared inside to tend to a quick chore. She hadn't actively discouraged him from spending time with her, but she certainly hadn't given him reason to think they had any future together.

"Don't think too hard on it, now," said the senator, as he heaved his large frame from his seat and moved to embrace his daughter. Louisa watched him struggle across the room toward her. It seemed the stress of the past years was catching up with him rapidly, making his fifty-three-year-old body resemble someone twenty years his elder.

"I love you, Louisa," he said as he kissed the top of her head. "I just want you to be happy and cared for. Won't you think about what I said?"

"I will, Father," she said, knowing that she would indeed have much to think about in the coming months.

EDNA WILLIS CROSSED into freedom the day after her fifth birthday. Even at that young age, she knew she was lucky. She was, after all, crossing into Illinois with both her parents. They'd been on the move for what seemed like forever to a five-year-old, though the adventure, as her parents called it when they spoke to her, would end in Washington, D.C. That's where her family, or what was left of it—an aunt, one older brother, and a cousin— had been living since escaping years earlier.

Her mother became a servant in a wealthy home, employed by a politician who was an active contributor to the Underground Railroad. The job was a good one—the politician wasn't home much of the time, and he had a young daughter just about Edna's age who once gave up a doll and half of a toy tea set to Edna for Christmas. Edna's mother refused the gifts, but did allow the two girls to play together on occasion with, of course, the politician's permission.

As Edna got older, she went to work with her aunt, a woman who kept Edna and her cousin Rosie busy washing dishes and scrubbing floors at the shoestring restaurant she kept. It was there a thirteen-year-old Edna witnessed her father's murder as he rose to defend her aunt from brutish advances from a drunken patron. The police didn't come, and probably wouldn't have cared if they'd been there anyway. So Edna watched her father bleed to death on a barroom floor while his murderer sauntered off down the street. Her mother was devastated, and though she had been a strong, healthy woman her entire life, her husband's death depleted her. Within a year, and most likely by her own sheer will, she was dead, leaving Edna with a few family photos, a silver cross on a red string, and a profound sense of injustice. The morning after her mother died, Edna took her mother's place in Senator Morrison's employ, and the room over the kitchen as her quarters. By the age of nineteen, she was running the household.

In the past, Louisa and Edna would sit and talk in the parlor like sisters after the house was settled for the night. Having both lost their mothers, their bond formed quickly, often able to communicate more with a quick grin, a roll of the eye, or a head nod than most could in hours of conversation. Their friendship certainly wasn't traditional, Edna knew that, but she liked working for the senator and spending time, albeit while she was working, with Louisa. Her job was far better than that of her cousin's, after all, and because of her position in the household, she was able to secure some time to herself, too.

On occasion, Edna would stop by The West End tavern to meet with friends who kept houses in the nearby affluent districts. The West End was no fancy affair, to say the least, but it served as an easy meeting place for ex-slaves and wayward souls looking for a place to ease their troubles. With Harrison Rogers keeping company with Louisa in the evenings, Edna was spending more and more time talking with Rosie, The West End's barmaid.

Edna saw him there—the man she'd seen outside the Morrisons' house the day Mordechai died. He was sitting on a stool, leaning against the bar. He downed a shot of cloudy gin from a dirty glass and leered at Rosie as she made her rounds.

She fixed her eyes upon the man. She had no idea how long she had been staring at him when his eyes wandered down the bar to meet hers. She reached across the bar and grabbed Rosie's hand, frightened and trying to look engrossed in conversation with her cousin. Even with her back to him, she knew that he hadn't looked away.

Rosie had seen him before. Once, she told Edna, he damn near killed a "fancy man" right in front of her. He had cleaned himself up a bit since then, it seemed to Rosie. Most likely he had come into some money, doubtlessly ill-gotten—though that was probably true for most of the West End patrons. Having spent most of her years tending bar in Murder Bay, Rosie had learned to trust her instincts, and she was always wary of men like this.

Edna returned to the bar the next weekend to celebrate her

first night off since the Morrisons began taking in wounded soldiers. Earlier that day, Oscar O'Brien said his good-byes and was
loaded into the back of a rented cart by his father and older
brother. The senator was attending a Union fundraiser with his
daughter and so released Edna for the entire evening. With the
hope of finding him again, Edna sat nursing her beer at the bar
while Rosie discussed her latest troubles with her landlord and
wiped beer glasses with a dirty rag.

Edna caught his eye as soon as he walked into the bar. She
held him in her gaze until he sat down beside her. His breath was
rank with alcohol, most likely from the saloon next door.

"Hi, there, fella, seen you in here a lot."

"Yeah, I come in here once in a while," he said, tapping the
bar three times and nodding to Rosie, who poured him a shot of
the usual. He turned toward Edna and leaned as close to her as
possible without falling over. "What you want, girl?"

Rosie walked over to the two of them, slid a gin in front of the
man, and stomped away.

"What do I want? I just want a friend," said Edna. "We both
come in here a lot. Thought I'd say hi." She began to play with
her string necklace, sliding her finger between the red string and
the smooth skin of her neck.

"What are you, contraband?" he replied.

"No, I'm a freewoman. Live uptown. Work for a wealthy family. House empty tonight. Awfully lonely this time of year, and
cold. You know what I'm saying?"

"I ain't got no money for no goddamn whore."

"I ain't no whore, mister. Just a lonely girl who's looking for a
little company."

Rosie had returned and was now staring at them both with a
look of utter contempt. The man was staring at Edna with the
same look, but he did this while slipping his rough hand around

her waist and quickly downing his gin.

"The name's Ronald Eddy."

"So, Ronny, are you comin' or goin'?"

"Let's go for a walk," he said and guided her to the door.

"Yes, sir," and she turned to wink at her friend.

Rosie watched the two leave the tavern and wondered if she'd ever see Edna again. *Well*, she thought, *that girl was warned.*

THE TWO WALKED through the grimy streets of Murder Bay and up 14th Street toward the better part of town. On Pennsylvania Avenue, they headed east. Conversation was sparse. The man was not much of a talker.

"I told you 'bout myself," Edna said. "Work as a domestic. What about you?"

"Well, I was in the army," he said. "That was before."

"You get wounded?" she asked.

"Yep."

"Which battle? Manassas?"

"Yep, that's the one."

"First or Second?"

"Huh? First or Second what?"

"Never mind."

They were walking down C Street now, and Eddy's dirty hand was firmly around Edna's shoulder. He was strong, and though she was leading him home, Edna felt his need to control her. She played to this and kept her hands in the pockets of her skirt. She searched the streets for any sign of life, but found none.

The streets were deserted. Eddy coughed as he reached into his greatcoat and unsheathed his knife. His hand moved up to the back of her neck. "How wealthy did you say your master was?" he slurred.

Edna's pulse jumped at the question. They approached the house, and she saw the recognition in Eddy's eyes. He halted momentarily as his eyes gazed up at the windows of the turret.

Edna ducked out of his grip, pulled the ice pick from her skirt, and drove it deep into the man's chest. Only the glass globe of the implement was visible, and it reflected light from the street lanterns onto Eddy's confused face. He stared at Edna, and she at him, as he fell to his knees on the sidewalk.

"That's for Louisa, you bastard," she spat at him. "And no one is my 'master.'"

He was still on his knees, but she was walking away now, back toward The West End where no one but Rosie would notice she had ever left.

ROSIE RAISED her eyebrows at her cousin as Edna entered the bar.

"I knew that soldier wasn't sick," she said under her breath, as she regained her barstool.

"What soldier?" asked Rosie.

"I told the police he wasn't sick. They wouldn't listen."

Rosie nodded in agreement. "They never do."

Edna's eyes met Rosie's. "If anyone asks, I never left this place."

"Honey," said Rosie, "no one ever asks."

The next day, the police gave the case the same amount of attention that would befit the murder of any army deserter and suspected killer during wartime: none. With no witnesses, there was little to investigate. Clearly, he had tried to mug the wrong person. The cash found on his body was used to bury Ronald Eddy in a meager grave in the pauper's cemetery. His other belongings—a rusty knife and a broken pocketwatch—were thrown into a wooden evidence box and forgotten.

. . .

HARRISON ROGERS DIDN'T have much time before his next
appointment. He had been running late all week, but he didn't
want to be absent from Louisa's thoughts for a single day. In his
hand he carried a small, satin-covered box. He jogged to the corner of 3rd and C, stopped, and walked to the front of the house.
Louisa was sitting in the front window of the parlor but disappeared as he struggled with the front gate. Edna stood in the open
doorway, wiping her hands on a dish towel.

"Good evening, Edna. How is the household tonight?" he
asked, as he entered the house.

"Fine, sir," Edna answered in the cheerful manner she
reserved only for Harrison. Since she'd known him, Harrison had
been striving to be liked — he always said what he thought was the
right thing, and if he couldn't think of what that was, he deferred
to abundant compliments; he was fast with a joke when the mood
warranted but could change his demeanor to somber just as
quickly. Edna liked him, but only in the way someone liked a
friend's silly younger brother. She'd never found him to be very
clever, but with the exception of her father and the senator, she
hadn't found too many men to fill that bill. "I'm sorry, but Louisa's
not feeling up to visitors now. I'll pass on that you called on her,
though."

Harrison moved past her into the foyer and began looking into
the parlor and the other rooms. "Edna, I'm not just a visitor to
you, am I?" he grinned as he removed his hat and held it and the
package in his hands. He sneaked a quick glance up the staircase.
"I couldn't help but see the lovely Louisa through the window. I
wonder if you could ask her to see me for a brief moment? I have
something for her."

Edna gave him a pitying smile—she suspected Harrison was the last person on Louisa's mind—and turned toward the kitchen. She disappeared down the hallway and, soon after, Louisa stepped into view. She was pale, but dressed in her usual way—dark hair parted down the middle and pulled tight to the back, a light blue day gown fitting tight to her waist and flowing over a minimum of dressing skirts. She led him to the parlor but did not sit down. She stood in the middle of the room and stared back at him with arms crossed, as if waiting for a reply to a question she hadn't yet asked.

Harrison was not deterred. "I'm sorry I can't spend the entire evening with you, my dear. I have a client who simply will not reschedule. But I did bring you this trinket, perhaps it will cheer you up."

She reached out to take the box and set it down on the fireplace mantle without opening it.

"Don't you want to see what it is, Louisa? It's certainly not as handsome as you, but I think you two will make a good pairing …much as the two of us would." He walked to the mantle, removed the box's lid, and looped onto his index finger an emerald ring with a stone that nearly glowed, even in the dusk of the parlor. "I know you haven't told me your answer yet, but until then, please wear this to know I will be with you always. I love you so."

Louisa's face showed little emotion, even as he drew near her and placed the ring on her right ring finger. Her mind was in another time, her arms wrapped around someone else. "It's beautiful, Harrison, but I already told you my answer. I know you spoke to Father already, but so have I. I want to become a nurse. I want to spend my time in a hospital helping people who need it instead of planning my social life. You're my dear friend, but I'm just not the one for you, Harrison. You should save your jewelry for someone else. It's only right."

Harrison placed his hand over hers to stop her from removing the ring. His jaw clenched, but he kept his voice calm. "Right?" he asked. "None of this, my dear, is right, most of all your decision. I understand the war has added a little bit to the plates of all of us, but your place isn't at the bedsides of men who cannot wash themselves—"

Louisa took a step back from him. "And how exactly has your 'plate' been made heavier? What is your burden? These unwashed men you speak of are risking their *lives* for this country, they're losing their limbs, their eyesight. They are dying..." She choked back a sob, and a tear from her right eye began tracing its way down her nose. "How dare you ridicule them? They need my help. They need me. I give them hope—"

Harrison just looked at her, his eyes welled with moisture. "But that's not all you give them, is it?"

Weeks of grief, anxiety, and anger burst from Louisa as her hand broke across his face. The outline of her thin fingers appeared scarlet on his left cheek. Stunned, Harrison held his palm to his face. That he had said something so atrocious to Louisa surprised him as much as it had her. "I'm so sorry, I should never have said that. Please, forgive me. I don't know—"

"I think it best if you go now," she said in a faraway voice.

He backed out of the room, quietly closed the door on his way out, and rushed off down the street. Louisa stood still in the room, letting the emerald slip from her finger and drop silently to the floor.

EDNA HAD HEARD the slap and, thinking the tables were turned, rushed into the parlor to find Louisa, a perfect shade of green, swaying from side to side in the center of the room. Edna struggled to guide Louisa back to the kitchen and helped her into a chair.

"That's one way to get a man to leave you," she said to her friend as she began pulling a variety of containers out of the cupboards.

Louisa shrugged her shoulders. "He said something he shouldn't have," she said, "but I probably provoked him. I don't know what's gotten into me lately. Father and I nearly had an argument the other day, and I found myself snapping at one of the other nurse's aides at Trinity this morning."

"Could be the weather. Cold one day, warm the next," Edna suggested.

"I don't know, that may be so. I haven't been feeling well."

"Or it could be your gowns are too tight and you're not breathing right. You've been lightheaded quite a bit." Edna was mixing pinches and spoonfuls of powders and liquids in a glass without hesitation. She stirred it a final time and handed it to Louisa. "Here, drink this. I used to make it for my mother. It worked every time."

Louisa held her nose over the glass and made a face. "It may have worked every time, but what for?"

"Oh, lots of things. Mix of weather, breathing problems...," Edna grabbed for Louisa's hand, "the baby sickness."

Every muscle in Louisa's body tightened at once. "I don't know what you mean," she stammered.

"Honey, you're having a baby, aren't you?"

Louisa nodded almost imperceptibly and began crying.

"Mordechai?" Edna whispered. Again, Louisa nodded.

The young women embraced. This time, however, tears flowed from both of them.

•   •   •

THE CONCOCTION had worked, and Louisa was feeling good enough to stomach some tea and biscuits before Edna began closing up the house for the night. Louisa sat in the kitchen, shredding remnants of a biscuit onto her empty plate and asking herself why this would happen to her.

Why did she betray her chastity before they exchanged vows? Why didn't she stay behind instead of going to a party while her love bled to death? Why would she have to bear a life of shame after sharing one wonderful night together? *Why did Mordechai have to die?*

The tears started again, but this time Louisa had tired of crying. She wiped her eyes with the back of her hand, took a long breath, picked up her tea, and walked to the front of the house. She knew Edna wouldn't approve of her carrying a cup and saucer around the house, especially into the parlor. *Well*, Louisa thought, *it's not as if I've done anything else I'm supposed to do.* And just as that thought finished, she tripped on the carpet, catching herself just before tea spilled all over the floor.

She looked down to see two things: first, she noticed the tea stain on her day dress, and next, she saw the last rays of light slip through the front window and reflect off a brilliant emerald that was lying at her feet.

Louisa picked up the ring and allowed herself to slump down into a chair. She closed her eyes and willed it all to go away. *We would have been engaged by now. We'd be getting married. No one would know that our baby came first, and we'd be a family. A normal family.*

The whinny of a horse from passing street traffic brought her back to the parlor, to the stain on her dress, to the ring she held in her hand. Her father would be heartbroken once he learned she was with child. She planned the events of the next year in her mind—leaving town, perhaps with Edna, so as to not bring shame to her father. Giving birth in a back room somewhere where she'd not be found out, somewhere where women "like her" hid and had their secret babies before returning home alone. And then she realized that she'd have to leave the baby behind. She would have to abandon Mordechai's child. She clenched the ring in her hand so tightly it dug into her palm. She couldn't give away their child. There was, as far as she could tell, only one option left.

The light from outside had all but disappeared, and Louisa sat in the dusky room listening to the night sounds from the street outside. Finally, she arose to go find Edna so she could ask her to remove the stain from her dress and tell her that she'd give her baby a normal family after all. Now that she'd decided what to do, the emerald ring fit perfectly.

Sunday, October 26, 1862

THAT FOLLOWING SUNDAY Louisa Morrison and Harrison Rogers were wed in a small but lavish ceremony after the last service of St. John's Episcopal Church.

Senator Morrison beamed the entire day, satisfied that he was able to make such quick arrangements. Just five days earlier his daughter had come to him confessing her love for Harrison. She wanted to marry as soon as possible, she said, because after a lifetime of friendship she wanted to begin the next stage of their relationship. Eugene Morrison couldn't have been happier, but was nervous that Louisa, not usually prone to such rash decisions, would change her mind. With a few promises made to several church members, including the Reverend Smith Pyne, Senator Morrison had the proper ceremony, the perfect guest list, and the ideal son-in-law.

Just two days would outshine this occasion in the senator's life: the day only four weeks later when Harrison and Louisa announced they were going to have a child, and the day they did. James Eugene Rogers was born on June 24, 1863, healthy and happy. All involved agreed that the parents were lucky given that the baby decided to come into the world several weeks early.

CHAPTER 14.

Monday, February 3, 1958

NORM CRAWFORD UNLOCKED the front door and made his way into the foyer of the old house. It was early, just after 7:30 in the morning, and it was the first time Crawford could remember having to unlock the door to Substation C.

Crawford knocked on Carey's door and pushed it open slightly to see if he was in. For the first time, he wasn't. *Good*, he thought. Crawford had been working long hours of late and had found himself alone in the house more often. Though he was happy for Carey, being alone in the house again was not altogether welcome. Over the last month, Crawford had heard footsteps outside his door, going up the stairs, even on the second floor. But each time he'd checked into it, no one was there. From time to time he had also felt the mysterious chills that Don Mullins had told him about. And two weeks before, he had seen his office out of the corner of his eye from the foyer and saw the room transformed into an elegant Victorian dining room. He turned around and the image was gone, replaced by the whitewashed plaster walls, old wooden desk, and stacks upon stacks of paperwork.

Sitting at his desk, Crawford picked up where he had left off Friday evening. He had been writing a proposal for portable radios. Officers could make more arrests if they didn't have to waste time in transit from making a collar to calling it in. He needed an average distance from arrest to call box. Based mostly

204

on guesswork, he had come up with four-tenths of a mile. It sounded good.

Crawford looked up immediately, as he heard the sound of a child laughing and the quick patter of feet on the stairs. His heart stopped for a moment, and he yelled out into the foyer, "Hello?"

He rose from his chair, rounded the corner of his desk, and crept slowly over to his door. As he peeked his head out and peered up the stairs, he could see the legs of a young boy scamper up the steps to the second floor. Crawford yelled a "Hello?" up the stairs. No answer. Taking no chances, he undid the snap on his shoulder holster and slowly climbed the stairs to the second floor.

Crawford stepped up into the second-story hallway. He looked all around. No one. He drew his revolver and moved slowly over to the first door on his right. Pushing open the door with his left hand, he carefully pointed his .38 at the ceiling with the safety on, in case it was just a kid trespassing. The room was dark and empty, diffuse morning light coming from the lone, west-facing window. Crawford checked behind the door and then exited the room, closing the door behind him. The next room also was empty. He closed the door and crossed the stairwell to the turret room. From the southeast windows he could see the Capitol dome. The walls were bare, as were the wood floors but for a few scraps of paper and debris. But sitting on the apron of the old brick fireplace was an ancient toy cannon.

Crawford bent down to examine it. It was heavy—made of iron, not of tin—and the wheels still turned. As he turned the cannon over in his hands, he realized that it looked familiar to him. It was just like the one Carey used on top of his desk as a paperweight.

•   •   •

THE RECURRING DREAM had ended the night Carey moved out of the house. While inhabiting the old house, it had become a routine. Lying on a cot in the turret room, paralyzed, bleeding. His hands reaching out. And always the dirty, bearded man with the black hat backed away from him, holding onto a gold pocketwatch, that malevolent smirk on his face. Standing in the doorway for a moment, he would turn and leave. And that was it.

It almost always woke him before dawn, so he never felt like he'd gotten a decent night's sleep. He'd forgotten what it was like until he spent the first night in his new apartment.

So when Carey arrived at 8:30 that Monday morning, he was in an uncharacteristically chipper mood—his hand was almost completely healed, he'd started shaving again (with a safety razor), and he'd gotten a good eight hours' sleep for the second day in a row.

He'd also taken Ruth out, first to lunch the previous Wednesday and then dinner on Friday. They'd hit it off and made plans to go out again this weekend. Things were starting to go Carey's way. His mind was far from the Finkels and the ghosts that haunted his office building.

The previous week the department had taken possession of the six brand-new Plymouth Fury Police Specials. They had automatic transmissions, two-way Motorola radios, and even air-conditioning. Carey had thought that last option something only for rich folks in Cadillacs. The additional six vehicles they'd requested had just been approved and were now on order.

Wednesday, he and Crawford had gone for a ride in one of the cars. It was comfortable and powerful, and it had that new-car smell that Carey had only heard about. Crawford and Carey had hardly pulled to the curb before the cruiser had been yanked from the patrol rotation and appropriated by an assistant chief who spent most of his time behind a desk. Much to Carey's dismay, Chief Correll hijacked another one, and Inspector Price took a third, after promising Carey that the remaining three would remain in the rotation. Nevertheless, at the end of the week, three more high-ranking cops were driving in air-conditioned splendor in the chilly days and freezing nights of winter in Washington.

This had greatly discouraged the men of the planning unit, but Carey had counseled them to keep their chins up. He pointed out that what happened had been somewhat inevitable. Privilege comes with power, after all, but there weren't enough high-ranking police officials in the department to steal all the cars they were acquiring. Besides, each of those officers had traded in his old car, and those cars were much better than the ones in the rest of the patrol rotation. The planning unit would achieve their goal of modernizing the department's fleet, one way or another.

After their Monday morning staff meeting, Norm Crawford lingered behind, waiting until Mullins and Kelsey had left the room with their doughnuts and coffee mugs and quietly pushed the door shut. He sat down in front of Carey's desk. Carey wondered why.

"How're you doing, Ben? You look good. Better. How's the new place?"

"Nice. Quiet."

"That's great," Crawford said, fiddling with the bottom of his coffee mug. "How's your, uh…research going? Uncover anything interesting?"

"Um…" Carey shifted uncomfortably in his seat. "You could say that."

It was clear to Crawford that neither of the men was eager to talk, so he dipped his toe in. "I guess you're glad to be out of this house."

"I'm glad to be sleeping in a real bed, in my own place, sure." Carey leaned forward. "Look, Norm, are you trying to ask me something?"

"All the time you spent in this house," he said, "you ever see or hear anything unusual?"

"I guess so." Carey paused, while Crawford remained silent. "It's an old house. I think it comes with the territory."

"Yeah, I guess…" Crawford said, weighing how much to confide in his friend. "I have to ask, though, Ben. You never saw anything you just couldn't explain?" Carey looked out the window, took a sip of coffee. "Because earlier this morning when I was in my office, I could've sworn I heard a little kid playing on the stairs." Carey felt a shiver down his neck, and Crawford continued. "So I got up to check it out, and I saw this kid running up the stairs. When I searched the second floor, though, no one was there." Carey nodded slowly. "Thing is, Ben, I saw him running up the stairs, but his feet never made a sound. That seem odd to you? Because it seemed odd to me."

Carey stared at him for a moment. "Yeah, that's odd, all right.…Was this the first time you saw something like that?"

"No."

"Me neither," Carey said, leaning back in his chair and eyeing the cracked plaster on the ceiling.

"So you think this place is…haunted?" said Crawford.

"You know when you called me here on Christmas morning?" asked Carey. Crawford nodded. "Well, when you told me that Wallace had shot himself the night before, I couldn't believe my ears. I'd been talking to Wallace when you called. And when I went back, he was gone."

Crawford suppressed a shudder. "Jesus Christ."

"Yeah."

Both men were silent for a while.

"So," said Crawford, "you think what you saw was Wallace's ghost? Is that what you're saying?"

Carey thought about the name he had given it, *Not Wallace*, and half-smiled. "I don't know what it was," he said. "He never showed up again. But there've been others…"

"The kid?" Crawford asked.

"I think so. I heard him on the stairs, too."

Crawford nodded again. "I forgot to tell you," he said, "when I searched the turret room upstairs, I found this." He picked up the paperweight on Carey's desk and set it down. Carey felt something heavy in the pit of his stomach.

"I've got some things to tell you," he said and proceeded to describe for Crawford everything that had happened to him in the house, and everything he'd learned about the house's history— Mordechai, the bearded man, Samuel Finkel, Brandon and Hilldrup, the Morrisons, Trinity Hospital, his nightmares, the night the officers saw the kid, the knocking in the basement, the incident with the straight razor, how he discovered Mordechai's name.

Crawford sat numb in his chair while Carey talked, his lips parted in an expression of stunned horror. When Carey was done, he bent forward, removed his glasses, and laid his head in his hands. "Oh, thank God," he exhaled. "I thought I was going insane, Ben. I didn't know what the hell to think."

"I know how you feel."

"How could you stand it? Living here with all this shit going on?" Crawford shook his head. "You should have told somebody what was happening, or at least…"

Carey raised an eyebrow at this.

"Yeah," Crawford said with an embarrassed laugh. "Never mind."

"Right."

Crawford drained his cup of coffee and sighed. "Is there any way I can help? I can't know about all of this without doing something."

"I was hoping you'd say that," said Carey. "Look, I've got a theory about what happened here. I think Henry Brandon sent his flunky Hilldrup down here to kill Mordechai. Somehow, they made his murder look like the result of his war wounds. I think that's why Mordechai's still haunting this house." Crawford just listened. "I just can't put all the pieces together. I need more evidence."

Crawford thought about it for a second and then asked, "When did Mordechai Finkel die?"

"In the fall of 1862. It must have been sometime after September 15—that's when Hilldrup received the payment from Brandon."

"Did you check the newspapers from September 1862?"

"No," Carey shook his head. "Would they still be around?"

"I think so," said Crawford. "I don't know about the *Post*, but I think the *Star* was around back then. Washington was a much smaller town in those days. I'm guessing they would have carried death notices and the like."

"Would they have papers that old at the library?"

"The papers wouldn't have survived that long," said Crawford, "but they should be on microfilm."

"Well," said Carey, not sure what microfilm was, "I'm not doing anything this Saturday."

IT WAS EARLY Friday evening, and Carey stood outside of Luigi's, a popular Italian restaurant near Dupont Circle. He waited for Ruth while a light drizzle fell on his head and formed a halo around the streetlamp above him. It was cool enough for Carey to see his breath, but not cold enough for the rain to freeze onto the sidewalk.

He had spent his lunch hour with Marie, discussing what to

do about getting legally separated, and then divorced. Marie seemed to Ben to be in an awful hurry about it. Since they didn't have kids or a mortgage, and neither one wanted to hire a lawyer, they agreed to file themselves. Ben had a friend in the U.S. Attorney's office who'd advised him on what they had to do.

As instructed, he'd brought along a list of everything he owned and everything they had bought together. His whole life amounted to two columns on a sheet of paper and the memories that accompanied each bullet point. He'd cooked her dinner for the first time the night their dining room table had been delivered—the pasta was underdone and the rolls were crispy, but she ate it all anyway, laughing the entire time. They'd purchased the bedroom set the week before he left for Korea, and they barely left the new bed until the morning he had to report for duty. The job of splitting up their belongings—the table to Marie, the bed to Ben—appeared to be just another business meeting to her, and Ben wished he could just as easily separate the furniture from the past each piece represented. The tables were turned now. Marie, having often told him he was too distant and mechanical, was dividing and conquering with military efficiency. Ben, meanwhile, fought the lump in his throat by nodding at whatever Marie said.

As he and Marie sat across from each other, divvying up their accounts, talking about which forms they'd have to file and how long it would take, Ben couldn't help think about the similarity to their first date: sitting across from one another over lunch at an inexpensive downtown restaurant. And yet everything was so reversed. That had been a beginning, full of hope and promise. This was the end—two lives that had been bound together forever were now coming apart so quickly and so finally.

When they got up to leave, their parting was cordial, removed. Ben didn't want to betray his emotions, and Marie seemed to not have any left in her at all. They walked out almost as strangers passing on the street. And it was this that gnawed at Ben during the afternoon.

He was not the same man who had courted Marie, nor the man who had stepped off the troop transport from Japan. He had been forcibly ushered from boyhood to manhood by mortar blasts, the still, pale bodies of his comrades strewn along ditches or crumpled over steering wheels, and the endless streams of hollow-eyed, displaced civilians. He returned from Korea with an understanding of the frailty of life, the importance of family, and the realization that his had changed forever. His father had passed away while he was overseas, and his wife was, in reality, little more than a stranger. He realized now that his marriage to Marie had been doomed the moment he returned home. She was still a child, despite her education. But he had grown up.

When he enlisted, they had written each other compulsively, and he had taken great comfort in her letters, knowing especially that she was there to help care for his father during his sudden, brief illness. She had then helped his mother to arrange the burial. He could not attend the funeral, as the army had fouled up his emergency leave orders. Carey was arguing with a staff sergeant in Tokyo while his father was being lowered into the earth.

He had been changed by the events of the last two months almost as much. The things he thought he could count on as absolutes he now knew were mere illusions. People were not always what they seemed, and neither was reality. Ben realized that he could only trust his senses so far, and this made him more flexible in his thinking, but at the same time more cautious.

So when he saw Ruth's face beaming up at him, he was comforted but not comfortable.

"Hello, stranger," she said. "You know where a girl might grab a bite to eat?"

"I've heard this place isn't bad," said Carey, pointing at the restaurant behind him with his thumb. "You have plans for dinner?"

"Actually, I do. I'm meeting a handsome young sergeant on the police force tonight."

"Oh, yeah?" he asked. "Is he bigger than me?"

"No, but he does carry a gun," she said, laughing. Carey just smiled and stared at Ruth for a moment. "Of course," she said, "we could talk about it inside…where it's dry."

"Oh, right," he said, shaking his head and pulling the front door open for her.

Carey and Ruth had gotten to know each other over lunch and dinner the week before. He had made a point of telling her at lunch that he was in the middle of getting a divorce. She had been sympathetic, but it did not seem to bother her. He was still a young man, after all, only twenty-eight, and he had a good job, in charge of three other officers.

Ruth Bergman was twenty-three and had graduated from Georgetown University with a degree in English literature eighteen months before. When she had begun her job search, her prospective employers only wanted to know one thing: could she type? She had no interest in being somebody's secretary. And although working at a department store was a far cry from dissecting the works of Austen, Hardy, and Thackeray, at least at Finkel's she could be a salesperson. She had some say in the way housewares was run, and she loved working with her customers. If nothing else, she could at least read during downtimes.

Carey had told Ruth about his family, about how his father died when he was in Korea, and his mother, who lived in a new apartment building in Bethesda. His stories from his days as a cop walking the beat had not disturbed Ruth—in fact, she had been fascinated by them. He had talked to her about wanting to work homicide someday, and how the planning unit was a great opportunity to prove his administrative skills and intelligence.

He had an easier time talking with Ruth on their third date than he had ever had with Marie. They talked with each other about everything, and she seemed truly interested in him. But he found the awkward silences more awkward with her for some reason. Ruth asked him about work, and they talked about their jobs over glasses of wine before ordering dinner.

After the waiter took their order, Ruth spoke up. "Hey, I almost forgot. How's your research going? You discover anything interesting about Samuel Finkel?"

Carey paused, considering his response. "Yes, I did. As a matter of fact, I took your advice and spoke to the PR man in New York about that."

"Really? What did he have to say for himself?"

"Eventually," said Carey, "quite a bit."

Carey went on to tell Ruth about Samuel Finkel's only son, Mordechai; about how he fought in the Civil War, was wounded, and was brought back to D.C.; and about Finkel's partner, Brandon, his employee, Hilldrup, and the strange payments recorded in the ledger. Carey told her about everything but the ghosts. He left that part out.

"Wow," she said, not noticing that the waiter had arrived with their entrées. "What made you start looking into all this?"

Again, Carey pondered his answer as he dug into his plate of linguini. "The place I work, it's not really an office building. It's an old house. A hundred-year-old Victorian manor. It was the home of a senator from New Jersey who took in wounded soldiers like Mordechai during the war. I think Mordechai stayed in the house. He may have even died there."

"Oh my gosh," she said. "That's amazing. How did you ever piece this all together?"

"A lot of time spent in libraries and dusty basements," said Carey. "And some luck."

"You really are going to be a detective, aren't you?" she said, making him chuckle. "So you think this Hilldrup guy killed Samuel Finkel's son?"

"It adds up," Carey shrugged. But the look in her eye told him she had another thought. "Why, what were you thinking?"

"Nothing. It's just that you said Hilldrup was a floor manager. I guess he reminds me a little of our Mr. Pulaski—not really the hired killer type, if you know what I mean."

Carey hadn't ever given Hilldrup that much thought. Yet she seemed to have captured the man's character in a few minutes. "Maybe," he conceded.

"I mean, if you were Mr. Brandon, would you send some manager to do a murder?" Carey shook his head. "Of course not. But you might send him to hire someone else to do it."

"That would also distance Brandon from the crime," he said, nodding.

"Exactly."

"How do you know so much about the criminal mind?" he asked, teasing.

"I like to read murder mysteries," she said. "You know, Agatha Christie, Raymond Chandler. It can't be Byron, Shelley, and Keats all the time, you know."

Carey looked at Ruth and smiled. It had been a long time since he'd had this pleasant a conversation with any woman who wasn't his mother. But as much as he wanted to go with his gut feelings, he wouldn't let himself.

"Ruth," he said.

"Ben."

"I think you can tell I like you very much," he said, and she smiled. "So I don't want to give you the wrong impression. But I don't want to rush things…"

"No," she said. "I understand."

"I guess what I'm trying to say is, I'd like it if we could just be friends for now. I don't think I'm ready for anything else. But I think maybe you deserve more than that, and I'd understand if that's not—"

"Ben," she cut in, "it's okay. If you couldn't tell, I like you, too. And I can always use another friend."

NORM CRAWFORD ARRIVED at the Southeast Neighborhood branch library on 7th and D Streets SE on Saturday morning, a few minutes past nine. He found the microform room next to the reference section and headed to the oak cabinet at the back of the room. It had about four dozen drawers filled with cardboard boxes of microfilm—roll after roll of 35-millimeter film containing back issues of the *New York Times*, *Wall Street Journal*, *Washington Post*, and *Evening Star*, all going back to the nineteenth century. Crawford removed two boxes from the *Evening Star*'s collection—*September 15, 1862–September 20, 1862*, and *September 22, 1862–September 27, 1862*—and carried them over to the microfilm reader.

Each issue consisted of four oversized pages, with no edition on Sunday. The paper carried news of the war; advertisements for coaches, tobacco, ladies' hats, and patent medicines; government announcements; and a heading, usually on page three, called "Local News," which was essentially a police blotter. Crawford scanned the front page headlines and then studied the local news section of each day's paper, starting with September 15, 1862.

Apparently, Crawford learned, criminals in 1862 were no smarter than the ones in 1958. After reading through a week's worth of century-old news, however, Crawford hadn't learned much else. He rewound the microfilm and loaded the next week's roll onto the spindle. Nothing happened Monday. Tuesday's paper covered Lincoln's Emancipation Proclamation, printing the text in full. Still no mention of Mordechai Finkel or even Senator Morrison, though.

Wednesday, September 24. *There it is.* Top story in local news. "Mordechai Finkel of the Tenth New York State Volunteers died Tuesday afternoon due to wounds received at the most recent battle of Bull Run. The reopening of a severe abdominal wound caused him to bleed to death. Mr. Finkel, a bachelor, was twenty-three years old and lived in Manhattan with his father. He was staying as a guest of Sen. Eugene Morrison (Rep.-N.J.), for the purpose of further recovery after being discharged from Trinity Hospital. He is to be interred this afternoon in a private ceremony." Crawford stared at the text, rereading it several times. *Jesus, Ben, this is real, isn't it?*

"You got here early," said Carey, putting a hand on Crawford's shoulder, causing him to flinch slightly.

Crawford got up from his straight-backed wooden chair and pointed to the text on the screen. "I just found what we were looking for, Ben."

"Found what?"

"Finkel died on September 23, 1862. The story's right here."

"Holy cow," said Carey, sitting down to read the glowing screen. "Yep….This is really good. But, unfortunately, it doesn't really connect us to the killer. It's clear they thought Mordechai died from his earlier wounds."

"I know, but it's something," said Crawford. "The timing at least provides circumstantial evidence for your theory." Carey nodded. "Anyway, I'd been looking through a bunch of nothing for an hour when I found this."

"Good thing you got here early then, huh?"

"Yeah, I couldn't sleep, so I thought I'd just come here." Crawford pushed his eyeglasses back on his nose and looked for a chair to pull beside Carey. "Let's check the next day's paper," he said. "Maybe they have more details. Finkel died in the afternoon, so they might have only had time to get the bare facts in Wednesday's paper. If there were more developments, they might be in Thursday's edition."

Crawford turned the dial and advanced the film, the text flying by Carey's eyes. "Here we are," said Crawford, scanning the items in local news. "Damn. There's no—"

"Yes there is," said Carey, placing an index finger under the small, backlit text. The third paragraph under the Local News heading from September 25, 1862, began with the headline, "N.Y. Man Found Slain":

> Metropolitan Police have identified a man found dead in NW as Mr. Aaron Hilldrup, of New York City. Mr. Hilldrup, an assistant manager of the Finkel's Department Store in Manhattan, was found in an alley near the Canterbury Music Hall. Police said that he was robbed and stabbed under the rib cage by an unknown assailant. His empty billfold was found beside him. Police are looking to question a transient named Ronald Eddy, who was seen talking with Mr. Hilldrup at The West End, a tavern on 14th Street SW.

"I'll be damned. She was right about Hilldrup," said Carey.

"Right about what? *Who* was right?"

"Brandon paid Hilldrup, right?" Crawford nodded. "But he didn't pay him to kill Finkel; he paid him to hire someone to do it. Most of the money wasn't for Hilldrup, it was for the killer. Brandon probably promised Hilldrup a promotion or a raise.

Hilldrup comes to D.C., finds some lowlife to do the job. He does it, Hilldrup pays him, and he heads back to New York."

"Except he never makes it back."

"No. The murderer must have found out Hilldrup was loaded."

"Right," said Crawford. "He could easily have hired someone for less than eight hundred bucks. Hilldrup's careless with his money, the killer finds out how much he's been holding out, and *wham*."

"It all fits," said Carey.

"So who is *she*?" asked Crawford.

"Huh?...Oh, nothing, I'll tell you later."

"Uh-huh."

"Norm, do you realize what this means?" said Carey. "We've just solved a hundred-year-old murder." He tapped the screen with his finger to emphasize the point. "Mordechai Finkel didn't die from his battle wounds. He was murdered by his father's business partner for control of the company. Brandon hired the job out to an underling who found a hit man. And Ronald Eddy was that man—the bearded man."

CHAPTER 15.

New York City
Saturday, December 11, 1865

IT WAS AT HOME that Samuel Finkel grew lonely. At work, in his seemingly endless battle with Brandon, he was engaged, driven, purposeful. At home, he was sad. He missed Marta. He missed his son. Not a minute passed, really, when he did not think about one or the other of them. He had become accustomed to this loneliness, but there was another feeling he could not shake, the feeling there was something he was supposed to do. Every day his evening ritual included running a mental list of his responsibilities, yet he couldn't place what it was that was nagging at the edges of his mind. His servant, Dinah, prepared the evening meal, and they ate together, in silence as usual, in the dining room of his Murray Hill mansion.

Afterward, Dinah drew his bath, and he undressed before the full-length mirror, a crutch under each arm. He stared with dismay at his reflection, his sagging jowls and rotund belly. He had been lean all his life; only in the last few years had his abdomen grown like this. Part of getting old, he decided, and dipped his toe into the bathwater. Satisfied, he carefully climbed in, wetting his crutches in the process.

The water was warm, and he worked up a modest lather with a bar of French soap. He found it difficult to relax, so he ran through his list one more time but, again, found no outstanding obligations. He added more water to the bath. *Hard to believe I*

220

ever lived without running water, he thought as he massaged the soap into his now useless legs. Few New Yorkers had running water and fewer still had a gas-fired water heater in the basement, he knew. He slid farther back in the tub and thought back to his childhood in Germany, his home in the suburbs of Bremen. Back then, he pumped water from a well into a bucket, and then carried that bucket to the bathtub for his father's bath, or his sister Anna's, or his mother's, depending on whose turn it was that night to bathe. The bathtub was in the backyard, behind their modest brick house, and beside the summer kitchen. His mother was very proud of her cast-iron stove, and the big pot of boiling water was the last ingredient in the bath, warming the otherwise frigid well water to a tolerable temperature. When the weather grew cold, they would drag the bathtub into the summer kitchen, and it became the winter bathhouse. *We had it good,* he thought. His parents did well by him and Anna.

Now he was in America, and he was bathing his own son, Mordechai, perhaps four or five, the boy splashing joyously in the clean, warm water. Samuel towel-dried the boy, paying attention to completely dry his thick blond hair, then playfully slapped the boy's behind and sent him scurrying to his mother. Marta sang softly as she dressed her boy, a lilting folk tune that Mordechai sang with her:

Fuchs, Du hast die Gans gestohlen [Fox, you have stolen the goose],
Gib sie wieder her [Give it back]!
Sonst wird Dich der Jäger holen [Or the hunter will fetch you]
mit dem Schießgewehr [with his gun].

He was tossing a ball with the boy now, on a playground, and several other children were playing nearby, with their fathers. The ball was crude, canvas stitched over crumbled bits of rubber, but with a swift underhanded swing, it carried quite a wallop. Mordechai caught the ball, although it clearly had stung his hands. He tossed it back to his father, not wanting the other boys to see his pain, wanting so much to be with others his age, wanting so much to be their equal.

Finkel opened his eyes and watched the steam swirl around the room. For as solitary as he was, his son thrived on attention. Mordechai was an only child and so found the most peace just being near his classmates. *He hates being the outsider,* Samuel Finkel thought. *He hates feeling left out.*

Hated. Past tense. The thought of Mordechai dead always shocked his father, and each realization hurt just as much as the time before. *I love you, son.* Samuel tried to send his thoughts toward his boy, feeling somehow connected as he traced the route from Manhattan to Washington. Too ill to travel so far from home, he had never visited his son's resting place. All he knew about the cemetery was its name—he didn't even know where his son's body was. Dinah's brother, God rest his soul, had been killed last year in Cold Harbor, Virginia, and was buried at the new national cemetery, on the hill overlooking the city. To think of all those soldiers watching over the capital for eternity, Samuel thought. *I wish Mordechai could be there with them to see this country at peace.* The thought caused him to bolt upward, and bathwater splashed out of the tub onto the tiled floor. Samuel watched the bubbles moving toward each other until they popped and disappeared.

He will be with them. I'll see to it that he isn't left out of that.

The nagging in Samuel's mind stopped, and for the first time in three years, he was able to smile.

•   •   •

Thursday, February 4, 1869

DINAH ENTERED Mr. Finkel's bedroom at nine A.M., after her repeated knocking had not been acknowledged. Her employer rarely emerged later than seven A.M., even on a weekend, and when she entered, she was already crying, knowing what she would find. But she was mistaken. Mr. Finkel was sitting up in his bed, his skin pallid, a tablet resting on his lap. His hand was shaking rapidly, and he was having obvious trouble writing. He looked up as Dinah approached him.

"I'm sorry to intrude, Mr. Finkel," she said. "I wanted to make sure you are doing well today. I knocked, but—"

"It's no trouble, Dinah," he interrupted with a raspy voice. His breathing was labored, and it took him great strength to speak. "I know, you thought I was dead. Well, you're just about right, I'm afraid."

Dinah looked panicked and searched the room as if a doctor might suddenly appear. She was twenty-four years old and had come to America from Aberdeen, Scotland, just eight years before. Though she had been employed by Mr. Finkel for the past six years, this was a part of the job for which she was not prepared. "Whom should I call? Which doctor should I alert?"

Samuel waved her off. "Doctors! I've finished with them. I'm old, Dinah. Anyone else I'd want to call has already departed for where I'm going." His chest heaved, and a loud, rolling cough emitted from his once strong body. Dinah nervously rested her hand on his shoulder and handed him a handkerchief. "But I do need your help with something. I'm changing my will this afternoon. My lawyer, Arthur Black, will be over later. I was writing down my notes here." He showed her pages of scribbles. "Your eyes are better and younger than mine, and I know I can trust you to keep my business to yourself."

"Oh, sir, you can trust me. You should hear what some of the other girls say about their employers. I never say a word, not one. Of course, I wouldn't have anything to say, anyway, anything bad that is. I mean—" She stopped herself from continuing by throwing her hand over her small mouth.

Samuel's laughter at this caused another coughing fit. When he finished, he was able to speak better than he had when Dinah had entered the room. "Don't worry, Dinah, you'd have plenty to say, and we both know it. People have been calling me a crazy old man for ten years. I know you've heard it. Hmph, imagine what they'll think when they find out what I'm up to." His grin was devilish. "Dinah, I've been a businessman—a shrewd businessman—for fifty-seven years. A man makes hundreds, maybe thousands of important decisions in that time. Sometimes people thought I was right, sometimes wrong. But you know, they all knew I was powerful....Now they just think I'm crazy. Well, I guess it's a little of both. You don't get this far without being a little of both, do you?"

Dinah shrugged. "I don't know, sir."

"Maybe not...maybe not..." He sat there without moving, and the smirk on his face faded. He had the watery blue eyes of an old man, with the lids flickering over them so that it appeared he rarely blinked at all. He stared out the window while Dinah listened to the clip-clop of the traffic on Madison Avenue. After a few minutes, she rose to move, thinking he had fallen asleep, but once on her feet, he came back to life.

"So we'll give them what they want, won't we? We'll give them a little of both." Samuel's attention now resembled that of what he had been, a firm man who commanded the attention of everyone he met. "They believe I'm crazy because I moved my son where he should be. My boy, oh, you would've liked him. Everyone liked him...."

"'Crazy,' huh? In this town you don't have to do much to be considered crazy anymore. Maybe I should've done more to deserve the title. My esteemed business partner, he's the one who started this whole thing. Brandon's been aching for control of Finkel's since day one. He'd steal from his own mother if she hadn't disowned him as a youth. He's good at the initial contact, but he sours once he's got you. And he had me…he had me.

"Everything Marta and I worked for was supposed to go to our son," Samuel smiled. "At least Marta didn't have to see that telegram….And I'll tell you this, I think that fiend nearly smiled when I told him what had happened in Washington. Without Mordechai, you know, Brandon stands to earn a great deal. He'll buy up my stock and gain control of the company. After that, who knows what he'll do?"

"But it's your store, sir," Dinah said in a confused voice. "Can't you give it to someone else?"

Finkel's grin returned and he winked at his companion. "Ah, my dear, you've put your finger on it. I can, but I won't. Brandon's clever and conniving; and he's also patient. He would cajole and coerce whomever I gave the shares to, and he'd win them one way or another. So I'm not giving them to anyone. Or to put it more precisely, I'm giving them to no one. That rat will never gain control of my company. Not ever."

Washington, D.C.
October 8, 1869

JAMES WAS A DELIGHT. A talkative and rambunctious six-year-old, he spoke English better than many of the lawyers with whom his father worked, and the boy spoke some French, as well. His hair was brown, and his blue eyes sparkled with preternatural wisdom. He was the prince of his mother's world, and Harrison brought the boy to work often to show him off to his partners.

It was a mixed blessing that James was able to grow up in the house his mother had. Just two months after his birth, Senator Eugene Morrison had collapsed while arguing on the Senate floor. His heart had given out. Once again, the position of making funeral arrangements had fallen to Louisa. She interred her father in the Morrison family plot, under the tree next to where her mother had lain for close to six years.

Harrison, Louisa, and James moved into the house on C Street soon afterward and doubled Edna's salary, giving her the chance to add "nanny" to the list of jobs she had provided since joining the household.

James became fast friends with a little boy from down the street, Aaron, and the two spent many long hours tossing rubber balls (and, as often as not, mud) at each other in the modest backyard.

After one such session, Louisa sent the neighbor boy home and dragged her filthy son into the bathroom. She pulled his muddy socks and shoes off his feet as Edna filled the tub with bucket after bucket of water drawn from the spigot down the street. The water was cool, and Louisa had taken a pot of it to the stove. With James now undressed, she poured the bubbling water into the tub and swirled it around with her hand. Satisfied, she placed James in the water and began to clean him with a washcloth and a bar of soap. The mud came off in gravy-like waves as she passed the cloth along his arms and legs. She sang to him as she dried him off.

A few minutes later, the boy was dressed in his nightclothes, complete with a little cap and cloth slippers, and was sitting in front of a plate of Edna's specialty: roast pheasant served alongside a crock of beans and stewed collard greens. James was not fond of the gamy meat, but ate it in tiny bites nevertheless, as he had worked up a powerful hunger and was afraid to confront Edna with a full plate at the end of the meal. He loved the baked beans, however, laced as they were with brown sugar and honey.

Afterward, his father retired to the parlor with a copy of the *Evening Star* while Louisa helped Edna clear the table. James, left to his own devices, did what boys of that age do, he went straight for trouble. On the front hall desk was an envelope full of odd-shaped papers and cards. Louisa had received the package earlier that day. It contained copies of a family portrait made in honor of Harrison's most recent promotion to partner in his firm. The photographs cost a great fortune, even to a family as well-off as the Rogerses were, but Harrison felt strongly about having enough to send to each of his siblings, proud as he was of his small but devoted family. To James, however, these cards were secret keys used by Union soldiers to gain information to Rebel hideouts. He grabbed one and began his search of the house, sliding it into any crack big enough to take in paper of such a heavy weight.

James ran up the stairs, searching for a Rebel to interrogate. He hiked over the beds and crawled through the heavy brush of woolen blankets and feather pillows. When he stubbed his toe on a bed warmer, he decided he was in hostile territory and so wandered down past Edna and his mother and into the basement. A ray of light from the kitchen illuminated the stairway and the far corner of the nearest room. Only "a little" afraid of the dark, James saw himself as the hero of battle, inserting his key between each of the whitewashed boards that subdivided the dank basement. He was just about to remove his key from yet another gap in the wall when he heard a *thud!* from behind him. With his hand still on the wall, James turned with a guilty look to meet Edna's stare.

"What are you doing down here by yourself? What do you have?" She stood with her hands on her hips, a large wooden spoon peeking out of her apron pocket.

The boy shrugged his shoulders and pushed the card all the way into the wall. "Nothing, ma'am."

"Uh-huh," she said, a little suspiciously. "Back upstairs with you, little man."

Thwarted as a Union hero, James turned his efforts to the soldier set he had received from his mother as a birthday present. The soldiers, their cannon, and its caisson came out of their wooden box and lined up at the front door. James dragged the toys across the carpet, making shooting sounds as he went, across the rug and onto the wooden floor. Here he stopped and regrouped his soldiers, and the artillery detachment began to ascend the stairway with a *thump-thump-thump-thump-thump*, the wooden soldiers barking orders to each other, the cannon pausing every so often to fire at an invisible enemy. The upstairs was still fairly well illuminated by the setting sun, and he brought his soldiers and their equipment methodically up the stairs, ensuring that no one was left behind.

The adults paid him no mind, and the brigade now set off down the hall, their commander on his hands and knees behind them, turning his cannon now to fire a round of canister into his bedroom near the top of the stairs. The Rebel soldiers in that room ran for their lives, terrified at the onslaught of Union forces converging on them from the hallway.

The brigade had conquered all the rooms but one, and James could see that the door was open a few inches, which surprised him because this door had been shut since he could remember. He pushed his cannon ahead of him as he crawled toward the bedroom door, the soldiers forgotten for the moment. It was cold in there, he could feel the draft, and dark too, much darker than the hallway, as if the curtains inside were pulled tight. But as he pushed the door open a few more inches, he saw that the curtains were indeed drawn open. It was nighttime in this room, and stars in the sky could be seen through the open window. He saw next, in the center of the room, a single chair, straight-backed, with decorously carved slats. There was a man—scared looking, naked from all appearances, sitting in a pile of blankets on the floor backed against the wall. His hair was dark, and he was holding something, a little box of some sort, in his shaking hands, and suddenly *pop!*—a flash of white light filled the room. James screamed and went running away from that cold, strange room, left his soldiers and cannon behind, and raced down the stairs and onto the lap of a startled Louisa.

James was trembling and talking about intruders and strange lights. Clearly, the boy's active imagination had gotten the better of him.

"Sweetie," Louisa said to him, "I think you're just tired. Let's go upstairs and get you tucked into bed."

James shook his head and burrowed closer into his mother's embrace.

"Would it make you feel better to have your father check upstairs and scare away the intruder?"

The child nodded, "Thank you, sir."

Harrison encountered no one upstairs, but found that the boy had somehow unlocked and opened the door to the turret room and left his toy cannon by the doorway. He bent down and picked up the cannon, wondering how the boy had gotten into the room at all. An icy breeze rushed at the back of Harrison's neck, and he quickly shut the door behind him. He locked it before returning downstairs.

THAT EVENING, Louisa lay in her childhood bedroom, the room she had returned to as a married woman shortly after she had given birth to James. She had told her husband that she wanted to be close to the baby at night in case the infant needed her, but long after James had outgrown the need for such protection, she remained on her own at night. Harrison urged her to return to the marital bed at first, but both had become comfortable in the roles—and the beds—they had made for themselves. Louisa did not despise her husband. On the contrary, she valued the security he provided for her and James. Harrison Rogers was successful in his career, but driven to spending days, even weeks, away from his family, working late into the night in his corner office. He no longer doted on Louisa as he had before, though Louisa didn't mind. In fact, outsiders, including her own husband, all admired how perfectly content she was. In the night, however, the truth of her life came to Louisa in a jolt that often kept her awake.

Outside, someone was shouting, a drunkard, no doubt. She climbed out of bed and peered through the window as two police officers set upon the man, leading him away by the arms. The gas streetlights of Washington illuminated the scene, and the man was hauled away amid great but solitary protest.

She wandered out of her room and crept into James's bedroom, where she listened to the steady exhalations of her sleeping child. She kissed him on the ear, and he snuggled deeper into his blankets.

She quietly shut James's door, turned toward her room, and froze. Out of the corner of her eye, she could see that the door to the turret room stood open a few inches, and a faint glow loomed into the hallway. She had not entered the room since the day she had seen Mordechai's body carted away. Having known how upset she had been, Harrison decided to keep the room locked for her benefit. She hadn't the desire to see it ever again. No doubt the room had been immaculately cleaned and rearranged by Edna years ago. *But who would be in there now?*

She stepped lightly, as she did not wish to awaken Harrison, whose room was adjacent to her destination. *It's just a room,* she thought, *a room my lover died in many years ago. My love, my only love. The father of my child.*

She pushed the door open, and the room was warm. Instead of the cot and wood chairs she expected to find, the room had been restored to what it had been before the war: a guest room with perfect appointments. Lace curtains covered the windows. There was a bed covered in silk pillows, a small upholstered rocking chair, and a desk. The desk held a single lit candle, which bathed the room in its golden warmth.

Louisa pushed the door shut and sat down on the edge of the bed, wondering who had lit the candle. *Edna, perhaps?* She didn't know, but she suddenly felt entirely comfortable, familiar, and she lay back on the bed. *Mordechai's cot had been right here,* she thought as she stared at the ceiling, *this is what he looked at while he was dying.* The flickering candle made brush-strokes of light and dark against the wall, and she thought of the night they had made love, the night that James was conceived, and how wonderful that experience had made her feel. And how it had changed her life forever. She closed her eyes and unbuttoned a single clasp on her nightgown. Her right hand slid inside the garment, against her stomach. He had been so warm, so close.

Her hand was moving downward now, probing places where only he had touched. After the initial passionate frenzy, Mordechai had lightly grazed her body with his fingertips, and it felt good. She pretended that Mordechai was in the room with her now, fantasized that he was lying right next to her, remembered what he had smelled like that night. Her left hand found its way inside the nightgown, she touched her right nipple, and gently squeezed it. She was moving the fingers of her right hand in circles now, and her body responded automatically. Mordechai had done this too, this circular motion that felt so good, always careful not to spoil the perfect rhythm, the perfect texture, the wondrous feeling.

She lifted her hands from where they had been, and now *his* hands were there, moving in a circle, exploring, teasing, then back up to where she liked it most, in that perfect circle. She felt him in the bed beside her but did not open her eyes. The smell was his, the feel of his nose under her ear, against her neck.

She could feel his mouth on her left nipple, sucking, teasing. She moaned, aware of the sound but unable to stop it.

I love you. I will always love you, he said. She could hear his voice, feel his breath against her ear. And then her senses overwhelmed her, and she bit her lip to keep from screaming as a tear ran down her face.

She kept her eyes closed for fear of breaking the moment. His hand was on her shoulder now, kneading the knot that had formed from years of stress and neglect. When her breathing finally slowed, she turned on her side, propped her head on her arm, and rested her hand on her lover's chest. She spoke to him in a low whisper.

"Where have you been? I've missed you so."

I've been here all along. I'm always here.

"I've been so worried you would be angry. I'm sorry—"

You did what you had to do.

"Have you seen your son? He looks just like you. He has your eyes. When I see him, I see you."

He's a beautiful boy. You're a wonderful mother to him.

Louisa craved his attention and reassurances. For the first time in a long while, she allowed herself to be perfectly comfortable. They spoke like that, hands entwined, for what seemed like hours.

HARRISON AWOKE sometime in the middle of the night to the quiet sound of conversation outside his bedroom door. He assumed that James was up and wandering around again, and that his wife or Edna was coaxing him back to bed. Long seconds rolled by, and the noise continued, so he rolled out of bed to inquire as to the problem.

He struck a match on his bedpost, lit the bedside candle, and opened his door. The hall was quiet. He walked to James's room and saw the boy's small hand resting on his pillow, the rest of him neatly tucked under layers of blankets. He turned to retreat to his room, thinking he must have been dreaming, when he began to hear the whispers again. They were coming from the turret room.

Harrison knew he had locked the door just this evening, but as he stood outside the room, he heard the distinct rustle of bed-clothes and a quiet giggle. Louisa's voice. He opened the door into the darkened room.

Louisa was on her right side in the middle of the bed with her nightgown pulled up to mid-thigh. Her eyes were closed and she was mumbling to herself, her left hand clawed and hovering a foot above the bed.

Harrison stared at his wife, and a deep fear gripped him. She looked perfectly contented, a look on her he hadn't seen since they were children. He knew he couldn't bring that level of comfort to her. He couldn't bring a flush to her face like she displayed here, by herself, in a room in which a stranger had died. Try as he might, he could not make his wife love him. He squeezed his eyes shut in pain and regret, but when he opened them, the sight was still the same.

"You should not be here," he said in a halting voice.

Louisa's eyes popped open, and her hand immediately went slack and dropped to the bed. She scanned the room in wild amazement, stopping when she met her husband's gaze.

"Have you gone mad, Louisa?" he asked her, placing his candle on the hallway floor and taking a step into the room.

She recoiled. "No, I haven't. We were just...we were..."

Harrison moved quickly to the bedside, grabbing her shoulders with firm hands and hoisting her to her feet. He turned her body to face the walls.

"Look around! There's no one here!" His voice grew louder, his tone more urgent. "You're alone, Louisa. Alone."

She tried to wrest free of his grip, but he was too strong.

"I'm not alone," she whispered. "He's here."

Harrison turned her around to face him. "Who is here?"

The answer came from the back of her throat before she could stop it. "James's father." Her eyes grew wide with terror as Harrison raised his hand and brought it down across her cheek.

He began dragging her toward the door, screaming, "You shouldn't be here, not in here." They were out in the hallway now, Louisa struggling for footing. "I told you never to go in there. I did this for you, for your own good."

He dragged her toward her room, his wife pleading with him not to hurt her child, not to hurt her boy.

"*Your* boy?" he said through clenched teeth as he released her to the floor outside her bedroom door. "I am that boy's father."

He stood in the hallway trying to calm down. Hands covering his face, he stumbled back to his room. He never saw Edna spying on him through the crack in her door, and he didn't hear Louisa's muffled footsteps as she crept into James's room.

Miraculously, James did not stir in his bed. Louisa listened again to his peaceful breathing. She uncovered his face from the blankets and stared at his familiar features. Tears sprang from her eyes, and she covered her mouth to stifle a sob. When she had calmed, she slid under the covers beside her sleeping child. He sighed deeply and wrapped his arm around her. The little boy smiled and mumbled. Louisa thought she heard him say, *Goodnight, Daddy.*

CHAPTER 16.

Sunday, February 16, 1958

CAREY STEPPED OUT of the train station and into the bright after-noon sun of downtown Bethesda. He walked over to the curb and hailed a cab. His mother had moved to the picturesque Maryland suburb four years earlier, after Carey's father died. The old row house in Columbia Heights, which Carey had grown up in, had suddenly seemed much too large for her. And she no longer felt safe on the streets after dark. The neighborhood was changing. So she now lived in a cozy one-bedroom apartment in a new mid-rise complex.

Charlotte Carey fixed a pot roast for Sunday dinner, and Carey ate it gratefully, his home-cooked meals consisting lately of scram-bled eggs and ham sandwiches. His mind was more at rest than it had been in a long time. But a memory kept itching him, and he had to scratch.

"Hey, Mom," he asked, while washing dishes for her to dry and put away, "do you remember that story you used to tell about the strange old man who played the organ at church?"

She paused for a moment, wrapping a dinner plate in the dish towel. "He died when I was about sixteen. But I wouldn't say he was a 'strange old man.'"

"But there was something odd about him, though, wasn't there?" Carey said.

"It's been so long since I told anyone that story," she said. "You must have been very young. You remember St. Paul's over on 15th and V Street?" He nodded. "I used to play the organ there. It was one of those big, old, three-manual organs with about thirty stops on the side. I was just in high school, but I was very good on the piano. I got the job because our parish organist, Mr. Gilchrist, died at the console while practicing one morning. The pastor came over to the school right away and asked if I would take over his duties for the weekend. I said yes and rushed right over after school to start practicing. Everything went well on Sunday, and the pastor asked if I would stay on permanently. Of course, I agreed to do it. They even paid me a little each week. Anyway, I'd been playing each Sunday for almost a year when I went in to practice one afternoon.

"I practiced every day after school the piece I was going to play on Sunday. That week I was playing a rather difficult piece I'd heard Mr. Gilchrist play many times, but which I was having trouble with. When I entered the church, no one else was around, but I could hear someone playing the organ in the loft upstairs. Whoever it was, was playing the piece I'd been practicing. Except they were playing it flawlessly. I climbed the staircase, and as I got to the top of the stairs, the playing stopped. I turned around to see who was there, and I saw Mr. Gilchrist, sitting in front of the organ smoking a cigarette, as he always did, just staring at that organ. I blinked my eyes, and he was gone."

"You saw his ghost?" said Carey, dumbfounded.

"It turned out that afternoon was a year to the day after he had died," she said. "I know you never believed in any of that stuff, but I know what I saw."

"No, Mom, it's not that," he said, sorry that he'd made her feel foolish. "I'd forgotten that was what the story was about. I don't know why I thought..." He stopped and shook his head. "What I'm trying to say, Mom, is I've seen things, too, since I started working in that old building. Things I never would have believed."

It was his mother's turn to look at him in disbelief. "Are you having fun with me?"

"No, I'm not kidding."

Carey told her about Wallace, about the bearded man and Mordechai, and about the boy, though he did not share his disturbing dreams or the incident with his razor. "I'd never experienced things like this," he said. "If these are ghosts, why have I never seen them before? Have you ever seen other ghosts?"

She nodded.

"How long have you…been seeing them?" he asked.

"Can't remember the first time," she said. "I just remember them always being there, even before I knew what they were. I don't always see them, sometimes I can just feel their presence. You remember Christmas Day? I waited for you outside on the porch because I didn't want to stay in that foyer. I felt like you had company you didn't know about.…I guess you did know."

"But why haven't I seen them before?"

"Ben," his mother said, touching his hand, "I don't think most spirits want us to see them, and they don't want to see us. They're stuck…stuck somewhere between death and the afterlife. They don't want anything to do with us, unless…"

"Unless *what*?"

"Unless they want something from us."

SINCE THE DAY that he and Crawford had come to the conclusion that Ronald Eddy had killed Mordechai Finkel, Carey had been keeping a parallel file to the notes he'd taken in Wallace's old sketchbook. He wasn't really sure what, if anything, he would ever do with it, but it satisfied his personal sense of order and desire to follow police procedure. Though he knew that no one would care, he wondered if he'd be able to prove his case to anyone else.

So he kept careful track of all his factual evidence linking the killers to the victim and the victim to the house. The supernatural evidence, from his own and Norm's eyes, from Wallace's sketchbook, he left out.

As February wore on, Carey and the rest of his unit threw themselves into their work. Having procured a dozen new vehicles, two-way car radios, more than fifty portable "walkie-talkies," and enough of the latest protective riot gear to outfit twenty officers, the planning unit had become an unqualified success in a short time. Deputy Chief Correll and Inspector Price, who had both benefited directly from the unit's efforts, commended Carey verbally and hinted at new opportunities for him if his unit continued to perform.

Crawford had become Carey's right-hand man, supervising the work of Mullins and Kelsey, and troubleshooting Department of Justice objections, while Carey took care of the big picture, setting the unit's goals and objectives.

Things had calmed down in the old house for the most part. Sometimes Carey and Crawford would compare notes about what they'd seen or heard. Aside from some unexplained footsteps and the occasional chill, neither of them had seen anything odd for three weeks. They were satisfied that they'd solved the mystery. Carey told Crawford about the revealing conversation he'd had with his mother. They concluded that they must have given Mordechai's ghost what he wanted. Perhaps the ghost of Ronald Eddy had been driven out as well.

Late one Friday afternoon, Carey had finished up his work and was absent-mindedly flipping through the Finkel file at his desk. Mullins and Kelsey had already gone home for the night when Crawford poked his head in Carey's door. "I'm taking off, Ben."

"All right, Norm," said Carey. "Have a good weekend."

"You too, Ben. You got plans?"

"Ruth and I are going out to a movie tonight."

"Oh, yeah?" Crawford said with an arched eyebrow. "You've been seeing her for what, a month now?"

"I guess, yeah."

"Why don't you and Ruth come over for dinner sometime?" he said. "I know Mary would love to meet your new girl."

"I don't know, Norm," Ben hesitated. "We're taking it slow right now. She's just a friend at this point."

"Ahh," Norm acted as though he understood, but couldn't hide a little disappointment. "Well, I'll see you Monday."

"Bye," said Carey, as Crawford waved and pulled the door shut.

The old photograph of Louisa, Harrison, and James Rogers was sitting atop the papers of the opened file folder. Carey picked it up and stared at the portrait, noticing anew how beautiful Louisa Rogers was. *I wouldn't mind being wounded so much if I'd had her for a nurse*, he mused. He traced a finger down the side of her cheek to her chin. He thought of Marie and frowned, slid the photograph back into the file.

Just then a slow knocking came at his door. "Come on in, Norm," he said, assuming Crawford hadn't left yet. No response. "Norm, that you?"

Knock…knock…knock.

Carey stared at the door. *Shit.*

From experience, he doubted this was an intruder, so he didn't bother to draw his revolver from his shoulder holster as he rose from his chair. He walked around his desk and toward the door. The knocking stopped. Carey watched as the doorknob began to jiggle and slowly turn. He backed up until his rear end hit the back of his desk. The door opened slightly and stopped. Carey then heard footsteps and the clunking sound of a crutch moving down the hall toward the kitchen. *Mordechai?* Unable to stop himself, he followed.

When he got to the kitchen, he saw that the basement door was open, inviting him down. But this time, Carey did not want to go. He stood at the top of the cellar stairs and pulled the light chain. A pool of light shone on the basement floor. There was no one down there. He switched the light off and turned away from the stairs.

Mordechai, his pale face drained of blood, stood directly in front of him, his eyes glaring at Carey, not more than six inches away from his face. He stepped forward and Carey recoiled, stumbling backward through the doorway. Losing his balance, he fell into the darkness of the stairwell. His arms shot out, fingers grasping at anything they could find, and his left hand managed to clamp down on the old wooden railing. The top of the railing came loose from the wall with a loud *crunch!*, but the bottom remained attached, and Carey held on to his precarious perch, his feet pointing upstairs to the kitchen, his head angling down to the floor below. He was scraped and bruised, but managed to pull himself up and climb back up the stairs.

Mordechai was gone.

Carey grabbed his coat and left the house without turning back. He rode the streetcar to his 16th Street high-rise apartment and walked around the block two times before his heart stopped pounding. As the scare from his latest encounter with Mordechai faded, his utter bewilderment grew. *What does he want from me now?* he thought. *This was supposed to be over.*

AN HOUR LATER, Carey picked up Ruth and took her to dinner. He was unusually quiet as they ate. They went to the Uptown Theater on Connecticut Avenue, one of the grandest of the old movie palaces in D.C. It had the biggest screen in town, and the movie was *The Bridge on the River Kwai*, which Ruth loved, but which could not distract Carey's preoccupied mind.

It was an unseasonably warm late winter evening as Carey and Ruth walked side by side down Connecticut Avenue after the movie let out.

"You seem quiet tonight, Ben," said Ruth.

"Do I?" he said. "Sorry."

"Anything on your mind?"

He stopped walking and turned toward her. "You know how I thought we'd solved the Finkel murder?"

"Of course."

"Well, I'm convinced we were right about Hilldrup and Eddy," he said. "But now I'm wondering if there's more to it."

"Really?" she said. "Like what?"

"I don't know. There's still so much I don't know about Mordechai. About the killer, too."

"Didn't you tell me once that Mordechai was buried at Arlington?" she asked.

"Yeah. His father had his body moved there a few years after he died."

"We could take a trip out there sometime. Try to find his marker."

They started walking again. Carey had thought of going to the cemetery before, but didn't consider it important enough to bother. "I guess it couldn't hurt," he said.

"You never know what we might find," she said, as they started down the avenue once again.

CAREY AND RUTH met at the Lincoln Memorial on the afternoon of the following Sunday, a cold, colorless March day. Across the Potomac was Arlington National Cemetery, and as they traversed

Memorial Bridge, rain fell in light sheets of mist. Carey didn't think he would learn anything he didn't already know by locating Mordechai's grave, but he was nonetheless curious.

Carey held a large, black umbrella above Ruth's head as they made their way up to the Administration Building. On this damp, chilly day, there were few other visitors. As they walked, they could see in the distance an interment service being held for an old veteran. A hulking hearse idled nearby, ahead of a line of private automobiles. Nobody else could be seen in any direction. Once inside, they found the visitor services desk and asked about locating a grave.

"Do you know the year of death?" the docent asked.

"Eighteen sixty-two," said Carey.

The man behind the counter was in his sixties, mostly bald, and wore thick glasses with black frames. He turned to a shelf filled with a dozen wide, leather-bound books, and slid out the one volume at the far end of the collection. The books were ledgers, containing the names and locations of the soldiers buried at Arlington, catalogued by date of death.

"Last name?" the man said.

"Finkel," said Carey, "first name, Mordechai."

The man opened the book, flipped forward to the appropriate page, and scanned the entries with his forefinger. "Section 2, lot 3818," he said matter-of-factly. "That's just beyond the Old Amphitheater. Not far from here. You can find it on the map over yonder." He pointed to a framed map of the grounds on the wall behind them.

"Thank you."

Carey and Ruth walked down the winding road, past the white columns of the Old Amphitheater and up a small hill lined with white, government-issue headstones. The rain had stopped, and a line of large oaks stood silhouetted black against the gray sky, with a few budding cherry trees straining to release their spring colors. They reached the hill's crest and looked out at the city in the distance, the top of the Washington Monument obscured by haze.

"It should be down here," Ruth said, pointing to a slope on their left bounded by a small group of evergreens. "Thirty-seven forty-two…thirty-eight fifty-four, this is the row."

Carey was silent as they walked, his mind mulling over the events of the past three months. Now that they were so close, he wasn't certain that he was ready to come face to face with Mordechai Finkel's final resting place. His soul was hardly at rest, God knew.

"Here it is," she said and stood before a plain white headstone under the gnarled arm of an ancient oak tree.

Carey stopped beside Ruth. He stared at the stone for a moment and then walked up to it, crouching down to get a better look. The white marble slab, like most of those surrounding it, was stained from age with dark gray streaks. At the top and center was a Star of David. Beneath it, in simple block letters, were the words—

MORDECHAI

FINKEL

NEW YORK

PVT US ARMY

JULY 29 1841

SEPTEMBER 23 1862

Carey's eyes traveled down the headstone to the cold ground covering Mordechai's earthly remains. *What more do you want from me, Mordechai? I'm trying to help you, but I don't know what more I can do.* Carey stood and sighed. This was more difficult than he'd imagined. Mordechai was no longer just a ghost or a name on an old piece of paper to Carey, but a flesh-and-blood man who lived and died. A twenty-one-year-old kid who was murdered by greed and left here to rot.

"He's really real, isn't he?" he said to himself as much as to Ruth.

"Yes," she said. "It's hard evidence, anyway....Police like hard evidence, don't they?"

Carey smiled and turned to Ruth. She looked up at him, hoping that he would take her hand, but he couldn't. They walked back down together to the entrance to flag a taxi.

MONDAY MORNING, Carey was late to work, arriving after Crawford, Mullins, and Kelsey for the first time since they'd started working together. After the morning staff meeting, Carey locked himself in his office with a cup of coffee and pored over the contents of his file and the notes he'd taken in Wallace's old sketchbook.

What am I missing? he asked himself. Mordechai had never terrorized him before last Friday. Mordechai had been the victim. It was he who had led Carey to the clues he'd found so far. *Was he trying to lead me back to the basement? The photograph?* Carey studied the photograph for the hundredth time and then flipped back through Wallace's sketchbook. Drawings of Louisa and James. But no Harrison Rogers. *Why?* Ronald Eddy and Mordechai were here. *What's the connection?* Louisa cared for Mordechai while he recovered. But he died before James was born, before she married Rogers—

The phone rang, breaking Carey's train of thought.

"Hello?" said Carey.

"Carey, it's Price. Got a minute?"

"Sure."

"Can you meet me for lunch today?"

"Um...yeah. No problem."

"Don't worry, it's on me. Well, the department, anyway," said Price. "Let's say twelve-thirty at Old Ebbitt's?"

"I'll see you then."

The Old Ebbitt Grill was one of the oldest taverns in Washington. On F Street between 14th and 15th, a block and a half from the White House, it was one of Price's favorite haunts. Price was sitting on the long, padded bench opposite the bar when Carey walked in. Carey pulled up a chair and sat down across from his boss.

"I already ordered for us," said Price. "I hope you like your steak well done."

Carey didn't, but free lunch was free lunch. He could see that Price had scotch, which looked tempting, but he decided against it and ordered coffee. Carey sat uneasily while Price reclined, swirling the ice cubes in his drink. James Price was a short, ruddy-faced man, with small eyes set too close together. But he was sharp as a tack, and Carey knew it. There was a reason Price had asked him to lunch, but only Price knew what it was.

Finally, Carey spoke. "So, what's up, Jim?"

"I was hoping we could sit down and talk for a while," said Price.

"Okay."

"Ben, the planning unit's been a great success. Nobody expected the results you've achieved, and it hasn't gone unnoticed. You're going to have more opportunities than you ever would've had otherwise. The question I have is, what do you want to do?"

"I don't know, it all depends on what's offered."

"That's not what I asked, Ben. What do *you* want to do?"

Carey paused. "The same thing every young cop wants, I guess. I want to work homicide, be a detective."

"That's good," Price said, nodding his head. "But you're right. That is what every young cop wants. And every middle-aged cop, for that matter. The way things are now, Ben, it could take ten years for you to get there, even if you score higher than everyone else on all the exams."

Carey nodded his head.

"The planning unit isn't the only section looking at strategic departmental improvements, Ben. You want to talk about homicide? Homicide is hopelessly backlogged and overworked. But we can't get the money from the feds to expand the number of detectives working it. So I've put in a proposal of my own." Price smiled at this. "It's something I've been discussing with Correll and the chief. Something I've been thinking about for a long time. Homicide has responsibility for all open cases. That means most cases sit on the books for years unsolved. As each detective's caseload gets heavier, the proportion of cases solved goes down. Homicide is hopelessly inefficient the way it's configured right now. They're disorganized, priorities get misplaced, shortcuts are made, evidence is lost or mishandled, never heard from again…"

Carey's mind suddenly clicked with what Price was saying.

"…We need a division to take over these cases. If an investigation goes over a year without making any significant progress, it passes over to this new division, a unit working solely on the toughest cases."

"That makes a lot of sense," said Carey, nodding.

Price got to the point. "If this proposal gets approved—and I have every reason to believe it will—I'm going to be heading it up. That means I'll be able to handpick the men working under me; I'll need men who are smart, resourceful, and ambitious. Are you interested?"

•   •   •

AFTER LUNCH, Carey returned to the office and popped into Crawford's office to fill him in on his lunch with Price. Carey pulled up a chair and told Crawford about what Price was planning, and how he had recruited Carey for it.

"What did you tell him?" asked Crawford.

"I said yes," Carey said. "And I also recommended you for a spot on the team."

"Homicide, no shit?" Crawford shook his head. "Ben, I never thought signing on to your planning unit would lead me there. But, yeah, I'm in."

"Nothing's definite, yet," said Carey. "It all depends on whether the feds will fund the reorganization."

"Sure, but it's a smart move. Price knows what he's doing." Crawford pulled a handkerchief from his pocket and began to clean his glasses. "A cold case squad, huh? If Price wants a cold case, we've got a doozy."

"Yeah, I didn't tell him about that."

"You should. We solved a century-old homicide. I mean, leave out the ghost story, of course, but—"

"I'm not so sure anymore," said Carey. "I mean, I'm confident that Eddy's our killer, but I think there might be more to it than that."

Crawford shifted uneasily in his chair. "So did you find some new bit of evidence, or did it find you?"

"Friday evening—just after you left," said Carey. "I heard footsteps in the hall, and I could tell it was Mordechai. I followed the sound into the kitchen, and that's where I saw him. Scared the bejesus out of me."

Crawford was white. "I thought it was over.…What do you think it means?"

"I don't know, but it felt wrong. Like he was angry with me."

"What do you think he's trying to tell us?"

"I think we're missing something. When I was having lunch with Price, he said something that got me thinking. *Evidence.*"

"What about it?"

"He talked about how poorly the evidence control room handles physical evidence, because they're so backlogged. Stuff goes missing, gets misfiled, lost, what have you. Some homicide files never get closed. What happens to the evidence?"

"If the case is closed, and the evidence goes unclaimed, it gets auctioned off, I think."

"What if the case never gets closed? Maybe they never nabbed Eddy for doing Hilldrup. There could be evidence, paperwork…"

"I don't know."

"Neither do I. But I'm going to find out." Carey got up to go and turned toward the door.

"Ben?" said Crawford.

Carey turned around. "Yeah, Norm?"

"When are they planning on tearing this place down, anyway?"

THE EVIDENCE/PROPERTY ROOM of the Metropolitan Police Department took up half of the basement of the Municipal Center, the MPD's sprawling new headquarters. From the look of it, though, they'd moved everything from the old evidence room without sorting through or reorganizing its contents. Carey was pleased to see that. For once, he thought, bureaucratic inefficiency was paying off in his favor.

The evidence room, with its old wooden shelving and rows of metal boxes, looked much older than the modern building that housed it. Carey, in his customary plain clothes, walked up to the sergeant manning the desk and flashed his badge, identifying himself as Sergeant Carey of the planning unit.

"Sergeant," the sergeant behind the counter said. "What can

I do for ya?"

"Well, I have sort of an odd question, if it's all right." The sergeant shrugged. "What happens to the evidence in an investigation if the case stays open for more than, say, ten years?"

"It depends," he said. "What crime are we talking about?"

"Murder."

"Well, if the murder goes unsolved, and no one claims the property, it could remain here for a long time. Until the captain releases the property for an auction."

"Okay," said Carey. "So how long could that take, conceivably?"

"That depends."

Carey could see where this conversation was headed. "All right, let's say a piece of evidence from an unsolved murder sits around for twenty years. Your cap releases the property for an auction, but nobody buys it. Does it get thrown away?"

"Well, first it would come back here," he said, "for final determination. Then, yeah, it gets incinerated. Unless…"

"Unless what?"

"Unless it gets misplaced or reshelved incorrectly," he shrugged. "We handle a lot of evidence here, buddy. And we don't have near the manpower we need to deal with it all. The older the evidence, usually, the lower the priority." Carey nodded. "So what's with all the questions? You need to look at something? What cases is the planning unit workin' on?"

"Inspector Price asked me to look into something for him," Carey lied. The sergeant straightened slightly. "Where would I look to find property from a murder case that was more than twenty years old?"

"Well, first check the files on the far wall. They're organized by case numbers, which go by date. Cases that old used a different numbering system. If you can find it in the file, it will tell you where to look. If it's not in the files, it's anybody's guess. But section F tends to have the oldest evidence relating to unsolved cold cases."

"Thanks."

Carey started with the wooden file cabinets lined against the green-tiled wall opposite the rows of shelves. He soon discovered the chronology of the files and went straight to the last drawer, containing the oldest extant files. The beginning of the drawer had cases from the teens. Not a good sign. Toward the back were a few cases from before the turn of the century. But nothing from before 1890.

Carey walked over to section F and started opening boxes, hoping to find something, anything—the older the better. What he found was a section unlike any of the others. Where every other section possessed a sensible, if not rigid, organization, section F was a kind of Lost and Found for property used in the commission of, or found at the scene of, any number of unsolved crimes. Carey meticulously sorted through dozens of boxes, working his way down to the end of the aisle which dead-ended at the opposite wall of the room. He knew the boxes contained evidence from pre-1900 cases, as the numbering system was similar to the few files he'd seen from that period. After an hour of opening musty metal boxes and searching through mostly worthless, rotting junk, he came upon the last six-foot, three-tiered shelf containing the last of the boxed property.

About half the boxes he saw, however, were made of wood and looked antique. Carey started with these. The numbering system was the simplest he'd seen: a two-letter code followed by three digits. The evidence inside these wooden boxes was tagged with paper and string, some of which had deteriorated. But on the slips of paper were dates and short descriptions of the items, such as an old fishing knife that read: JUNE 13, 1868—SERATED KNIFE FOUND LYING NEXT TO VICTIM—WM. O. HOOD—MATCHING WOUND TO BELLY: PRESUMED HOMICIDE. Carey rifled through almost every box without finding anything relating to Hilldrup's murder. The next box he found was the last. He opened it, but did not see what looked like evidence from a crime. It was more of a junk drawer collected from the streets of D.C. The contents did not correspond to the number on the box, nor to each other. There were items from 1883, 1864, 1907, and many other years—fountain pens, skeleton keys, combs, a pair of gloves, and a broken pocketwatch. The watch was gold-plated, though most of the plating had worn off. It had tall, Roman numerals on its face and delicate scrolled hands.

Carey read the tag and held his breath: OCTOBER 18, 1862— GOLD POCKETWATCH, WITH MONOGRAM, FOUND ON VICTIM— RONALD EDDY—PRESUMED STOLEN: HOMICIDE. He turned the watch over and could make out the letters well enough to read the monogram: HRD.

Carey wondered what its significance was. It wasn't Mordechai's watch, nor Hilldrup's. Regardless, it showed that Eddy had been murdered himself about four weeks after he killed Mordechai, and that his murder had never been solved. He searched the rest of the box, hoping to find another clue, but this was it. He grabbed the watch and walked back to the front desk.

"You still here?" the sergeant said.

"I'm done now," Carey said. He laid the pocketwatch on the counter. "I need to know if I can sign this item out."

The desk sergeant picked up the watch, looked it over, and then read the tag. He gave Carey a look of disbelief. "You've got to be kidding me. *Eighteen sixty-two?*"

"That's what it says, all right."

"For chrissakes, this should have been tossed years ago." The sergeant leaned forward, "Listen, you're not going to report this to Inspector Price, are you?"

"Well," said Carey, "that depends."

. . .

CAREY RECLINED on his new tan couch and looked at the accumulated evidence from his unofficial investigation laid out on his coffee table. He had it organized as if to tell a story: Wallace's sketches on the far left; the names of the soldiers released from Trinity Hospital into the care of Senator Morrison to the right of that; next, the ledger entries showing the $800 payment to Hilldrup; the newspaper account of Mordechai's death, then Hilldrup's murder; the pocketwatch; and last, the photograph of Louisa, Harrison, and James.

Louisa...so beautiful. Wallace had really captured her in his sketches. *How old was she when she nursed Mordechai? Only eighteen. Mordechai was just twenty-one. So young.*

An idea hit Carey just then. When he'd been in the hospital in Korea, he couldn't count the number of wounded guys who'd fallen in love with the nurses who cared for them. *What if that's the connection?* He picked up the notebook and turned to the page that had his notes on Louisa. She married Harrison Rogers in October 1862, and James was born eight months later. He remembered thinking that they'd wasted no time. Maybe they had to get married. Or maybe, to be more precise, *she* had to get married.

Had Mordechai and Louisa been lovers?

If they were lovers, then James was most likely Mordechai's son. It was an interesting theory. But Carey wondered, *How in the world am I going to prove it?*

CHAPTER 17

Friday, September 23, 1932

LOUISA WAS RESTING in her mother's rocking chair, watching the curtains dance in the warm breeze. With the cross breeze, the turret room was the coolest room in the house on a day like this, but Louisa would have been sitting there even if it weren't. She rarely left the room anymore; there was little reason to do so. She had enough to think about just sitting there, alone with her memories.

She glanced into the hall and could see a young James playing at the top of the stairs with his soldiers. That was how she always remembered him, even though he had grown into an extraordinary man. He had stayed in the house with her until he turned twenty-five, a bright salesman who left to take an executive position in Chicago's venerable department store, Marshall Field's. She had missed him greatly, even though he'd visited as often as he could. He had met Emma, a young switchboard operator, soon after he moved, and their three children, Wilson, Mary Louise, and Abigail, had all grown up in the Midwest.

James had died over four years ago, shortly on the heels of his wife's passing. He had been buried in his own family's plot in a sprawling cemetery just west of the city he had grown to love. After the crash of '29, and with their parents both gone and their financial values low, the children and their families decided to try their luck out west. She had received word from Wilson nearly a year ago. He and Abigail's husband, Joe, had found work running a general store outside of Los Angeles. Mary Louise and her husband,

Albert, had been able to purchase a bit of land just north of San Francisco. The grandchildren were close with one another, and they were happy. James would have been proud.

A creak on the stairway floorboards gave Louisa the hope she would see James walking up the stairs to greet her. Instead, Edna popped her gray head around the corner.

"You want some company up here?" she asked. "I have lunch almost ready for you."

"Edna," Louisa replied with a smile, "how many times do I have to tell you not to wait on me? I can fix my own lunch. You should sit and relax."

"Hmph, you old people are so crotchety." Edna walked to the room and sat down on a small sofa. "Well, I'll just take a little breather. You know, in case you need anything."

Louisa playfully rolled her eyes.

Edna reached out her hand and rested it on her friend's shoulder. "Are you all right today? I know this day is hard on you."

"Yes, it is," Louisa said. "Seventy years today."

Edna nodded. "Been a long time."

Louisa turned to Edna. "We have gotten old, haven't we, Edna?" Edna smiled in agreement. "You remember what we talked about last spring? I don't know how much longer my heart can hold out."

"Don't talk like that, Louisa," said Edna, furrowing her brow.

"It's all right, Edna. I'm not afraid anymore," Louisa said. "If I do go before you, you must make certain that my will is carried out to the letter. You're the only one who knows how important it is to me."

Edna nodded and said, "I will, Louisa. You know I will."

Louisa gazed out the window at the Capitol dome and let out a long, peaceful breath.

.   .   .

LOUISA HAD BECOME a widow thirty-three years into her marriage. After their confrontation, Harrison rarely spoke to her anymore, pulling into himself more and more. Once James had grown up and moved away, his loneliness only intensified. Toward the end, he had taken to talking to himself and refused to sleep without a lamp burning at his side.

One day, Louisa and Edna returned from the market to find Harrison in his study, slumped over her father's old mahogany desk, a pool of blood around his head, clutching a pearl-handled revolver in his dead hand.

After all their years together, she felt nothing but pity for Harrison. He had tried, for his part. She knew it wasn't his fault that he had fallen in love with her, nor was it his fault that she would always love another man. She was a great prize to him. But once he had won her, he found that the thing for which he had yearned for so long was something he could never have.

"You did the best you could for him," Edna said after a few minutes of silence. Louisa wasn't sure which man her friend was talking about, but she guessed it didn't matter. She had done her best for both of them.

"I miss him, Edna. After seventy years, I miss him like I did that day. I'm not even sure of the passage of time anymore. I'm getting to questioning my own mind, getting my years crossed, my thoughts confused." She turned to face Edna, looking into her eyes. "Sometimes I'll be sitting here and I see something out of the corner of my eye, and when I turn, it's gone. I see *him*, Edna. One time he was standing right in front of me, smiling but with tears in his eyes. He looked exactly the same, but I was old. I don't know, maybe I was dreaming."

"Maybe," Edna said, "maybe not. The spirit world isn't that far away from us. You two were connected. I haven't seen him, but that doesn't mean he's not around here somewhere." She squeezed Louisa's hand. "Maybe you have both of us lookin' out for you."

If I had to go through the years with someone other than Mordechai, Louisa thought, *I'm glad it was you.*

CHAPTER 18.

THE MORNING STAFF meeting over, Carey stopped Crawford as he was walking out the door and asked him if he was free for lunch. "Yeah, I am," he said.

"Chinese okay?"

"Sounds good to me."

Shortly after one o'clock, they headed up to Chinatown and stopped in at The Golden Dragon. It was a chilly day, and they ordered beef lo mein, sesame chicken, and drank hot tea.

The waiter brought out two small bowls of hot and sour soup, and as they sipped their soup from porcelain spoons, Carey brought up the case.

"I had an idea," he said.

"Yeah?" said Crawford. "Let's hear it."

"I'd been thinking about Louisa and the boy, and if there were more of a connection there than her being his nurse. What if…" Carey raised his spoon for emphasis "…what if Mordechai and Louisa had been lovers?" he said. "And the boy, James, was Mordechai's son?"

"What makes you think that might be the case?"

"She was his nurse. She was a beautiful young woman, he was a handsome young soldier—"

"Before he got crippled."

"She could've seen past that," said Carey. "But, more importantly, the timing works. The boy was born just under nine months

257

after Mordechai died. It's possible that Louisa's husband was not the real father. I think it might be what we've been missing."

"Well, maybe. But how does that change anything with respect to Eddy and Hilldrup?"

"That I don't know."

As they mulled over Carey's theory, the waiter brought out their entrées, which they began eating. Crawford said, "Did you find some new evidence that brought you to this conclusion?"

"No," said Carey. "It's just a hunch."

"Well...*wait a minute*," Crawford said, pointing at Carey with a piece of beef held in the air between two chopsticks. "Didn't you go over to the evidence room last week?" Carey nodded. "Did you find anything there?"

Carey reached into his coat pocket. "I was saving this," he said. "It's interesting, but I'm not sure it's useful. Just don't drop it into your noodles." Carey handed the pocketwatch across the table to Crawford.

Crawford held the watch in his hand and read the tag. "Holy cow," he said. "Don't those guys in evidence ever throw anything out?"

"Sometimes they do, sometimes not. It depends."

"So Eddy was murdered not long after he did Finkel, huh?" Crawford turned the watch over. "Did you see this monogram?" Carey nodded. "What do you think it means?"

"I have no idea."

"H-R-D," Crawford said, rubbing the smooth back of the watch with his thumbs. "What was Louisa's married name?"

"Rogers," said Carey. "Why?"

"Wasn't her husband's name 'Harrison'?"

"Yeah, but the monogram's HRD, not HDR."

"Ben," Crawford said, shaking his head. "You don't own anything with a monogram on it, do you?"

"No, I don't, but what's your—?"

"In a monogram, the first initial is on the left, middle initial's on the right, and the last name initial goes in the center, like this." Carey looked sheepishly at him as Crawford handed back the watch. "It's possible that 'HRD' is Harrison Rogers, if we could confirm his middle name."

"I should have figured that out," said Carey, shaking his head. Crawford shrugged sympathetically. Carey held the watch before him, angling it to let the light from the window play on the letters etched on its back. "Although, even if this watch did belong to Rogers, I don't know what that would mean."

"It might tie Eddy to the house," said Crawford, nudging his glasses up the bridge of his nose. "But you're right. I don't know what it means, either."

THE D.C. TRANSIT STREETCAR teetered down Pennsylvania Avenue, throwing sparks from its electrified third rail, which lit up the undercarriage of the trolley as it sped away from the Capitol on another damp, chilly evening.

Carey sat against the window of the car, looking out at the buildings but lost in his own world. What did the monogram mean? If the watch had belonged to Harrison Rogers, had he had something to do with Eddy? Or had Eddy just found the watch in the house? That didn't seem likely. Even if Rogers had visited Louisa and left his pocketwatch, he wouldn't have left it in one of the soldiers' rooms. Would Eddy have taken the time to ransack other rooms in the house for valuables? And if he did, wouldn't the police have been wise to it?

So many damn questions raised, Carey felt like he had fewer answers than he did before. Hilldrup and Eddy were connected, Carey felt certain. Yet what was this connection between Eddy and Rogers? Or was it just coincidence? Crawford had volunteered to look up information on Harrison Rogers at the Office of Vital Records. Now Carey wished he'd gone with him, but he was exhausted. The combination of his job, this ongoing investigation, his divorce, and a new relationship had left Carey drained mentally and physically.

As the streetcar turned up 15th Street, Carey closed his eyes and tried not to think. But his mind wouldn't let go. If HRD were indeed Harrison Rogers, he knew that it meant something. Rogers was significant. Carey couldn't see it yet, but he felt something jelling out of this new information, something that Mordechai wanted him to see.

CRAWFORD WALKED WEST down D Street, bracing himself against the cold wind that had whipped up. He had found quickly what he was looking for at the Office of Vital Records. Harrison Deane Rogers was the full name of Louisa's husband. Born in 1840, he had been a lawyer in New Jersey and Washington, D.C., and the only son of Sarah Deane and Tyler Rogers, a one-time congressman and assistant secretary of the Navy during the Civil War. Harrison had thrived as an attorney in Washington and had also run, unsuccessfully, two times for Congress from New Jersey. He and Louisa had no other children after James. He died in 1895.

Crawford was returning to 301 C Street to look through Carey's file. If he was going to help Carey solve this puzzle, he needed to know what he knew. As Crawford approached C Street, the wind began to whip harder, and he could feel the first few stinging drops of rain as they hit his face.

Substation C was completely dark when Crawford arrived, not a light on in the house. He opened the door and quickly turned on every light downstairs. He walked into Carey's office, sat down at his desk, and opened the bottom drawer.

He removed the file folder and notebook and cleared off the surface of Carey's desk so that he could spread out and review the materials—Wallace's sketches, Carey's notes, Bogart's documents, the old photograph, and his own notes on Harrison Rogers. As Carey had said, Wallace had never seen, or at least had never drawn, Harrison. And neither he nor Carey had seen the man— unless Harrison was the ghost in the bathroom who had "attacked" Carey. He looked closely at the photograph. Louisa really was beautiful. The boy definitely took after her. Harrison had a haughty air, his chin thrust forward and head tilted back slightly. His dark mustache and goatee were shaved into thin lines around his pursed mouth. The skin on his cheeks was deeply pock-marked and rough. His thin, aquiline nose led to a broad forehead and long, dark hair that was slicked back behind his ears. The eyes seemed gray and out of focus to Crawford, as if staring at nothing and no one. It was not a pleasant face, to say the least.

Harrison and Louisa's families had both come from the area surrounding Princeton, New Jersey, and both of their fathers had taken up residence in Washington in elected or appointed federal office since the children were young. It would have been inconceivable that the two, so close in age, did not know each other. Both Senator Morrison and Secretary Rogers were Republicans and abolitionists; they must have been at least casual friends.

As Carey had postulated about Mordechai's attachment to Louisa, so Crawford began to wonder about Harrison. If he'd grown up with her, seen her blossom into womanhood, what feelings would he have harbored for her? Crawford knew Eddy's motive—the same as Hilldrup's and Brandon's: money. But Crawford had been a cop long enough to know that passion was just as often a motive for murder.

What if Carey had been right about Mordechai and Louisa?

If Eddy was connected to Harrison by his pocketwatch, the connection could have been made indirectly, through Mordechai— Eddy's assignment, Harrison's rival.

It was getting late, Crawford knew, and he thought of putting Carey's things away when he heard the sound—a desperate, breathless sobbing that pierced the silence of the old house. It was coming from upstairs and bade Crawford, against his better judgment, to investigate.

AT FIRST CAREY did not recognize the room. But the room hadn't changed, only his perspective:

He stands looking over at the soldier from just beyond the foot of his cot. The soldier is sleeping, and a well-dressed gentleman stands beside the cot, staring intently down at him. He leans over to examine the soldier's wound and loosens the dressing with his forefinger. The man removes something from his gray waistcoat, a small, four- or five-inch jackknife. He slowly moves the knife over the open wound and plunges it in. The soldier's eyes open, and his face contorts in great pain. He struggles, but the man holds the soldier down with all of his weight, while the soldier's hands scrape and tug at the man's chest. The soldier manages only to pull the man's watch and chain loose from his vest pocket. But the man doesn't seem to notice. Soon the soldier stops struggling, and his body lies motionless, the hand still holding the watch clenched in a tight fist.

The man rises and wipes his hands with a handkerchief. He returns the kerchief to his pocket and turns his face to the window—

Carey awoke with a start. He threw off his covers and turned on the lamp on his bedside table. He was scared. He didn't know why, but he felt he had to go over to the old house right away.

• • •

CRAWFORD DREW his revolver and climbed the stairs to the second floor. The sound was coming from the turret room. The door was open, and Crawford could barely see in, the room lit only by the streetlamp outside. He was able to make out the silhouette of a woman sitting before the center window, her body shaking with each sob. He stepped into the room and searched the wall with his hand for a light switch, but found none.

He holstered his weapon and approached the woman, whose back was to him. As his eyes adjusted to the darkness, he saw that she was very young, with long, dark hair and fair skin. She sat on a stool that was engulfed by her long, billowing skirts. She wore a long-sleeved bodice underneath a blue petticoat. Crawford drew closer, wanting to understand what was happening. Tears spilled from her cheeks onto her hands, which were facing palm-up in her lap. They were stained red, and when she turned to face him, he realized that her hands and the front of her dress were covered in blood.

Crawford recoiled from the specter before him. It was Louisa, and she rose from her stool, staring directly into his face as she approached, pleading silently.

You shouldn't be here.

Suddenly she stopped, and her eyes, now wide with terror, shifted to a point above his left shoulder. Crawford wheeled and saw a man—his face wrinkled and gray as death, eyes sunken into his head. He lunged toward Crawford from out of the darkness. Stumbling backwards, Crawford reached a hand out to balance himself. But there was nothing there to stop his fall. He tumbled into the window pane, breaking through the plate glass and plummeting through the air toward the ground below, a scream escaping his lips as he fell. His momentum carried him onto the spikes of the wrought-iron fence in front of the old house.

Suspended six feet above the ground, Crawford's still body lay impaled across the top of the fence. Lacerations from the broken glass crossed the back of his neck and arms, and two black iron spikes punctured his lungs and protruded barely an inch through the front of his blood-soaked shirt.

THE TAXI PULLED UP alongside the two squad cars parked outside 301 C Street. Through his rain-spattered window, Carey couldn't make out much of what was going on. He paid the cabbie and opened his door, staring in shock at the police tape across the entrance and the building lit up like an open house.

He ducked under the yellow tape covering the opening in the gate, and a uniformed officer in a black raincoat stopped him. Carey flashed his badge and said, "Sergeant Carey."

The officer shined his flashlight on Carey's ID and then into his face. "Jesus," he said, "that was fast." The officer let him pass. It was then that Carey noticed the ambulance drivers and the photographer walking around in the tall grass and mud in front of the porch. He recognized the police photographer from his old precinct; he was packing up his gear and shaking his head. The drivers were leaning over something, and Carey heard one of them say, "Morgue. It's a DOA." They were standing over a body lying on a stretcher. The body was covered with a white sheet.

The turret towered over them, its windows aglow, but for the middle one, which had been shattered. The two ambulance drivers raised the stretcher and began rolling it toward the gate. Carey approached the two men and stopped them. "I'm Sergeant Carey," he said. "Who is this?"

"I don't know," the older one said, a cigarette dangling from his lips. "But he's gonna be late for dinner."

Carey pulled back the sheet to reveal the man's face, but was not prepared for what he saw. It was Crawford. He looked as though he'd been dipped up to his chin in blood. Carey could see cuts down the side of his neck and two gaping holes in his chest. He hadn't seen anything like it since Korea. He covered Crawford's face and tried to catch his breath. He stared at the ambulance driver. "This is Sergeant Norman Crawford," he said. "He's a cop, you dumb sonofabitch."

The driver grimaced and looked down at the ground. "Sorry, Sergeant. I didn't know."

"What the hell happened?" Carey snapped, trying to control himself.

The younger driver spoke up, "We found him...he'd fallen from the second-story window. He was hung up on those spikes," he gestured toward the wrought-iron fence. "We found him like that."

"Jesus Christ," Carey turned away and shut his eyes, trying to maintain his composure. He'd lost his wife and his best friend in the course of a few weeks, and now the unreality of it all came crashing down on him. There was nothing interesting or mysterious left about this house or its former inhabitants. It had tried to kill him once before. *Now, because of me*, thought Carey, *Norm is dead.*

"You knew him, Ben?" the photographer asked.

"Yeah," Carey said.

"I'm sorry," he said and turned away to finish doing his job.

Carey knew he had to move, do something. He turned and ran up the front steps to the porch and burst through the open door. He could hear voices coming from his office. Three or four other officers, and they were arguing about something—

"—happened once before. You don't know that you saw anyth—"

"I know what I saw, goddamnit!"

"Take it easy, fellas…"

The three officers fell silent upon noticing Carey standing in the doorway. Carey recognized the two beat cops, Officers 5991 and 6025. The other was a young cop he'd never met. "The man who's lying dead out there," Carey said, his voice shaking now, "was Sergeant Norm Crawford. He was a good cop. He was my friend….I don't know what you're arguing about, but I can guess." Carey, regaining his composure, looked each of the officers in the eye and said, "I'd appreciate it if you told me everything you know about what happened here tonight."

Officer 5991, Jim Girardi, was sitting on the edge of Carey's desk and looked over at his partner, who was sitting down. "It's your call, Mike," he said.

Officer Mike Kelly, 6025, began: "Officer Girardi and I were walking our beat, coming down C Street around the corner from here. It was raining, and we heard a noise. It sounded like breaking glass followed by a man screaming. We ran over to investigate and found him…like that. When I looked up to the second floor, I saw someone, a man, standing in the window of the turret room. The light wasn't on, but I could see his face by the street lamp."

"You got a good look at him?" asked Carey.

"Yeah, I did," said Kelly. "Jim didn't see him, but I did. He was tall and thin with gray hair—an older man, in his fifties or sixties, maybe. And he was staring down at the victim…Sergeant Crawford, I mean. He stood there for a moment before backing out of the light. I told Jim I'd seen someone, and we rushed into the building. We searched the house room by room, everywhere we could, but there was no one here. There was no way he could have escaped without us knowing. He just disappeared."

"I see," said Carey. "Has anyone called Inspector Price?"

"He's on his way," said Girardi.

"Thanks," said Carey, who made his way over to his chair and sat down. He looked down at his desk and saw the papers and documents from the Finkel file spread across the top of it. He sighed heavily and wiped the moisture from his forehead with the palm of his hand. "If you fellows will excuse me for a moment," he said. "I've got to call Sergeant Crawford's wife." The officers looked at each other and started out the door.

Kelly, the last one out, stopped in the doorway and turned to Carey. "Sergeant," he said, "about our report…"

"What you told me here tonight was for me," said Carey. "You put whatever you have to in your report. I won't question it."

Kelly nodded and closed the door. Carey stared at the documents on his desk for a minute. He found Crawford's notes and began reading them: "Harrison Deane Rogers (H.D.R.)…b. 1840, d. 1895…father Tyler Rogers, Ass't Sec'y of Navy…Harrison lived/practiced law in N.J. and D.C.…Morrison/Rogers family friends?"

Next to them was the photograph of Louisa, James, and Harrison. Carey knew he'd have one more question for Officer Kelly. But his first task was the one he dreaded most. He picked up his phone and dialed Crawford's number.

"Hello? Norm?" a woman's anxious voice answered.

"Mary, it's Ben.…I don't know how to tell you this…"

BY HALF PAST MIDNIGHT, the rain had let up. One of the officers at the scene dropped Carey at his apartment, where Ruth was standing outside waiting for him.

"I told you not to come," he said, furrowing his brow at her. "Do you know what time it is? You shouldn't be out here by yourself."

"Ben, I'm all right," she said. "I was worried about you. I didn't want you to be alone after what happened."

"Ruth…" His shoulders dropped, and Ruth moved in close enough to put her arms around him. "I'm sorry. I'm glad you came," he said. "Come on, let's get inside. It's cold out here." Ruth stood by him as they rode the elevator to his third-floor apartment. Carey remained silent as they got off the elevator and walked down the hall. He unlocked his door and let her in. Ruth had been here several times, had even helped him pick out some of the decorations.

"Sit down, Ben," she said, leading him into his living room. "I'll fix you a drink." She poured him a scotch and fixed herself a brandy. She handed him his glass and sat down next to him on the sofa. "Ben, do they know how it happened?"

"No," he said, "but I have a pretty good idea." Carey had called her from his office and told her that Norm had fallen from the second-story window, that he was dead. He had left out the details. He tasted the scotch. It burned his throat a little going down, but the warm sensation felt good. "Norm was working with me on the Finkel case—he called it moonlighting. But there's something about the case I haven't told you."

Ruth tilted her head slightly at him. "What?"

"The reason we were looking into Finkel in the first place." She knitted her eyebrows, confused. "That old house is where Mordechai was murdered, in the second-floor turret room above my office—the same room I slept in after Marie and I split up. But there's more…there are spirits—ghosts, presences, whatever you want to call them—that still live there. I've seen them; so had Norm. They showed us clues. We wouldn't have known about Finkel, or any of this, if not for them. I never told you because I knew you'd think I was crazy."

Ruth was staring at him, her mouth open. She shook her head. "Ben Carey," she said, "how could you think that of me? I know you. I believe you. You're the most rational, sane man I've ever known. If you say you saw a ghost, I believe it."

"Norm fell out of a window in the same room. I got him involved in this—the planning unit, everything. He's dead because of me."

She gently turned his face to hers with her hand and said, "Don't ever say that, Ben. It's not true. Norm was a grown man. You were a good friend to him. You're not responsible for what happened to him."

Carey leaned forward, covering his eyes with his hands. Ruth could see the tears streaming down the side of his face. He wiped his cheeks with the back of his hand and let out a bitter laugh. "We solved it," he said, "for whatever it's worth now."

"You solved it?"

"We were trying to piece it together," he said. "Why was Harrison's watch found on Ronald Eddy? What was their connection?" He paused and set his drink down on the table. "When I was staying at the house, every night I had the same bizarre dream. In the dream, I was Mordechai, lying in the room dying, and Ronald Eddy was staring at me, backing away, clutching that gold watch. Since I moved in here, the dream had stopped—until tonight. Except this time it was different. This wasn't the same dream. The whole time I'd been dreaming of what happened *after* Mordechai's murder—Ronald Eddy leaving the house with Mordechai's watch. But it wasn't *Mordechai's* watch, it belonged to the killer. In my dream, for the first time I saw who it was. It was Harrison Rogers."

"Louisa's husband?"

"Yes, but he only married her after Mordechai died," he said.

"But why would he kill Mordechai?"

"Mordechai and Louisa were lovers. She was pregnant with his son, James. But Harrison had been in love with her for a long time. He found out about Mordechai and Louisa's affair and killed him, making it look like his wound had simply reopened.

On the same day, Ronald Eddy was sent by Hilldrup to do the job, but Harrison had gotten there first. Harrison stabbed Mordechai in the stomach while he was sleeping. He woke up and tried to fight him off, but was too weak. During the struggle, he grabbed Harrison's watch. When Eddy came in later, Mordechai was already dead. He stole the gold pocketwatch from the dead man's hand and left to collect his fee."

"Oh, my God."

"Earlier tonight, I learned something else. One of the cops on the scene arrived just after Norm fell," he said. "He saw a man in the window. When they searched the house, he had disappeared." Carey pulled an old photograph from out of his pocket. "The officer gave me a description of an older man. When I showed him this, he identified him—the man in the window was the same man who's in this photo, only older." Carey showed Ruth the portrait of Harrison Rogers, and she let out a gasp.

"He didn't want us finding out what he'd done," he said.

"How did you find out about Mordechai and Louisa?" she asked.

He sighed and shook his head. "I guessed," he said and shrugged his shoulders. "It's the only part of the solution where I have no evidence. I doubt I ever will. But I'm sure of it. I only wish it were of some good now."

"You may not see it," she said. "But I do." She put her hand on his. He closed his eyes and tried to chase the image of his friend lying dead on a stretcher from his mind.

THE NEXT THREE DAYS Carey spent in a haze of sadness and remorse. He asked for time off from work, and Price gave it to him. The truth was, Carey wasn't sure if he'd ever be able to set foot in the old house again. His worst fear was of confronting the ghost of his dear friend and partner, Norm Crawford.

The funeral was scheduled for that Thursday afternoon. Crawford, who'd been a combat veteran and was a policeman killed in
the line of duty, was to be buried at Arlington National Cemetery.

The entire police force, Police Chief Murray, as well as the
District of Columbia's three governing commissioners all turned
out to honor Norm Crawford on a cloudless, warm, early spring
afternoon. Inspector Price spoke at the funeral, followed by Carey
and Crawford's older brother, George. A battalion of police
motorcycles followed the hearse carrying Crawford's body and led
a procession of a hundred or more cars.

Carey was dressed in his full police uniform that day. Asked by
Mary to be a pallbearer, he helped carry Crawford to his grave.
The reverend said his piece, "Ashes to ashes, dust to dust…,"
while Carey and the rest of the mourners choked back tears. The
day was inappropriately bright and sunny. Trees and flowers were
starting to bloom. It was the kind of beautiful spring day Washington was known for.

A stream of well-wishers consoled Mary Crawford, who stared
absently at her husband's coffin. Carey and Ruth were among the
last to walk up to her.

After Ruth gave Mary her condolences, Carey took her hand.
"If there's anything I can ever do," he told her, "you let me know.
Norm was like a brother to me."

Mary nodded to Carey, forced a weak smile, and returned her
gaze to the coffin.

"It's a beautiful site," he said, gesturing with his head toward the
trees all around, the view of the Potomac, unsure what else to say.

"I'll be buried with him when my time comes," she said, dabbing her eyes with a handkerchief.

"That's a comfort," he said, patting her hand. "I'm glad they
allow spouses in the cemetery. I wasn't sure."

"My body will be laid over his," she said. "My name will go on the back of his tombstone. That's how they do it here."

Carey fell silent and continued to hold her hand awkwardly, until it was time for him to take his leave.

As Mary and her other family members walked back to their cars, Carey took Ruth by the hand and started walking north in the direction of the old Custis-Lee mansion and the amphitheater.

"Where are we going?" she asked.

"I need to see something," he said and continued on in silence.

They approached Section 2 of the cemetery and started up the hill, stopping underneath the ancient oak tree, whose leaves were now budding. He walked up to the grave of Mordechai Finkel and stepped around it to see the other side.

"It's here," he said simply.

Ruth was several steps behind and gave him a curious look, as if to say, "What?" As she walked up beside him, he was pointing to the words engraved on the back of Mordechai's grave marker. The words read—

LOUISA

ANNE

MORRISON

BELOVED OF MORDECHAI FINKEL

MOTHER TO HIS SON, JAMES

JANUARY 14, 1844

APRIL 9, 1933

EPILOGUE.

Tuesday, August 26, 1958

ON TOP OF ELIAS BOGART'S sprawling pile of mail sat a bulging nine-by-twelve kraft envelope sent from Washington, D.C., by Sergeant Ben Carey. Bogart picked up the package and sat down in his leather chair, propping his feet up on his desk. He opened the envelope and pulled out a large manila folder with a letter clipped to the front of it. The letter was dated August 22 and read:

> Dear Elias,
>
> I'm returning the file you lent me, along with a few documents I unearthed, which I thought might be of interest to you. I did some more digging and found some quite interesting information. I took the liberty of mimeographing some of the documents you gave me. It turns out your instincts about Mordechai Finkel were right. I shared the file I created with my superior officer, Inspector James Price, who takes a special interest in these types of cold cases.
>
> Suffice it to say that, if you're still interested in "shaking things up" at your company, this file should put you well on your way. Note in particular the photographs attached to the inside of the folder...

Bogart opened the folder and undid the paperclip on the two photos. He looked at the engravings on the two sides of the white marble tombstone for a few moments, before realizing what it meant. The expression of shock gave way to a devious smile that started on his mouth and slowly spread across his entire face.

CAREY HAD RETURNED to work, counting the days until his unit would be moved to another location. A new officer was assigned to take Crawford's place, an older sergeant named Dick Rozek, who had some accounting experience. Carey moved Rozek in with Mullins and Kelsey, refusing to make anyone else take Crawford's and Wallace's old office. He never again stayed at the office past dusk. He bought himself a new briefcase, and he learned to take work home when he needed to.

In June, Price's Cold Case Homicide Squad was approved by the Department of Justice and established at MPD headquarters. Price selected three of the most experienced homicide detectives and two sergeants to staff the unit. Carey left the planning unit and joined Price's new homicide squad in August. The planning unit was given to another sergeant and moved over to the fifth precinct house the same month.

The first rule of homicide is that the first forty-eight to seventy-two hours are critical in solving the crime. If there are any witnesses, they will be easier to find and their memories will be more accurate during the first two to three days after the murder. In two-thirds of the homicide cases that are solved, the police arrest a suspect within twenty-four hours of the crime. If the case goes unsolved longer than two days, the chances that it will ever be solved drop sharply.

Carey's new unit took over murder investigations that had gone unsolved for over a year, cases that other experienced detectives could not solve. He had passed the required detectives' exam and transferred over to the homicide division, of which the cold case squad was now a part. He was learning to investigate murder cases under the tutelage of some of the MPD's best homicide detectives.

ON FRIDAY, OCTOBER 24, 1958, bulldozers tore down the old Victorian house at 301 C Street NW in a light, misting rain. Few onlookers bothered to notice this decrepit old building being demolished, but among them were Detective Ben Carey, Ruth Bergman, and an old gray cat.

The good and the bad things this house represented to Carey were slowly being knocked back down to earth. It seemed long ago now, the events of the previous winter. Carey could scarcely believe that he'd really seen and heard all that he'd recorded in Wallace's black notebook. Like a dream, the events faded away into memory faster each day he was removed from them. Now, when he saw something in one of the windows or moving across the exposed second floor, it was a trick of the light or swirling dust, no more mysterious than a cloud that resembles a face floating in the sky. Ronald Eddy and Harrison Rogers no longer existed. Louisa and James had no more reason to haunt this place. Perhaps James would know his father, and Louisa would be reunited with her one true love.

And somewhere, Mordechai would finally be healed.

ABOUT THE AUTHOR

 DAVID R. HORWITZ was born in Washington, D.C., in 1964, the first son of a D.C. police officer and a piano teacher. Raised in suburban Maryland, David read voraciously, wrote short stories, and biked to D.C. whenever he could. He played guitar and violin, performed in variety shows, and wrote silly songs inspired by a range of songwriters, from Stevie Ray Vaughn and the Grateful Dead to Billie Holiday and Cole Porter.

In college, David studied journalism and Russian, wrote for the school paper, and earned his degree in information systems management. He landed a job as a clerk typist with the federal government, taught himself computers, and rose through the ranks. Nine months after placing an ad in *Washingtonian* magazine, David married the author of the best reply. He inherited an orange tabby cat and later named another Monkey Boy (after a character in *Mister Boffo*). When he was hired as a lead programmer in 2000, he and his wife, Deirdre, bought their first home — a century-old former dairy farm in rural Minnesota.

Motivated by his passion for military history and inspired by Robert Girardi's novel, *Madeline's Ghost*, he wrote in earnest on nights and weekends. David's dream of writing full-time ended when he died in 2004. He left behind his wife of ten years, parents, sister, brother, five nephews, niece, and manuscripts that would become the Ben Carey mysteries.

A NOTE ON THE TITLE

The title *Murder Bay* refers to an area in nineteenth-century Washington, D.C., near the White House that was notoriously known for its brawlers and brothels.

A NOTE ON THE TYPE

The text of this book was set in Electra, a typeface designed in 1935 by the renowned designer and illustrator William A. Dwiggins (1880–1956). A standard book typeface since its release due to the evenness of design and high legibility, this face cannot be classified as either modern or old style. It is not based on any historical model, nor does it echo any particular period or style. It avoids the extreme contrasts between thick and thin elements that mark most modern faces, and it gives a feeling of fluidity, warmth, personality, and speed.

Printed and bound by Thomson-Shore, Inc.
Dexter, Michigan

Designed by Top Five Books